Legacy

≈ of the ≈

BRAVE

Deborah Kelly

Legacy

⁓ of the ⁓

BRAVE

Deborah J. Kelly

TATE PUBLISHING & Enterprises

Published by Tate Publishing & Enterprises, LLC
127 E. Trade Center Terrace | Mustang, Oklahoma 73064 USA
1.888.361.9473 | www.tatepublishing.com

Tate Publishing is committed to excellence in the publishing industry. The company reflects the philosophy established by the founders, based on Psalm 68:11,
"The Lord gave the word and great was the company of those who published it."

Published in the United States of America

ISBN: 978-1-61566-907-3
1. Fiction / War & Military   2. Fiction / Historical
10.02.18

Dedicated to the memory of *Frau* Edith Long, my German teacher, whose testimony inspired me to write this story.

I would like to thank Ed and Gretchen Thomas for their generosity in allowing me to finish this story at their beautiful retreat, my family and friends for their encouragement in this endeavor, and my husband for his undying love and support.

Cast of Characters

Howard Apgar: radio operator on the Peterson crew

David Bellerive: flight engineer on the Peterson crew

First Lieutenant Albert Camistro: officer and copilot on the Peterson crew

Herr Hahn: owner of farm on the south side of Eigeltingen

Georg Hartmann: Leyna Künzel's uncle, brother of Leyna's mother

Frau Huber: wife of the area *Kreisleiter*

Second Lieutenant Randall Kellam: officer and navigator on the Peterson crew

Onkel Klaus: member of the German Underground

Herr Krueger: owner of the bakery in Engen

Leyna Künzel: object of main character study

Stefan Künzel: Leyna's brother

Ada Lehmann: friend of *Frau* Huber

Sergeant Roland Lidgard: right waist gunner on the Peterson crew

Second Lieutenant Frank Owen: officer and bombardier on the Peterson crew

Captain Hanke Metzger: German officer assigned to watch the Künzel farm

Lynn Milliken: ball gunner on the Peterson crew

First Lieutenant Bernard Peterson: officer and pilot of the Peterson crew

Frau Seiler: friend of the Künzel family

Jack Sims: tail gunner on the Peterson crew

Doris Taylor: Rand's girlfriend

Sergeant Roy Wheeler: left waist gunner on the Peterson crew who evaded capture

Tante Zelma: member of the German Underground

Prologue: Spring 1984

It was late on a Friday afternoon as the gray-haired professor drew a close to her lecture in second semester world history at the Christian university lecture hall. She stood tall, with shoulders back, and the students seemed to appreciate her melodic and expressive voice. She knew well that staying awake in an afternoon history class was always a challenge, and she did her best to bring the subject to life.

"As we draw this chapter on World War II to a close, I would like to ask you to read ahead this weekend to the next chapter. That will give you some good background, as next week, all week, we will be engaging in two character studies from this time period. You won't want to miss this. Have a great weekend, and I will see all of you, Lord willing, on Monday afternoon."

With that said, she dismissed the class. There were a couple of students who made their way to the front of the room to ask her questions about makeup work. They were all greeted with the same clear eyes and charming smile. For an older woman, she was remarkably beautiful. After answering each question, she packed her bag, climbed the stairs, and stepped out into the sunny spring afternoon. Some sweet smell from a nearby flower riding on the breeze, touched off a memory, and made her smile. She loved springtime.

Monday afternoon came quickly. The professor took roll, and then she looked up with amusement at the last two rows of the lecture hall that were usually empty. "And, I would like to welcome our guests this afternoon. Some of you I recognize from previous semesters. Welcome back," she began.

"Today, we begin our 'living history week.' We will study two individuals: one a twenty-three-year-old American Army Air Corps officer stationed at Wendling in Norfolk, England, and the other a nineteen-year-old German girl who lived four miles or so east of Engen in the Hegau. We will meet both of these individuals at a very crucial time in world history: March of 1944.

"Our young man is Randall. Rand was born and reared in Dubuque, Iowa. He was the eldest of four children who were born to a middle-class family. Rand's father was the county sheriff. His paternal grandfather operated a rather large farm of 250 acres, west of Dubuque."

The professor scanned the faces of the students quickly, and then she continued. "To give you a brief background on this young man before we join him in Wendling, he grew up in a loving and hard-working family, spending much of his time as a boy working with his grandfather on the farm. His father was a deacon in their local church, and Rand attended there regularly until he went away to New York to the university. He held the distinction of being the first one in his family to attend college.

"It was at this time that he began to question his purpose in life. At the same time, the dark clouds of war were rapidly approaching the American continent. You will recall that after December 7, 1941, there was a general call for enlistment that was wildly received by most young men eager to defend their country. Rand was one of those men.

"As soon as he graduated from college, Rand joined the Army Air Corps. After months of specialized training in many places, including Florida, Texas, New Mexico, and Colorado, he and his crew received their orders. They were shipped overseas to Wendling Air Force Base in eastern England and attached to the 392nd Bomb Group, 577th Squadron, which flew the historical B-24s, also known as Liberators. You will recall the euphoria with which England received their American counterparts and the opening up of air bases all across England to accommodate their newly declared allies."

The professor moved to the overhead projector and slid a photograph onto the glass. A striking but haunting image, frozen in time, shot onto the screen at the front of the lecture hall.

The professor breathed in slowly. "These young men comprise the Peterson crew. Now I will introduce you to each of them. On the front row, from left to right, you will find the officers of the crew: the bombardier, Second Lieutenant Frank Owen; First Lieutenant Albert Camistro, who is the copilot; our subject, who is a second lieutenant and the navigator; and on the far right is the pilot, First Lieutenant Bernard Peterson."

The professor took a pencil in hand. "On the second row, from left to right, we have the left waist gunner, Sergeant Roy Wheeler; the tall one is radio operator Howard Apgar; the next one is the flight engineer, David Bellerive; then right waist gunner, Sergeant Roland Lidgard; the tail gunner, Jack Sims; and the last one here on the right is the ball gunner, Lynn Milliken." The professor paused a moment and walked across the length of the platform.

"Our second object of study this week is a German girl by the name of Leyna. She is the more difficult of the two studies, a little withdrawn, a little beyond her years. She too grew up in a good home, on a farm east of Engen. 'Engen, Tengen, and Blumenfeld are the most beautiful towns in the world,' an old Baden proverb says." The professor looked out to the crowd and put her hands together. "Now, I suppose we should depart from history for a moment to geography. How many of you have been to Germany?"

Out of a room full of over two hundred students, only two hands were raised. The professor nodded. "All right. How many of you know where Stuttgart is?"

Only one hand went up. The professor cleared her throat. "How many of you have been to Disney World or Disneyland?" she asked with a telling smile. As she suspected, almost the entire hall was filled with hands. "The castle in the magic kingdom," she continued, "was modeled primarily after mad King Ludwig's castle, Neuschwanstein. Neuschwanstein is in the Bavarian Alps in the southern part of Germany. Leyna lived almost two hundred kilometers from that castle and thirty kilometers from the northern border of Switzerland.

"Her father was a farmer and a Lutheran pastor in a heavily Catholic part of Germany. As Adolph Hitler rose to his position of power, as we have already studied, the mouths of any dissenting factors were quashed, and Hitler became the dictator who told the people of Germany what they could and could not stand for and who was to be treated with respect or disdain.

"Leyna's father unwittingly became part of a movement known as the Confessing Church. Now, the Confessing Church was a group of believers who refused to bow to the demands of the Third Reich, specifically concerning the exclusion of Jews from worship and leadership in the church. They also opposed the exaltation of the Aryan race in practice.

"For his part in the Confessing Church, Leyna's father was arrested and removed from their home, along with her elder brother. Her brother was pressed into the German infantry. Her mother, perhaps broken by the effects of the war and the removal of her husband and son, began to suffer from memory loss and delusions. It was not long before her health began to fail. So, it fell to Leyna to care for her mother and to run the family farm. As the war progressed, she was required to provide a higher percentage of the crop yield to the government, leaving precious little for sustaining their lives.

"Recall the conditions into which the allies stepped when they liberated the concentration and POW camps." The professor paused for a lengthy moment and then swallowed hard. "Conditions all over Germany were similar the year before victory and her armies arrived." The professor lowered her eyes for a second.

"Now, we are ready to join our first study, in his bunk, on the air base, north and east of London."

Evening, March 17, 1944

Rand Kellam was a well-respected member of the Peterson crew. He had held the position of second lieutenant for nearly a year and served as the navigator on the B-24, *Ready, Willing, and Able.* He stood a little taller than most of the men in his barracks. He had light brown hair, a handsome smile, and a charming personality.

On this particular Friday evening, most of the men had gone into Beeston. Rand had stayed behind to catch up on his letter writing and to try to get some extra sleep. They had been slotted to run their seventeenth mission in the morning. He wrote to his parents, and then he shifted on his bunk and began a letter to his girl in New York.

He wrote about the volleyball game they had played that day, the cold and damp weather, and about his bunkmates. It was always a task not to write about anything top secret. All of the mail from the boys in England was censored anyway.

He did not write about what was really on his mind. That was something he had learned to share with no one. He never wrote about his missions. On the days his crew would fly, they were always up in the early hours of the morning. Breakfast consisted of fresh eggs from the farm in the middle of the airbase. Next they would head off in the darkness for their briefing, where they were always told that flak was expected, and there was a great likelihood that some of them would not return.

From there, they would catch a ride out to their aircraft. It seemed like it was always cold and foggy. Sometimes, they would wait in their Liberator for over an hour only to have their mission cancelled due to bad weather. Rand was always relieved to go back to his bunk and back to sleep.

He did not write about how he felt inside each time they taxied out to the runway to line up for take off, each time they sped down the runway, blowing the fog away with their propellers. He never mentioned the tedium as their plane climbed high in the sky and circled around for what seemed like hours, trying to make formation with the rest of the Liberators. Then there was the roar of the engines and the rattling of the B-24 as they all took off over the English Channel into enemy territory. Sometimes the sky was clear and blue. Sometimes it was fraught with clouds and the terrible unknown.

He usually got a sinking feeling that went straight into his heart when the flak started bursting around them. He never wrote about the enemy fighters he shot at with the nose gun or the times he was called upon to make another dead reckoning of their position because the pilot had lost track of where in the world they were in all of the commotion. He never mentioned the sound of the bombs dropping or the smoke he had seen rising from the destruction. Nor did he ever describe what Germany looked like from twenty thousand feet up, with its towns and green patches of farmland.

They had several close calls on previous missions when anti-aircraft fire hit their engines. A couple of times, they were not sure they would make it back to England alive. One time Lieutenant Peterson had called for a vote whether to head for Sweden to be interned for the remainder of the war or to try to make it back to Wendling. The vote was unanimous for Wendling, and they were all relieved when they made touchdown safely. Every mission was the same in some respects: a mixture of freezing cold that cut to the bone, terror that went straight to the heart, and the desperate hope that nothing would go wrong. He was glad at least to be part of a top-notch crew. In spite of the fear he always felt, he was proud to be serving his country.

At ten o'clock, some of the boys came back from town, half drunk. Rand tried to stay out of their way. He closed up his letter to Doris and climbed under the covers for the night. At eleven thirty, the copilot, Lieutenant Camistro, stumbled into the bunk below Rand, thoroughly arousing Rand from his sleep.

"Where have you been, Al?" asked Rand in an irritated whisper. "We have to be up at oh four hundred for the mission."

"I got caught by the MPs trying to sneak back in," replied the lieutenant rather loudly, slurring his words.

Rand tried to hush him. "Get to sleep, you crazy bird." Rand rolled over and tried to go back to sleep. He shook his head. Last time Al had gone to town, he had stayed out all night with some new gal he had met at a dance, and when he finally returned to base, he got a severe tongue lashing from their colonel and two days in the brig. Each man was required to complete twenty-five missions before he could return to the states. Al was two missions behind the rest of his crew.

Morning, March 18, 1944

At five in the morning, the crewmembers for mission fifty-three out of Wendling assembled for general briefing. Rand never found it hard to concentrate in spite of the early hour; perhaps it was the lump in his stomach that kept him alert.

As usual, the commander entered the room, followed by the intelligence officer. Everyone in the room stood at attention. The intelligence officer bid the men good morning and began the briefing by uncovering the target map for the day. It was a good minute before the moans in the room faded into silence. The target was deep into Germany, and everyone knew from experience that it was going to be a horrendous journey.

Rand summoned all of his mental powers as the officer talked about their target for the day, showed the expected resistance on a map, and pointed out their secondary target. Lieutenant Kellam looked across the room. Their copilot was nodding off.

The briefing room was crowded this morning. There were a total of twenty-eight aircrews present, consisting of ten men each. Following the general briefing, Rand attended the special briefing for the navigators. Then he joined the rest of the crew as they all went back to their lockers to pack them up in case they did not return, and suited up. The sun slid coldly up over the eastern horizon, and the fog clung hopelessly to the frosted grass on the ground.

Rand slipped into his fur-lined flight boots, grabbed his flak helmet and vest, goggles and parachute, and then caught a ride out to the hardstand where Lieutenant Peterson was already doing his preflight ritual on *Ready, Willing, and Able.* He tossed his packet of papers and instruments up and climbed in the bomb bay doors. The airplane smelled like a musty mixture of oil, gasoline, and hydraulic fluid. Rand's eyes caught sight of the patches that the mechanics had made to their aircraft following the Gotha raid. He brought his mind forward and secretly prayed that this mission would be nothing like that one.

"What time is liftoff?" Rand asked the gunnery sergeant, who was checking the bombs carefully.

"Nine thirty," replied the sergeant, who didn't even bother to turn around.

Rand got his maps and instruments all situated on his navigator's table as the rest of the crew made their way to the bomber. None of the ten men really spoke to each other much during this part of the operation, though by now they were a close-knit group. There was a certain understanding they all had. They had seen enough planes return with crewmembers dead or dying. They had all returned to the Nissen huts to find that the belongings of other crewmembers, who were missing in action and never returned to safety, had been cleared out.

Lieutenant Peterson gave him the usual rap on the shoulder. "All set, Lieutenant?"

"All set, Lieutenant, sir" replied Rand. He plugged in his heated flight suit just to make sure it was working and zipped up his jacket.

Before long, *Ready, Willing, and Able* was rolling down the runway at top speed. The pilot lifted the heavy bird carefully into the March morning. The sky was as clear as a mountain lake. Rand listened to the whir as the nose wheel retracted. They circled around until everyone was assembled. At ten thousand feet, Lieutenant Peterson gave them all word, and Rand secured his oxygen mask on his face.

As they leveled off over the English Channel at twenty thousand feet, Rand looked off to the south. On their right wing, at various altitudes, were twenty sets of B-24s in twelve ship formations. Overhead and to the north was a long bomber stream of B-17s in formation. Above all of these groups flew the friendly fighter escorts.

Rand breathed into his mask and flexed his fingers inside the gloves. If there was ever a moment that he was proud to be a part of the fighting men of his country, it was then. Nothing could describe the scene he was witnessing that morning in the air over Europe, all the machines roaring toward their targets with one purpose in mind: to put an end to the tyranny.

The snowy peaks of the Swiss Alps soon glistened brightly against the dark blue horizon. There were no clouds to hide them as they sped to their bombing target on Lake Constance. Rand checked their location. Their twelve-airplane formation slowly tightened. They were flying along the Swiss border. In a few minutes, they would turn to the south and then west and drop their load on their primary target for the day: the Dornier airplane assembly plant at Friedrichshafen, where the Hindenburg and the Graf Zeppelin had been built during a more peaceful period of history.

Rand took in another deep breath. The cold was beginning to set in. It was thirty degrees below zero. The icicles on the inside of the plane glistened in the bright sunlight. Rand watched as their lead crew began their right turn. The lead crew was on their twenty-fifth and final mission and was the best of the 392nd.

"Flak ahead," called the ball gunner.

Rand breathed in deeply and braced himself for a blow. A second later, the flak was bursting all around their formation. The concussions from the flak bursts sent chunks of metal from the B-24 zinging through the aircraft. One ship on the left side of *Ready, Willing, and Able* fell to the earth in flames.

"I've got a reading," came the bombardier over the interphone.

"It's all yours, bombardier," said the pilot as he gave over control of the aircraft to the bombardier. Lieutenant Owen opened the bomb bay doors and, minutes later, successfully sent the payload whistling overboard.

Suddenly, they took a hit to their first engine. Then everything began to fall apart.

"Fighters at three o'clock," yelled the waist gunner.

Thirty seconds later, the rounds from the German fighters were bouncing off and into the body of the B-24.

All of a sudden, a twenty-millimeter shell exploded in the navigator's panel. A piece of shrapnel flew through the air. Rand felt a sharp sting as he took a direct hit above his left eye. He looked back at the pilot through the astrodome and wiped the blood from his face. In spite of the pilot's attempt to pull more power from the other engines, they were beginning to fall behind what was left of their group.

"We've got blood all over the nose," called back the nose gunner. "We're leaking hydraulic fuel."

"Pilot to navigator. I need a fix!" yelled Lieutenant Peterson over the interphone. "To Switzerland."

Rand wiped the blood from his forehead again and took a reading on his instruments. His mind was busy trying to block out the pain in his head and the thought that they were in desperate trouble. It wasn't easy for him to concentrate. From his vantage point, he could see the number one engine on fire. He saw the bright sunlight pouring through the holes in the side of their airplane and he could smell fuel. Rand bent over, snatched his pencil off the floor panel, and focused on his calculations. He needed to give their pilot a fix—and fast.

Following another round of pelting from the enemy fighters, Rand tried to report some coordinates to the pilot, but the line was silent. He turned around. The copilot motioned from the cockpit that the interphone was dead. Even if he shouted at the top of his lungs, they wouldn't be able to hear him above all of the noise. Rand grabbed a portable oxygen container, his parachute, and his papers and scrambled up the tube to the cockpit. From the cockpit, he saw a whole swarm of enemy fighters perched at high noon about to swoop down for another kill. Where were the friendly fighters? Lieutenant Peterson made another desperate call for cover.

Holding tightly to the back of the pilot's seat with his left hand, Rand rattled off some coordinates to Lieutenant Peterson.

From the cockpit, he tried to sight the other bombers from their group, but they were scattered all over the sky. One bomber just below them was almost completely engulfed in flames, but was still flying. As the enemy fighters dove on what was left of the bomber group, the pilot sent Rand to the bomb bay to see what the commotion behind them was all about. Lieutenant Peterson was afraid they were on fire.

Rand scrambled back to the bomb bay, where the left waist gunner was screaming for help. The right waist gunner, Sergeant Lidgard, had taken a bullet in the thigh and was rolling in pain on the spent casings on the floor and shouting hysterically.

Suddenly, the whole ship made an eerie bolt upward then to the side. Rand grabbed hold of the side of the airplane as he was tossed to the ground. The right engines went dead, and as they did, the plane began a slow but steady descent. Rand scrambled back to the cockpit as fast as he could go.

"We're not on fire yet," he shouted to the pilot.

The pilot looked back at Rand for a second and then nodded toward the copilot with a look of grave concern. Lieutenant Camistro had been hit in the stomach by a stray bullet from one of the German fighters, but he was still alive.

"I'm trying to feather the engines," shouted Lieutenant Peterson. "If I can't get them to go, I'm afraid we're going to have to bail. Go tell everyone to get ready."

At that moment, the copilot started arguing with the pilot about who was going to fly the plane into the ground. Rand turned around and ducked out of the cockpit. Since the interphone was out, he had a lot of ground to cover. He pulled the nose gunner out first, then cranked up the ball gunner, and lastly made his way to the tail gunner.

When Rand got back to the bomb bay, he glanced over at the left waist gunner. He was buckling on his parachute. Rand swallowed hard, grabbed his parachute, and, with steady hands, he latched it securely onto his torso. Then he grabbed the parachute for the right waist gunner and helped him slip into it.

Just before Lieutenant Owen opened the bomb bay doors and just before the pilot gave the signal to abandon ship, Rand began to tear their orders and navigational papers into little shreds. Fuel was leaking inside the compartment, and although his orders were to burn the papers at all costs, he was not willing to seal the fate of every man on board by lighting a match.

The nose gunner went out the camera hatch before the bail-out bell went off twice. Lieutenant Owen manually cranked open the bomb bay doors. Before he jumped out, Rand looked up to see the pilot scrambling down from the cockpit. Lieutenant Camistro had apparently won the argument. He was going to fly the plane so the others could get out, but Rand had no time to ponder this heroic action.

Rand gave the injured waist gunner a gentle push. Roy Wheeler, the other waist gunner, was the next to dive headfirst into the rushing air, followed by the bombardier and then closely by Rand.

The whole world was spinning around Rand Kellam like a merry-go-round. His mind was spinning too. How could he go from flying a mission to dropping through the air from thousands of feet up?

Finally, he gained his bearings, and when he did, he saw *Ready, Willing, and Able* flying slowly away to its sure demise. He remembered well now what their trainer had said. He would wait to pull his cord until he was closer to the ground. This would aid in his chances of escape or survival.

Rand glanced at the fast-approaching earth and pulled his cord. The cord came clean off of his vest, and for a moment he panicked, until he felt the gentle swoop of the parachute above him. If it hadn't been for his situation, he might have noticed the peacefulness that surrounded him. It was quieter than he expected.

He hit the ground hard in a small clearing between two bands of tall trees. Not far off, to his left, the bombardier, Second Lieutenant Frank Owen, had landed and was burying his parachute on the edge of a grove of trees. Rand wiped his eyebrow free of blood and stood up in a daze.

He glanced at his watch. It was two in the afternoon. Where were they? He looked up to see four B-24s heading west toward home, high in the sky. His heart sank to his feet. They were leaving without him. He had felt terribly far from home in his warm bunk back at Wendling, but that was nothing to compare with the distance that now separated him from freedom. He gathered his parachute and shot into the snowy woods with Lieutenant Owen.

Afternoon, March 18, 1944

Leyna Künzel had spent the morning loading the wagon with twenty bales of hay and driving the horses to the Hahn farm on the southeast side of Eigeltingen, a small town not far from Engen. The barn on the Hahn farm had burned two weeks earlier. Because they were able to save the livestock, they now faced a feeding crisis and needed hay for the animals. Leyna had agreed to bring over a load of feed in exchange for some much-needed *Reichmarks*.

It was almost two o'clock in the afternoon when she was on her way home, but she was still carrying nearly half of the bales she had brought. *Herr* Hahn did not take the full load, and had paid her mostly in potatoes. She was still a little upset with *Herr* Hahn when her thoughts were interrupted by the sound of airplane engines. Leyna urged the horses on but watched the air war above. She couldn't tell which planes belonged to which side, but they all made a tremendous roar.

Leyna turned the horses west to go through Eigeltingen. As she rounded the corner by the inn, she heard a terrible explosion farther in the distance. Five minutes later, not far from the quarry, she saw a group of farmers with pitchforks in hand pushing an American airman toward the inn. She stared at the American.

She had seen her first American in an air raid shelter last fall in Frankfurt. She had been visiting her cousin when the sirens went off. She and her cousin took cover with the rest of the neighborhood, and as they descended into the lower part of the shelter, they passed by some German soldiers who were guarding an American prisoner. He had a bandage clear around his head, and his eyes were ringed by black and blue circles. The rumor in the shelter was that he had been shot down by a German fighter.

Leyna stared at him periodically during the raid, until the lights flickered and went out.

Hitler had spent a lot of time and effort to warn the German people about these American and British airmen who would swoop down on the Germans, killing innocent women and children. To the Germans, these evil men were known as *Terrorfliegers,* or terror flyers.

Leyna looked on. The farmers and the parade of curious townspeople were shouting at the American, spitting on him and cursing. The American was limping along, with blood streaming down his leg, trying to shield himself from the occasional blow. Leyna closed her eyes, pulled her scarf closer across her face, and looked up at the road ahead.

She was approaching a thick patch of forest. She was on the road to Engen now. Up ahead was a small clearing where the Dornsberg River cut through the heart of the forest. Long ago, someone had built a stone bridge over the river. As the wagon drew close to the bridge, Leyna slowed the horses. She glanced off to her right to look down at the river. There was snow on the ground, and the trees were still bare from winter. The cold and clear water was tripping over the smooth rocks in the riverbed.

Leyna's heart skipped a beat as her eyes caught a curious sight about a stone's throw distance downstream. There, caught fast in the trees, was a white blanket. No! It was a parachute!

Leyna slowed the horses to a complete stop, secured the reins to the wagon, and stood straight up. Her heart began to pound. As she looked closer, she could see the figure of a man caught up in the trees. He looked like a *Terrorflieger!*

Leyna glanced over her shoulder and then down the road to the west. She reached up and fastened her scarf around her face. Other than the wind blowing, it was strangely silent. As fast as her feet would take her, she jumped down from the wagon, over the bank by the stream, and into the snow. She hurried downstream along the east bank until she arrived at the spot where the man and the parachute were hanging.

Leyna looked up into the thicket of bare branches. There, a good arm's length above her, hung the *Terrorflieger,* suspended by his harness. He was staring down at her with frightened eyes, all tangled in the tree and badly wounded. His right leg was dangling at an unnatural angle, and he was missing his boots. They must have blown off on his way down.

"*O nein,*" she said.

Leyna looked back toward the road. There was no sign of anyone. She had no time to waste.

"I am here to help you," she said with conviction in German. "Do you speak German?"

To her surprise, he replied in German. "A little."

Leyna stepped from side to side, quickly surveying his situation in the trees.

"I must get you down before someone spots you or they will most likely kill you," she said hurriedly while fumbling for something in her pocket. As she pulled out a large pair of scissors, she heard the distinctive sound of a gun click that came from deeper in the woods, beyond the dangling American. Leyna froze. A moment later, she dropped the scissors into the snow and took a slow step backward. She was certain that the next sight she would see would be German soldiers.

Rand was quick to follow the bombardier into the forest. Lieutenant Owen was pleased to have the navigator by his side, but Rand was still in shock from all that had just happened and couldn't seem to get his bearings. At least they had landed in what looked like a rural area and, for the time being, were safely hidden in a forest. After no more than a minute's rest, the two fugitives took off in what Rand thought was a westerly direction.

Rand reached up and felt in his pocket for his survival pack. In the pack was a candy bar, a couple of cigarettes, a tiny compass, some Belgian money, and a small map of Europe. His escape photo, a picture of him in an ugly, charcoal gray suit and a stiff white shirt, suitable for use in a fake identification, was tucked securely in the folds of the map. He had hoped that he would never have occasion to use it.

Before too long, they began to emerge from the forest. Not far ahead, Frank spotted a fellow airman stranded in the trees. His back was turned to them. The two men slowed their pace and made their way cautiously toward the parachute in the trees. They were not sure if any Germans had found him yet, or if he was still alive.

In survival training, the instructors had told them all plainly that if they were to get shot down and were to survive, they should immediately surrender to anyone in uniform, even a postman. Not surprisingly, the German civilians, if they got to the airmen first, were known for executing their own form of justice on the *Terrorfliegers* who had inflicted pain and death on their friends and loved ones caught in the bomb sights.

As soon as Lieutenant Kellam and Lieutenant Owen got close enough to the waist gunner hanging in the trees, they saw a German boy in oversized trousers and a long coat, his face half covered by a scarf, running directly toward them. Rand and Lieutenant Owen retreated back into the forest. They were too late.

Rand looked over at Lieutenant Owen, who was leaning up against a tree and breathing heavily. He wasn't sure if they should stay and risk capture or go back the way they had just come. Rand looked down into the snow. Their footprints would betray them for sure.

Lieutenant Owen reached into his jacket and pulled out his handgun. The decision to stay had been made without any discussion. Rand drew in a deep breath. He was a little surprised that Frank was carrying a weapon, as very few airmen chose to, fearing that upon capture, the weapon might be turned on them.

He glanced at the German boy, who was now only a couple of yards away from where they were hiding. The boy reached into his pocket, and it looked as if he would pull out a weapon. Frank cocked his gun and pointed it directly at the boy.

Leyna stood as still as she could. She was surprised to see two more Americans emerging from the woods. One of them was pointing a gun at her. Leyna swallowed hard.

The injured American caught in the trees attempted to twist around to see why Leyna had backed away.

"Frank!" said the injured American hanging in the trees. "For heaven's sake, put the gun down. He's going to help us."

Leyna looked over at the two Americans who had come out of the woods. The American on her left was quite tall, with light brown hair, and had a wound on his head. He looked about the age of her brother. The American to her right was the oldest of the three and appeared distrustful of her. He was leaning on his left side against the tree, pointing the gun at her. Though they were probably trying to hide it, she recognized fear on the faces of all three men.

"How do you know he's going to help us?" asked the man with the gun, looking skeptically at her.

"Because he said so," replied the man in the tree.

Leyna waited, staring into the eyes of the man with the gun while she listened to the injured American in the tree speak words that she did not understand. Slowly, the man with the gun lowered his hand.

"He was going to cut me down," said the American in the tree. "Give him a boost up here."

The tall American stepped toward Leyna. Leyna took another step back. He bent over and handed her the scissors, and then he pointed up to the man hanging in the tree. The man with the gun limped toward her. In one swift motion, the two men lifted Leyna up.

The cords from his parachute were wrapped around the branches in a tangled mess. She worked quickly, sawing with her scissors on the cords that were holding the injured man prisoner. Soon, he dropped to the ground in a heap. Before they lowered her to the ground, she grabbed hold of as many of the upper lines of the parachute as she could. When she came down to the ground, she brought the chute down with her, along with a bunch of dead branches.

With skilled motion, Leyna severed the parachute lines from the tangled lines with her scissors. The injured man now lay groaning on the snow-covered ground. The other two men were looking at each other, not sure what the next step would be.

Leyna kept glancing toward the road. She was certain someone would come looking for these men, and when they did, she would be caught with them and most likely shot. Right then and there, she made up her mind.

"Quickly," she said. "We must go to my wagon."

The injured man tried to roll over while the other men exchanged words of confusion.

"Shh," said Leyna suddenly.

The men fell silent. Leyna shot a look of panic toward them. Through the cold winter air, she could hear the clear sound of a motorcycle in the distance. She looked down at the parachute in her hands.

"*Sich verstecken,*" she cried, and motioned for the two men standing to lie down next to the injured man. They moved quickly, once they understood what she was asking them to do. Leyna spread the parachute over them, kicked snow on top of the edges, and then grabbed a stack of dead branches that had come down with the parachute.

As quickly as she could, she ran back to the road and to her wagon. By the time she stepped over the bank and onto the road, a motorcycle with a sidecar, most likely from the field headquarters in Mühlhausen, had already pulled up and stopped next to her wagon. They were heading toward Eigeltingen.

Leyna clutched her pile of sticks and walked toward them, stopping to settle the horses. She was hoping to draw their attention away from the river. A young sergeant was driving the bike.

"Have you seen any *Terrorfliegers* or parachutes?" he shouted quite sternly and hurriedly over the noise of the motorcycle.

Leyna swallowed hard, hoping they could not hear her heart pounding. "Yes," she replied honestly, reaching up and pulling her scarf down, away from her mouth. "The people by Eigeltingen have caught a man," she said pointing east. "They are holding him with pitchforks."

"What are you doing with those sticks?" asked the sergeant next.

Leyna stared back at him, not knowing what to reply.

"Stop with your useless questions to the *Fräulein,* and drive on to Eigeltingen," commanded the older man in the side car.

Leyna caught a glimpse of the sergeant's suspicious look as he drove off. She took in two deep breaths and threw the sticks into the back of her wagon. Her hands were shaking now. She glanced down the river to the spot where the men were hiding. She had half a thought to leave them there. She knew deep down that she was asking for nothing but trouble if she were to help them.

With the motorcycle safely out of sight, Leyna wrapped the scarf back around her head and went swiftly to the men under the parachute. On her way, all she could think of were words she had heard her father say many years ago. She knew that if her father were there, he would do the same thing.

"Come quickly," she said, out of breath. "We must hurry." Leyna bent over and tried to help the injured man to his feet.

The tall *Terrorflieger* gathered up the parachute and hastily buried it. The husky, older man took hold of the injured man's other arm and, together, they helped him up. Before they could make any progress toward the wagon, the injured man went into a dead faint. Leyna struggled to keep him from falling.

From behind them, the tall airman came along, scooped the limp body of the injured man over his shoulder, and headed straight for the wagon. They made their way as quickly as they could over the bank and onto the road. With one big groan, the two men tossed their comrade into the wagon and, without any further delay, scrambled into the back.

Leyna hastily covered the men with the blanket she had used to wrap around her legs to keep warm and then arranged the remaining hay around them. She took her place back at the front of the wagon on the seat, untied the reins, and started the horses up slowly.

Once they had made it farther down the road, she breathed in deeply. So that was why *Herr* Hahn did not want all of her hay. The Lord knew she would need it on the way home to hide the men. Leyna tightened the scarf around her face. It was cold. *What have I done?* she thought.

On the slow journey home, she had plenty of time to think about what she had just done, where she would hide them, how she was going to feed them. She rocked herself gently on the wagon seat, mumbled to herself, and tried to calm her beating heart.

She knew that she had just committed treason, and she knew the penalty for treason in Hitler's Germany. She knew there would not be a sympathetic eye or ear for hundreds of miles around. Then she heard a still, small voice. "My grace is sufficient for thee." Just as quickly as it had come, it was gone.

They were soon at the crossroad. Leyna steered the horses on the road to Bittelbrunn. Not long after she had made the turn, an older man on a bicycle passed very close to Leyna's wagon with great speed, startling her. The man was wearing a green hat, steering with one hand, and carrying an old pistol, a Luger, in the other hand. Around the next bend, Leyna saw exactly why he had been in such a hurry.

Herr Gersten had captured a short American flyer and was walking him down the road toward Aach with his hands tied behind his back and a rope around his neck. A small parade of children was following, shouting in broken English, "For you the war is over." Women who had gathered around the flier were throwing rocks at him and hitting him with sticks.

Leyna glanced over her shoulder to be sure her cargo was still covered. Then she urged the horses on. In fifteen more minutes, she pulled the wagon down a short, tree-lined dirt road toward a dark brown barn that sat to the left of the driveway. Beyond the barn, among a grove of trees, stood an old, two-story farmhouse with a steep roof. When she got to the barn, Leyna hopped off the wagon, opened up the two doors, and then carefully guided the horses as they pulled the wagon inside. She looked both ways before she shut the doors tight and latched them closed.

She let out a short sigh and then returned to the wagon, pulling the scarf off her head. Her hair fell down past her shoulders. The three men under the hay and the blanket had not moved a muscle. She wondered if they were dead. They were so still.

"You are safe for the time being," she said in German as she removed the hay and pulled the blanket off of them. The injured man did not move. The tall American let himself down slowly over the side of the wagon. The other one sat on the edge and swung his feet over the side. Then they looked at her. This was the first time they really had a chance to see her face.

They saw now that she was not a German boy. She was a little on the petite side, with long, wavy, light brown hair, and she was wearing an old pair of overalls. Her eyes were clear blue and set right above high check bones. Her chin was nicely rounded, with a dimple in the middle; she had inherited that from her father. To the Americans, her face seemed kind and beautiful. Though she was older, she didn't look a day over sixteen.

Lieutenant Owen looked at Lieutenant Kellam. They were both thinking the same thing. She did not know that, hiding behind the scarf, the Americans had thought she was a boy.

Leyna turned away from their gaze and proceeded to unhitch the horses, leading them both back to the stalls. She put up the harnesses, and then she returned to the wagon. The two airmen were now peering out of the window by the barn door. Leyna climbed into the back of the wagon and gazed at the injured man, who had regained consciousness while being jostled in the wagon. He was looking quite pale.

"*Terrorflieger,*" she began tenderly, speaking to the injured man in German, "I will go into the house to get some bandages and medicines. I cannot let you into the house just yet because my mother is inside. Do you understand what I am saying?"

The injured man opened his eyes in pain.

"*Ja,*" he replied.

"Good," she said. She looked up at the other two men with her big, blue eyes, grabbed the parcel of potatoes from *Herr* Hahn, and then headed out the side door, closing it securely behind her.

"She called you a *Terrorflieger,*" said Lieutenant Owen, making his way to the side of the wagon after she had left. That was the only word he had understood. "That is not a good sign."

"Roy, how do you know German?" asked Rand, who was still looking out of the window for any sign of German soldiers.

Roy stirred a little but remained under the blanket on the wagon. "My grandmother was German," he said, with a hint of pain in his voice.

"What did she tell you?" asked Lieutenant Owen.

Sergeant Wheeler moved his head from side to side and took a shallow breath. "I don't know. Something about getting something, and her mother is in the house."

Lieutenant Owen shook his head and looked at Rand Kellam. "We don't even know where we are."

Rand took another wipe at his forehead. He was still bleeding, and the pain was only getting worse. "At least we are alive," he said softly. "I wonder if the rest made it down okay."

"Well, did you hear all of that commotion a ways down the road? That was Rolly being mobbed by those Krauts," said Lieutenant Owen. "I saw him through the crack in the wagon."

Rand shook his head. "Keep your voice down," he urged.

Suddenly, the side door opened, startling all three of them. Leyna had returned with a pitcher and a basket. She looked like an old farmer dressed in her brother's clothes, but now she had rolled up the sleeves of her red-checkered shirt and had pulled her long, wavy hair back into a ponytail. She set down the pitcher of water and her basket of bandages in the back of the wagon and then climbed up the spokes of the wheel and sat down beside the injured sergeant.

"*Terrorflieger*," she began again, but this time Sergeant Wheeler interrupted her. "It's Roy Wheeler, ma'am. *Meine Name ist Roy*," he said.

The German girl smiled shyly. "Roy," she said. "I am Leyna."

Roy turned his head to the side. "That is Lieutenant Rand Kellam," he said pointing to the tall airman with the injured eye who was standing by the window. "And this is Lieutenant Frank Owen."

Leyna nodded at both the men; then she turned her attention back to Roy. He had the face of a little boy, but his face was now contorted in pain. She tried to choose her German words carefully, since she did not know any English and because she did not know how much he really understood her.

"Roy, I'm going to try to straighten out your leg, but it is going to hurt. I have only worked on animals. I am not a nurse."

Roy nodded his approval, and she carefully took his leg in both hands. With a sudden motion, she twisted his leg back into line. Roy let out a good yell. Frank looked away. Rand came away from the window and tried to quiet Roy in vain. Leyna hopped out of the wagon and searched the barn for a piece of wood to make a splint for him.

She used her scissors to tear apart Roy's pant leg. Then she washed the wounds, applied a salve, and wrapped his leg up with cloth on the splint. She reached up and wiped his forehead with a wet cloth. He was sweating, and it was not warm in the barn at all.

He took a deeper breath than usual and began to cough. Leyna covered his mouth, but when she took away the cloth, it was full of blood. She looked up quickly at the other two men with concern in her eyes. She knew what this meant. Internal bleeding was not something she could put a bandage on. Leyna hesitated a moment, and then she felt around on his chest until he reacted in pain as she touched the right side of his rib cage. He had hit the edge of the airplane on his way out.

"There," she said at last, as she tried to sound positive. "You are all back together. After I fix up the other *Fliegers,* I will get you something to drink."

Leyna jumped down out of the wagon bed and motioned for the navigator to follow her. She took him over to the window, where she sat him down on a milking stool and examined his head in better light. She closed his eyelids, carefully washed out the wound over his left eyebrow, and wiped up the blood. Then she took a tweezers in her right hand and tilted his head slightly.

"*Es tut mir leid,*" she said softly. In the next moment, she yanked a piece of metal out of his forehead as quickly and directly as she could. Rand, who was more expecting her to put a bandage over the wound than cause him more pain, let out a quick yelp. Leyna covered the wound up by holding a cloth to his forehead.

"*Es tut mir leid,*" she said again.

Leyna set the tweezers down in Rand's hands. He picked up the chunk of metal and gazed at it with his right eye. Leyna removed the cloth from his forehead, applied some salve, pushed the skin together, and began to tape up his wound in a criss-crossed pattern.

"What does she keep saying?" shouted Rand to Roy.

"She's sorry," replied Roy weakly. "She's not a nurse. She has only worked on animals."

Frank Owen, who was still sitting on the side of the wagon with arms crossed a couple of feet away from them, let out a small laugh. "Then she'll do fine with us," he said.

Leyna looked up at the lieutenant, not sure what had just been said. When she had finished with Rand, she went over to Frank. He just shrugged.

"Do you speak any English?" he asked her as she walked up to him.

Leyna cocked her head at a funny angle. "What did he ask me?" she asked Roy, still keeping her eyes on Lieutenant Owen.

Roy did not answer.

"*Ich spreche kein Englisch,*" she replied, having recognized only the word *English* in his question. "*Ich spreche etwas Französisch.*"

Suddenly, Roy let out a faint laugh. "If you speak any French, you can try it on her," he said through a couple of groans.

Lieutenant Owen pointed to his right foot. Leyna stooped down and removed his boot. He winced. Even with the sock over his foot, she could see that it was swelling. It was most likely a sprain. She took a piece of cloth from her basket and tore it into four strips. Then she wrapped the strips around his ankle, tied them up in a brace, put his sock back on, and replaced his boot. She noticed that the sole of his boot was coming off.

Leyna set aside the basket with the bandages and walked slowly over to the window at the back of the barn, next to the empty pig-pen. She put her arm on the window ledge and looked up at the blue sky through the cobwebs that had collected on the window.

"Now what do I do with them, Lord?" she whispered. She had, all of a sudden, felt frightened. The gravity of her situation was sinking in. There she was, alone with three enemy soldiers, one of them terribly wounded. Leyna turned to the men, whose eyes were on her. She shook her head slowly and sighed. How was she going to tell them what she was thinking?

She walked over to the wagon and peered over the side. "I must go to *Frau* Huber's house to fit her for her new dress. She will be furious with me if I am not there by four. Do you understand what I am saying, *Terrorflieger?*"

"*Ja,*" replied Roy after a moment.

Leyna patted him on the arm and left the barn. Lieutenant Owen and Lieutenant Kellam quizzed the sergeant on what she had said. He told them he wasn't sure.

Lieutenant Owen hung his head. Rand Kellam went back

over to the window by the barn door and stared out. There was nothing like the feeling of evading capture, only to be cooped up in a smelly, cold barn, possibly for days or months, only to be found later and shot. Both lieutenants were thinking this, but neither said anything out loud.

After what seemed like a long time, Leyna returned with the bandage basket full of bread and cheese. She had refilled the pitcher with cold water from the well. She had also changed into a long, gray dress with buttons sewn down the entire length of the front and had pinned her hair up. She looked quite stunning.

She handed the basket to Lieutenant Owen and the pitcher of water to Lieutenant Kellam; then she put on her coat and folded up a long piece of cloth into the basket on the bike that was leaning against the south wall. She checked her pockets for her scissors, pins, and tape measure, and then she pulled the bike to the door.

"Where is she going?" asked Lieutenant Owen with a hint of frustration in his voice. "When will she be back?"

Leyna turned her head and brought her eyebrows together. She did not understand a word he had just spoken.

Roy tried to sit up in the wagon. He propped himself up on his elbow, and then he coughed.

"When come you again?" he asked in the best German he could muster.

"I'll be back by sunset," she replied. "Then I'll put my mother to bed and bring you into the house for the night. I am sorry that I cannot do more for you."

Roy nodded and slipped back down into the wagon.

"She'll be back when the sun goes down; then we can go into the house," he said to the men between breaths.

"Thank you!" said Lieutenant Kellam as he raised the pitcher to her.

Leyna smiled in return. She imagined that she knew what that meant. She buttoned her coat, put her scarf around her head, and pulled her bike onto the gravel outside of the barn.

Early Evening, March 18, 1944

On her way to *Frau* Huber's, the wind tugged at the scarf on her head. Leyna breathed in big gulps of cold air. She had somehow become numb to the world in the past couple of years, numb to the war and the darkness all around her, numb to her own feelings. She realized now that the events of the day had jolted her from the safety of her indifference. Now, for their sakes, she was going to have to wage her own private war.

Frau Huber lived on the outskirts of Engen. Her brother was the governor of Württemberg-Hohenzollern, and her husband was a representative for their district. Leyna had been sewing for the woman and her family for four years or so. She was a rather large woman, and the financial status of her husband allowed her the privilege of affording custom-made clothes.

Leyna drifted past the front gate of the Huber's house. She laid her bike against the fence on the side of the house, removed the half-finished dress and some sewing supplies from the basket, and walked around to the front door. She did not have a watch, but she knew by the shadows cast by the sun that she was late.

Frau Huber opened the door and greeted her coolly. "I was beginning to wonder if you had forgotten, child," she said with a scold in her voice as she beckoned Leyna to come in.

Leyna removed her scarf with her free hand. "I apologize, *Frau* Huber," began Leyna. "I had to go out to see *Herr* Hahn with a load of hay, and it took me longer than I thought. But I have brought your dress, and I think it is going to look lovely on you."

Leyna followed *Frau* Huber into the front room. *Frau* Huber turned and gave her a look out of the corner of her eye.

"I am counting on you to make me look good, Leyna," she said quite sternly.

Leyna tried to smile in return. *Frau* Huber was always overly serious about her appearance, and Leyna was sensitive to that. Leyna could never quite figure out how, especially in time of war, *Frau* Huber could get her hands on the nicest fabric and afford to pay a seamstress. Still, it did not matter to Leyna. She was the one who benefited from *Frau* Huber's vanity.

Leyna followed *Frau* Huber into the front room. It was there that Leyna saw *Frau* Lehmann sitting delicately on the red parlor couch, sipping a cup of tea and eating a pastry.

"*Frau* Lehmann," Leyna said with a nod in greeting.

"She is going to watch my fitting, Leyna, if you don't mind," said *Frau* Huber.

Leyna set the shell of the dress down on a chair and arranged her sewing supplies, along with the scissors and tape measure, on a nearby mahogany table. While she fitted the magistrate's wife, she and *Frau* Lehmann talked together as if Leyna were not even present. Their conversation was solely about the Americans who had been shot down and captured. Someone had told someone who had told them all about it. Leyna put her head down and tried to concentrate on her work.

"I have heard that there are several still missing," said *Frau* Lehmann in a dreadful tone. "You should keep your house locked at all times."

Leyna stifled a yelp as she poked herself with a pin and she looked at *Frau* Lehmann.

"I should see if someone can escort you home in safety, Ada," replied *Frau* Huber at this news. "We can't let you out on the streets with those types of animals loose amongst us."

Leyna worked her way around the hemline of *Frau* Huber's dress, and then she stood back a moment.

"It's simply lovely, Leyna," said *Frau* Lehmann with delight. "You will have time to do a dress for me before the dinner party?"

Leyna turned to *Frau* Lehmann. The last thing she had time to do was another dress.

"I can try to fit it in, *Frau* Lehmann," she said with a forced smile. "Are you serious?"

"Oh yes, my dear. You don't think I will let *Frau* Huber have the best dress for the evening?" she said in jest.

Leyna turned her eyes back to *Frau* Huber's dress. "I will do the hemming and take some tucks on this side," she said, thinking out loud, "and then I will attach the sleeves, and it should be ready for you to wear."

"I am not happy with the sleeves, Leyna. I would like them to be shorter," said *Frau* Huber, raising her chin a bit.

"Certainly," Leyna replied.

"Will you deliver the dress to me by next Wednesday? I would like to have it by then," said *Frau* Huber.

Leyna nodded affirmatively, even though this new request moved the deadline up a full week. She helped *Frau* Huber out of her dress, gathered her sewing supplies, and put on her coat and scarf. *Frau* Huber escorted her to the front door.

"Thank you," said *Frau* Huber as she opened the door with caution and peeked out. "I don't think it is very safe for you to be going all alone," she said under her breath.

Leyna stepped outside and turned to her with a smile. She pulled the scissors out of her pocket. "I always carry these, *Frau* Huber," she said. "And I am sure God will go with me."

Frau Huber crossed herself and wished Leyna a safe journey. Leyna was happy to finally be on her way home, though she was nearly frozen by the time she turned onto the dirt road leading up to her house. She was relieved to see nothing stirring around the farm, for she had pictured a swarm of German soldiers and a firing squad awaiting her.

After Leyna left on her bicycle, Lieutenant Kellam hopped up into the wagon to check on Roy. He helped Roy sit up enough to take a couple sips of water. Lieutenant Owen looked at the bread in the basket.

"I bet she's going to turn us in," he said despondently. "And the next thing we'll see is a squad of German soldiers."

Lieutenant Kellam wagged his head.

"I think if she were going to do that she wouldn't have bothered fixing us up."

"Do you reckon the food is poisoned?" asked Lieutenant Owen. He hadn't forgotten the briefing where they were told that if they were shot down, they should not accept any food because it might be poisoned.

"I'm willing to take a chance," said Rand. "I'm hungry."

Lieutenant Owen handed them both a piece of bread and some cheese and then watched Rand begin to eat. The three ate in silence until all of the food in the basket was gone. Lieutenant Owen hobbled over to the lookout window and leaned against a post. Rand helped Roy lay back down, where he seemed to be more comfortable, and covered him up with the blanket. Then he jumped down and walked around the barn. The equipment and the animals were all a very familiar sight to him. Under better circumstances, he would have thought he was back at home.

He surveyed the animals in the barn and picked up an item or two that he recognized from his grandfather's old shed, surprised that he recognized the implements.

"I need to sit down, Rand," said Lieutenant Owen wearily. "You want to watch for a while?"

Lieutenant Kellam put down the planer in his hand, navigated past the stalls, and took up watch at the window by the barn door. Lieutenant Owen made himself at home on a pile of hay, propping his leg up against the side of a stall and rubbing his ankle every now and then.

From the lookout window, Rand could see down the driveway, across the field in front of the barn, and over to the grove of trees by the side of the house. After several minutes of watching out the window and not seeing even a dog go by, Rand began to wonder why they were worried that someone was going to find them. It appeared that their rescuer had hid them well. Rand looked back at Roy, who was lying quite still in the wagon. Then he looked up at the opening to the hayloft.

Rand climbed the ladder to the loft and looked around. It was cold. Now that the excitement was over, he was beginning to feel the effects of his sudden impact with the ground. His shoulder and his left leg were feeling stiff and sore. He curled up on his right side on a pile of straw and tried to go to sleep.

Though his body was worn out from the events of the day, his mind was still running around like a dog chasing his tail. He had made a promise to God while he was still in the plane and tearing up their orders. He wondered now if he would have the chance to keep it.

He thought about the lead crew on their twenty-fifth and final mission. He had not seen them go down, though it seemed like an awful lot of ships were hit that afternoon. There were so many airplanes falling from the sky that he had quickly lost track of the others in their formation. He hoped that their lead was landing safely back at Wendling and celebrating. He could picture it all clearly in his mind.

For some reason, Rand had been at the hardstand when the crew of the *Sweet Eloise* had returned from its final mission the last day of February. Their aircraft was shot to pieces, and they had landed on three engines, but they had each earned their ticket back to the states. He remembered the celebration that ensued as the ten men emerged out of the bomb bay doors. There were handshakes and hugs. They were jumping up and down for joy, and someone had a bottle of whiskey.

In the middle of all the commotion, Rand had noticed the copilot on the tarmac toward the rear of the aircraft. The angle of the sun that afternoon hit the copilot directly in the face. Amid all of the noise and jubilance, there he was on one knee, with tears streaming down his cheeks, saying a prayer.

Rand had stopped his congratulations long enough to watch

the copilot rise to his feet with a smile on his face to join the celebration. Rand did not know the copilot was a man of faith. He had felt a twinge of guilt at seeing this display of gratitude. He recalled the story of the leper who returned to thank the Lord for healing him. One thing was for sure now: Rand would never get to celebrate the completion of his twenty-fifth mission.

Rand rolled over on his left side and let a couple of tears roll down onto the hay. Unlike his father, he did not function well with uncertainty, and now this was to be his life, his every moment. He was torn between wishing he had perished with the aircraft, wishing he had been captured, and glad that he was at least in hospitable hands. How would his parents feel when they got the telegram informing them that he was missing? What would Doris do?

Sunset, March 18, 1944

Leyna pulled up to the house on her bike and laid it down right outside the back door. She glanced quickly toward the barn, and then she decided to go inside with *Frau* Huber's dress right away. Her mother was sitting in the front room in her rocking chair, with a brown blanket over her legs, hunched over and staring at the floor.

"I just got back from *Frau* Huber's, Mother," started Leyna, a little out of breath, as she put her sewing supplies up on the shelf in the kitchen. "She said to give you her greetings."

"Did you, dear?" came a frail, high-pitched voice from the other room.

Leyna walked over to the door between the kitchen and the front room and put her hand up on the doorway.

"I am almost done with her new dress. I think she is pleased." Leyna took a closer look at her mother. She looked very pale.

"Can I get you a cup of coffee? I'm going to start some dinner now."

"That's fine, dear. I have a cup of coffee right here," said her mother in return.

Leyna squinted her eyes. There was no cup by her chair. She turned toward the kitchen to put on a pot of coffee. When she had filled the pot with water, she walked over by the window and pulled up the trap door. A rush of cold air hit her in the face. She reached down into the cooler box her father had made in the crawl space and grabbed a pile of potatoes and two half-rotten onions. The trap door shut with a thud.

"I took the hay over to *Herr* Hahn this afternoon, and he paid us. I'll have enough money to go to town this week," said Leyna as she was putting on her apron.

Her mother did not reply. Leyna walked over to the doorway

with a potato and a paring knife in hand. Her mother had drifted off to sleep again. Leyna sighed quietly. Her mother was looking so old and worn out. She wished that there were something she could do to make her more comfortable. Leyna turned back to the sink and flipped on the radio. The gentle and serene sound of the Leipzig orchestra playing Bach drifted from the speaker.

She peeled the potatoes in record time, and then she cut them up. She reached for the onions, diced them up, and tossed them into her black skillet with a slab of butter. She added a little flour, salt, and some vinegar. On top of the onions, she sprinkled the rest of the leftover bacon; then she added all of the potatoes. If she had had any sugar left, she would have added some of that too, but it had been a long time since they had seen any sugar.

Leyna washed her hands and dried them on her apron. She went out the back door and grabbed a couple pieces of wood for the stove, cradling them in her arms. What would she tell her mother about the men? Her mind was running up one wall and down the other, trying to figure out how to get them inside the house without upsetting her. She was certain that her mother would be frightened of them, even if she did not recognize them as Americans. Leyna's eyes lit up as she came to a consensus. She looked out toward the barn. It was getting dark outside.

In half an hour or so, she fed her mother some dinner, served her a cup of coffee and then helped her to bed. Her mother seemed very tired and more withdrawn than usual. Leyna kissed her lightly on the forehead and wished her a good night, but before she got to the door, she heard the usual question.

"Where is your father? Tell him that I want him to come in for the night."

"Yes, Mother," Leyna replied as she closed the shutters and the blinds on the bedroom windows.

Each household was required to abide by the blackout regulations that were strictly enforced, even out in the country. Leyna turned out the light and quietly shut the door to her mother's room.

She went quickly to her bedroom, pulled the mattress off of her bed, and dragged it to the attic door. With great effort, she pulled the mattress up the stairs and deposited it in the middle of the attic floor. She pulled the shutters closed and drew the blinds. *With the two beds already in the attic under the eaves and my mattress, at least this will be better than sleeping in the woods or in a prisoner-of-war camp,* she thought. She dashed to the back door, slid on her boots, and stepped outside.

By now, it was dark, and it was very cold. Leyna looked out toward the road. The Künzel farm was on a plot of land that was bordered on two sides by forest, on the north by the road to Bittelbrunn, and on the east by their fields. The nearest neighbors were half a mile to the west on the other side of the hill toward Engen. She picked up her bike and walked it toward the barn.

When she opened up the back door to the barn, she did not see or hear anything stirring. She flipped on the light switch. She found Lieutenant Owen on the other side of the wagon, sitting on the floor, looking pensive. She went to grab the pails to milk the cow, but they were not in their usual place in the water bath. When she made her way to the cow stall, she found that Lieutenant Kellam was finishing up milking the cow. She noticed that he was milking two udders with one hand. The other pail that was sitting beside him was already half full.

He said something to her. She tried to remember how to say thank you in English but said it in German instead.

She turned to feed the other animals, but when she got to the troughs, they were all busy eating already. She went back to Lieutenant Kellam. He looked up at her with his big eyes. She smiled a weary smile.

"They need water," he said.

Leyna hesitated a moment. "Ah, *Wasser,*" she said.

After she had drawn water for the animals, Leyna took one of the pails from Lieutenant Kellam and poured the contents into the milk can sitting in the water bath. Then she grabbed the other pail and motioned for him to follow her. She found Sergeant Wheeler in the same pitiful state as she had left him.

"Little *Terrorflieger*," she began. "It is time to go inside."

She helped him sit up. He began coughing up more blood. Leyna looked to the other two men in distress.

"*Herr* Wheeler," she began, swallowing hard. "You need a doctor. Do you understand me?"

"*Ja*," he replied.

"I think you would be better off in the hands of the German soldiers than here with me. I am afraid you will die if you stay here." Leyna hesitated. "I can take you into town. Surely they will bring you to a doctor."

"*Nein*," replied Roy emphatically.

It was by his determined response that Leyna knew that he understood her. "I don't want you to die like this when you could have help," she tried again.

"I want here to stay," he replied in German.

Leyna looked up at the two men, who were puzzled at their conversation; then she motioned to Lieutenant Owen to come and help. The two airmen lifted their comrade out of the wagon and followed Leyna quickly out the side door. It seemed like a long way to the house, even though it was not.

They all piled inside the back door, carrying mud from outside along with them. Leyna put the pail of milk aside and closed the back door. She motioned for the men to remain in the back room, then she stooped down and began to remove their boots from their feet. She took the socks off of the sergeant's feet. They were muddy and soggy. When they were all in their bare feet, she motioned for the men to follow her.

From the back room, Leyna led them left into a hallway and up four stairs. She opened up a narrow door to the left and climbed up a second set of stairs to the room in the attic. The stairs were narrow and steep, but the men pulled Roy up with only a little difficulty. Leyna flipped on the light switch.

They laid Roy on the mattress in the middle of the floor. He was coughing again. Leyna covered him with a blanket. At least it was warmer in the house than in the barn. Lieutenant Owen sat down on the edge of one of the other beds and put his fingers together on his hands. Leyna looked from one lieutenant to the other. No one knew quite what to do next.

"What did she say to you in the barn, Roy," asked Lieutenant Owen.

He waited quite a long time, and then he replied. "She, she said I was dying and asked me if I wanted to go to a doctor."

Lieutenant Owen looked over at Rand Kellam, who was standing by the German girl.

Rand looked down at the floor. This was one of those situations for which the military had not prepared him. Rand knew the state of affairs looked grim for Roy, but he wasn't ready to admit that Roy was on death's doorstep.

"Are you hungry?" she asked the sergeant.

"Not much," he replied with difficulty.

She looked at the other two men and motioned for them to follow her. When they had all reached the bottom of the attic stairs, she pointed at the door to her mother's room.

"*Meine Mutter schläft,*" she whispered and laid her head in her hands.

They both seemed to understand. She led them back to the kitchen and offered them a seat at the kitchen table. She quickly pulled the shutters on the kitchen window closed. After she had taken two plates and two glasses and set them on the table, she took the skillet from the stove and spooned a portion of potatoes onto each plate. She followed that up with a glass of fresh milk and a fork each.

Then she sat down, folded her hands, and bowed her head. She missed the look that was exchanged between the two American airmen as she began to pray. By the time she said "amen," they had both bowed their heads. As the two men dug into their food, Leyna got up and started a pan of broth for Roy. She thought that he might have an easier time eating the soup.

The two airmen exchanged a few words of conversation initially but then ate on in silence. Leyna switched the radio on again. At first, it was playing some violin music, but all of a sudden, a man's voice came over the speaker in a screaming tirade. Leyna abruptly turned it off. Both men looked up at her as silence filled the room. Leyna put two fingers to the top of her lip, just below her nose.

"*Herr* Adolph Hitler," she said, not hiding the disgust in her voice.

The two men looked at each other and then hung their heads. The whole situation somehow seemed like a bad dream, until the voice of the dictator woke them all up. They were really in Germany, and they were really in danger.

Leyna turned to stir the broth on the stove. It seemed to her that the Americans were not at all as bad as Hitler had made them out to be. She suddenly felt sorry for them. Though she was doing everything possible to help them, she could see the distress in their eyes. She wondered for a moment where they were from.

Leyna picked up the skillet from the stove and offered the men more potatoes. At her third offer, Lieutenant Owen picked his plate up again, eager for more. Lieutenant Kellam reached out with his hand and stopped her from putting more on his plate.

"Frank," he said, "I think she is waiting to eat until we are done."

Lieutenant Owen hesitated a moment and then took his plate back, smiled, and gestured that he was done. Leyna looked at Lieutenant Kellam and offered him some more. She did not know what he had just said to Lieutenant Owen. Rand declined more food with a brief shake of his head. Then, just as he had predicted, Leyna took out a plate for herself and finished up the small amount of potatoes that were left.

Lieutenant Owen got up and hobbled across the kitchen floor. He stopped in the doorway to the front room, next to where a picture of the Künzel family was hanging on the wall.

"Is this your father?" he asked Leyna.

Leyna looked up and guessed at his question.

"That is my family: my father; my brother, Stefan; my mother; my sister, Liese; and me."

The lieutenant took the picture down from the wall and brought it to the table. He pointed at her mother, and then he pointed toward the bedroom. Leyna nodded. Lieutenant Owen pointed at Liese. Leyna breathed in deeply and bit her lip. How would she communicate this to the Americans?

"She is in heaven," she said softly, pointing up.

Lieutenant Owen looked up. She was not in the attic. Lieutenant Kellam spoke up. "Heaven? She's dead?"

Leyna shrugged. "*Tot*," she said. "From Scarlet fever."

Lieutenant Owen moved on. He pointed to her brother, Stefan, next. Leyna sat back in her chair and frowned.

"He is in the German army," she said with a salute.

Lieutenant Owen seemed to understand. Lastly, he pointed to the man with the mustache.

"My father," she began. "He has disappeared. We do not know what has become of him. He is most likely dead." Leyna shrugged.

The two men looked puzzled.

"I'll never forget the day they took him away from us," she went on. "He was wearing his favorite blue coat and he told us not to fear. The Lord would be our shepherd." Leyna paused a moment. "I haven't seen him in four years."

There were little tears forming in her eyes now as she stared at his picture. When she looked up, both men looked away. Somehow, she thought they had understood her. At least they didn't ask any more questions.

Leyna cleared the plates, and then she disappeared with the big kettle that had been boiling on the stove. When she came back a few minutes later, she beckoned for the men to follow her. She took them to the room by the back door, pointed to the bathtub, and gestured for them to give her their clothes. This was perhaps the most surprising thing that she had done, and the two men did not know what to make of her request.

Leyna was quite insistent. She opened up a wardrobe door and pulled out two shirts and two pairs of overalls. She held the first pair up to Lieutenant Owen. They seemed to be the right size. The second pair was too short for Lieutenant Kellam. She pulled out the only other pair of pants in the wardrobe. They were still too short but longer than the others. She handed these clothes to the men and left them with a towel each and a small piece of a bar of soap, closing the door firmly behind her.

By the time the men emerged from cleaning up, Leyna had finished washing the dishes. She took their clothes from them; pulled up the rug by the back door; opened up a trap door; and tossed the clothes down into the hole, along with their boots and Sergeant Wheeler's muddy socks. After replacing the rug, she took a broom and swept the floor.

"She's a smart girl, Rand," said Lieutenant Owen, straightening out his trousers. "At least now we look more like civilians."

Leyna offered both of the men a pair of thick socks, and she took a pair up to Sergeant Wheeler. After Leyna had fed some broth to the sergeant, she set to work ripping out the hem on Lieutenant Kellam's pair of pants. She motioned for him to lie down on the bed, and propped his leg up over the bedpost. It was while she had the needle stuck in her teeth and as she was tying a knot that she heard a knock at the door downstairs.

It was not a soft knock, and it startled her. Since her father had been removed from the community, no one ever came by to visit. Leyna's eyes grew big. Everyone in the room froze. Leyna stuck the needle into the side of the mattress and, without a word, she moved toward the door and flipped the light out.

At the bottom of the stairs, she closed the attic door. She took in a deep breath, said a quick prayer, and went to the back door. Whoever was there was knocking more insistently now. She hoped that they would not wake her mother.

Leyna tried to steady her heart as she put her hand on the

doorknob. She took a quick look around. There was dirty bath water but no other sign of the men. She opened the door slowly.

"Good evening, *Herr* Captain," she said, greeting the German officer who stood before her in his smart, gray uniform. She tried to smile pleasantly, though he was not smiling. There were two soldiers flanking him. She recognized the officer. She had seen him often in town, and he was acquainted with her father. He was a solid man with broad shoulders and a handsome face.

Captain Metzger broke into a perfect smile at last.

"Good evening, *Fräulein* Künzel. I am here on a rather unpleasant task," he began in a medium tone but silky voice. "I don't know if you are aware, but we had some American invaders who were shot down in our quadrant today, and there are still three that are unaccounted for."

Leyna raised an eyebrow, pretending to be surprised. "*O nein!*" she said.

"In the interest of safety, we are doing a thorough search—house by house."

Leyna's heart stopped beating for a moment. She dug her tongue into her teeth. "*Herr* Captain," she began. "I saw two of those *Terrorfliegers* today."

Captain Metzger was immediately interested, and he leaned forward slightly. "Where?"

"Oh," she said continuing, "they had captured one in Eigeltingen and then the other one was just outside of Aach."

Captain Metzger's face fell a little. "We know about those. They have been secured, and tomorrow they will be on their way to Frankfurt for interrogation." The captain tucked his right hand behind his back. "Now, I am going to have my men search your barn, *Fräulein* Künzel."

Leyna nodded. "Please do. I would be quite uncomfortable if you didn't."

Captain Metzger searched her face. Leyna remained steady as the two soldiers turned around and made their way to the barn.

"Won't you step in out of the cold for a moment," she offered the officer as a courtesy.

Captain Metzger did not hesitate, but stepped inside the door and into the back room. He looked around the room until his eyes lit upon the dirty bathwater in the tub; then he looked back at Leyna.

"I haven't taken my bath yet, *Herr* Captain," she said. "My mother is in bed."

"How is your mother?" he asked mechanically.

"She is not doing well, *Herr* Captain," replied Leyna. "Most days, she does not even know where she is."

"I am sorry to hear about that. How is your health?" he asked, turning to her suddenly. "You are looking a little pale."

"I think it is just the cold weather, *Herr* Captain," she replied quickly.

The officer brought his eyes full circle around the room and then turned them to Leyna. He kept them on her for what seemed like an inappropriately long time.

"What were you doing in Eigeltingen?"

Leyna put her lips together for a moment. "I took some hay over to *Herr* Hahn this afternoon," she said without any emotion. "Did you know that their barn burned down?"

The captain did not respond, but kept his eyes on Leyna. Leyna steadied her heart. Below the officer's feet were the clothes and shoes of the Americans. Above his head in the attic was the enemy for whom he was searching. What irony that he was so close to his prey.

Suddenly, his men knocked on the door. The young man with the square face saluted his officer and then proceeded to report that they had found blood in the wagon in the barn, but there was no sign of the Americans.

Leyna's heart sunk. She looked Captain Metzger straight in the eyes. He wanted an explanation.

"Minka must have had her kittens," said Leyna with a shrug. "I don't know why, but she always has them in the wagon."

Captain Metzger brought his right hand to his chin, and then, to Leyna's relief, nodded at last, appearing quite satisfied with her explanation.

"Right," he said turning to his men. "Search the house."

Leyna drew in a quick breath as the two soldiers pushed past her. She had seen his offer to search the barn as a courtesy, but his command to search the house was a clear invasion. "Please, *Herr* Captain," she began with alarm. "Do not disturb my mother. She is asleep and she will be unbearably distressed if you wake her."

Captain Metzger looked at Leyna without pity. He was not moved by her plea. Leyna looked down at the floor as the grave reality that she was about to be caught helping the enemy began to settle in. She listened in agony to the sounds of the soldiers pouring over her house, waiting for the inevitable word that they had found the men. Suddenly, a high-pitched scream pierced the air.

Leyna shot past the Captain and ran to her mother's side. As she had feared, her mother was screaming in terror at the sight of the soldiers who had entered her room. Leyna ran to her side to calm her.

"I won't go! You can't take me away! I've done nothing wrong!" shouted her mother hysterically.

By this time, Captain Metzger was standing in the doorway of her mother's bedroom. Leyna slipped an angry look at the Captain.

"It's all right, Mother," said Leyna calmly. "They aren't going to take you anywhere."

As Leyna was holding her mother, trying to quiet her down, she heard one of the two soldiers speaking with the Captain.

Captain Metzger looked at Leyna with suspicion. "Why is the mattress missing from the other bedroom, *Fräulein?*"

"It is upstairs, in the attic," said Leyna without pause.

"And what is it doing up there?" asked the Captain as he narrowed his eyes.

"Where else would you store a mattress?" replied Leyna.

"Private?" called the Captain. "Have you searched the attic?"

The soldier shook his head.

"Then do so at once," barked Captain Metzger.

Leyna clung to her mother and closed her eyes as she heard the private going up the attic steps. She had not expected it to come to an end so soon. If only she had hidden them somewhere else. If only she had left them in the woods.

"Nothing up there, Captain, but her mattress," reported the private as he descended the attic stairs.

Leyna tried to hide the surprise that she felt as she looked at the disappointed Captain.

"Are you certain?"

"Yes, *Herr* Captain."

"Then we are finished here…for now," said the Captain smugly as he turned to leave.

Leyna left her mother and followed the men to the back door. She did not understand how the private could have overlooked the three men in the attic. She felt a little faint.

Before he stepped out into the night, Captain Metzger turned abruptly to Leyna. "You will phone me if you see or hear anything suspicious?"

"Of course," she replied automatically.

Captain Metzger lifted his hand and brushed her cheek with his glove.

"Good night, *Fräulein*," he said in an intimate tone.

Leyna dared not lean away.

"Good evening," she replied more formally.

The officer stepped outside, and he and his men marched back to their car.

Leyna shut the door, and then she leaned with her back against it. She closed her eyes and waited to hear the sound of the engine turning. Then she waited for the sound of them driving away. She finally peeked out the window. They were gone.

Leyna fell to her knees and bowed her head to the floor.

"Dear Lord," she whispered with trembling lips. "Please forgive me for bearing false witness about the cat. Why did you send the Americans to me? How can I keep them?"

All was still for a moment, and then she lifted her eyes. It was as if God had lifted her fear away. By some miracle, he must have hidden them, and they were all still safe.

Leyna glanced up the attic stairs as she went to tuck her mother back into bed. It was a good ten minutes before her mother was calm enough to lie back down. Leyna fought off the anger she felt at the Captain for upsetting her mother so. After reassuring her one last time, Leyna turned off the light and closed the bedroom door.

She went quickly up the attic stairs. When she turned the light on, she could hardly believe what she saw. Her mattress was propped up against the wall behind the door and there was no sign of the men anywhere. She stooped down to look under one of the beds but all she saw was a blanket.

"They are gone," she said clearing her throat. "You can come out now."

At first nothing in the room stirred, but then she heard a groan from the other side of the room. The blanket she had seen under the bed began to move.

"Who was it?" asked Roy weakly as he rolled out from under the bed.

"A German officer and two men," she said seriously. "They are looking for you."

Sergeant Wheeler translated for the other two who were scooting out from under the beds and brushing the dust off of their trousers. Lieutenant Owen threw his head back and let out a big sigh.

"They found your blood in the wagon," she continued. "I told them it was from the cat having her kittens."

Roy looked up at her and managed a smile.

"You're—" he began, but was interrupted by a cough. "You're wonderful," he said, looking straight into her eyes.

"I am just glad they didn't find you. They came very close," she returned.

"What was the screaming?" asked Lieutenant Kellam with concern.

Leyna waited for Roy's translation. "They frightened my mother," she replied, "but she is fine now." Leyna bit her lip and hoped that her mother wouldn't remember anything about it in the morning.

She waited for the sergeant to translate for the lieutenants, and then she motioned for Lieutenant Kellam to put his leg back up on the end of the bed and she resumed un-hemming his overalls. Leyna was eager to put what had just happened out of her mind. A wave of relief came over her and when it did, she could not seem to steady her hands or sew a straight line.

The clock on the wall in the kitchen read nine thirty by the time Leyna had wished them good night and began to mix up some bread for the morning. When she had finished mixing the dough and had put away the dishes from dinner, she went to the back room and emptied the bathwater out the back door. She pulled the rug away from the trap door and retrieved the airmen's clothes.

She knew very well that if she were caught with these items, they would all be in danger, but she could not bring herself to throw them into the stove. She ran her hands along the buttonholes. Then she sat down in the rocking chair in the kitchen and began to remove the insignias and the buttons from their uniforms. She threw the insignias into the fire in the stove. She removed their pockets and placed them aside. The buttons she planned to put on *Frau* Huber's new dress.

Sunday, March 19, 1944

By the time the sun was completely up, Leyna had already milked the cow, fed the animals, and collected four eggs from the chicken coop. She had also set the lieutenants' uniforms in a bath of black dye in the barn.

When she returned to the house, she found that her mother was up and dressed and was making a pot of coffee. Leyna took a long look out of the kitchen window to make sure no one was outside. She set the eggs in a bowl and kissed her mother on the cheek.

"Mother, I am going to fix breakfast, and then I will call the workers in and we will eat," said Leyna cheerfully as she paused to see how her mother would respond.

"Workers?" exclaimed her mother. "What workers?"

"The men who are here to help us on the farm."

Leyna's mother turned, made her way to the table, and sat down beside Leyna.

"Oh, yes. The workers," she said with a confused look on her face. "I did not remember that they were here. Your father will be very glad for the help."

Leyna sighed. She hoped that the presence of the men would not upset her mother, but she knew she was taking a chance. So far her mother had said nothing to her about the events of the previous evening, and she seemed undisturbed by it all. Leyna went to the stove and pulled a loaf of bread from the oven. After she had sliced some bacon and some cheese, she made her way up the attic stairs.

As soon as the men heard someone on the stairs, they got up from their beds. Lieutenant Kellam hit his head lightly on the roof as he got up. Sergeant Wheeler didn't stir.

"*Guten Morgen,*" said Leyna politely with a shy smile.

"*Guten Morgen,*" replied Lieutenant Kellam, rubbing his head.

Leyna was pleased with his greeting. "And how is our patient this morning?" Leyna knelt down next to the sergeant. He was pale and sweating heavily. She saw a trail of dried blood that ran down the side of his mouth. Leyna looked away for a moment and closed her eyes. Lieutenant Owen said something, but Leyna did not understand. She stood to her feet. Since the sergeant was not really conscious, she would have to try to explain her plan to the others without his help.

"*Meine Mutter,*" she began "*ist in der Küche.*" Leyna pointed downstairs.

Lieutenant Owen nodded his head, indicating he understood her.

"*Wir gehen nach unten.*" She motioned toward the stairs.

Lieutenant Owen nodded.

Leyna pointed at both of the lieutenants, and then she raised her finger to her lips to silence them. Then she shook her head.

"*Nein. Nicht ein Wort,*" she said.

Lieutenant Owen looked at Lieutenant Kellam. "I think she doesn't want us to speak. Maybe she told her mother we are deaf."

Lieutenant Kellam chuckled at the thought.

The lieutenants followed her timidly down the stairs and into the kitchen. First, they saw a gray-haired lady at the table, drinking a cup of coffee. She got up slowly when she saw the men and greeted them with a feeble smile. To Leyna's relief, they just smiled shyly at her and nodded.

"You do know, Mother, that they cannot speak," began Leyna, a little relieved. "But they will still be good workers." She reassured her mother with a pat on the arm.

"What do you mean, child?" asked her mother, perplexed.

"I mean that they cannot speak. If you try to talk with them, they cannot answer you."

Leyna searched her mother's face, hoping that she would just accept the nonsense she had just said without question.

"The poor dears," she finally replied. "There was a boy down the street from us who was deaf. He was a sweet boy. I always felt so sorry for him. He spent a lot of time in the woods, but he could never hear the birds chirping."

Leyna sighed. Sometimes her mother's memory was sharp and clear. The two Americans sat down at the table following her mother's example. Leyna put the bread, bacon, cheese, and coffee on the table. Her mother bowed her head and began to pray. During breakfast, the lieutenants were careful to maintain silence, even though her mother tried speaking to the men several times. They simply returned her questions with a polite look.

"Where do the men come from, Leyna?" asked her mother finally.

Leyna put her coffee cup down. "I'm not sure, Mother," she replied honestly.

"They look like they are from the north," said her mother. Then she went on to tell Leyna about some friends she had had in school who were from north of Hamburg. When her mother talked about old times, she got a certain young look in her eyes, but in the next sentence, her mother was back to her confused self.

Leyna offered their guests more bread and cheese. Her mother finished her cup of coffee.

"I think I will go back to bed," said her mother wearily.

"Are you not feeling well today, Mother?" asked Leyna.

"Not as good as yesterday," she replied.

"Do you want me to bring the radio in so you can listen to it?"

"That would be wonderful, dear," replied her mother as she rose from her chair.

Leyna unplugged the radio in the kitchen and followed her mother into her bedroom. She heard the lieutenants behind her as they climbed the steps to the attic. When she returned to the kitchen, she cleared the breakfast dishes.

She knew what her plans were for the day, but her concern now was what the men would do, cooped up in the attic. Perhaps they could occupy some of their time by playing a game. Leyna set off for the front room. It seemed like ages since she had sat down at a table to play a game.

With a box full of dominoes in hand, Leyna climbed the stairs to the attic. She handed the box to Lieutenant Kellam who was seated on the bed closest to the door. At first he just looked at the box, but then he opened the lid and dumped the dominoes onto the floor. A minute later he and Lieutenant Owen began a game.

Leyna checked on the sergeant; then she descended the stairs and closed the attic door. It was Sunday. She thought it was very important to go about her regular routine. Leyna grabbed her Bible, her coat, and her scarf, and headed outside.

The air was chilly, and her nose was frozen by the time she arrived in Engen. She parked her bicycle next to several others in the driveway at the Schaeffer's house. The warm smell of freshly baked bread welcomed her as she stepped inside. She found five other people already assembled in the Schaeffer's living room. After she greeted each one by name, she took a seat next to the window on the other side of the deacon, who led the Bible study that morning.

While they waited for two other ladies to arrive, the talk was mostly about the American planes that had been shot down the day before. Leyna crossed her legs and slid her Bible from one side of her lap to the other. She tried not to look anxious, but she found it impossible to concentrate on the Bible lesson that morning. Maybe she shouldn't have come. What if the captain showed up at her house again while she was gone? Leyna swallowed hard and flipped the pages in her Bible to the next passage.

When the service was finally over, they sang one last song. Leyna got up from her chair immediately to head home but was stopped by *Frau* Seiler, who asked her how her mother was faring. Leyna tried to forget the things that were haunting her mind for a few moments, but when she left the Schaeffer's house, she couldn't remember what she had told *Frau* Seiler.

Leyna returned to the farm just after noon. She went immediately to the back room and spent a little time searching for her father's razor. She had noticed the faces of the two men who were present at the church service that morning. The Americans would need to be clean-shaven so as not to raise suspicion if they were ever seen. She finally found her father's shaving instruments in the back of a cupboard in a box. She spent quite a while sharpening the blade, and then she summoned the lieutenants to the kitchen table.

There were a few awkward moments as she tried to explain to them what the items were and why she thought they should use them. Unbeknownst to her, the lieutenants knew what the items were, but neither of them had ever used a straight razor. Leyna finally figured out what their hesitation was. She examined the faces of both men from a distance, and then she took a towel and wrapped it around Lieutenant Kellam's neck and turned to mix up some foam. Rand started to protest. Lieutenant Owen chuckled.

"You're worse off than I am, Kellam," he said.

"That thing's sharp enough to slit my throat," returned Rand.

Leyna brought the foam, a brush, and an old mirror to the table, along with a pan of water. Lieutenant Kellam backed away from her. Leyna handed him the foam and the brush. Finally, he reluctantly smeared it on his face. Then she handed him the razor. Lieutenant Kellam took the razor but shook his head. Leyna smiled. She figured the Americans probably had some other mechanism for shaving by the way they were looking at the straight razor. Leyna held out her hand, asking for the razor back.

"I'll show you," she said. "It's not difficult."

Lieutenant Owen seemed amused by it all, but she could see that Lieutenant Kellam was not. At last, he reluctantly surrendered the razor to her.

She carefully tilted his head, and then she began giving instructions as she carefully shaved the left side of his face. The lieutenants understood nothing of what she said, but they watched as she skillfully gave him a shave. Her father had once injured his right arm in an accident, and Leyna had shaved him for three months while his arm healed. After she had finished Lieutenant Kellam successfully, she turned to Lieutenant Owen.

"Now it's your turn," said Rand.

After their shave, the men returned to their game of dominoes. Leyna spent the remainder of the day working on *Frau* Huber's dress. When dinner was done, Leyna re-dressed the sergeant's leg and the wound above Lieutenant Kellam's eye. Leyna was concerned but not entirely surprised that Sergeant Wheeler's condition had not improved. By sunset, he would not even drink water anymore.

After Leyna had found some appropriate shoes from her father and brother's wardrobes, and after dark, Lieutenant Kellam and Lieutenant Owen both accompanied Leyna to the barn. Lieutenant Kellam helped Leyna with the animals, milking the cow while she fed the animals and drew the water for them to drink. Lieutenant Owen hobbled back and forth across the floor, stretching his legs. They were both happy to be out of the house if only for a few minutes.

Leyna was relieved to sit down in the rocking chair that evening and read from her Bible. There had been no surprise visit from the German officer, and so far, she managed to put food on the table.

While she was reading, Lieutenant Kellam came into the kitchen, startling her.

"I'm sorry," he said sincerely when he noticed the look on her face.

Leyna breathed in deeply and tried to smile. He went to the pump at the sink and helped himself to a glass of water. Leyna turned back to her reading. Rand leaned against the kitchen cabinet and drank his glass half empty. He was pretty sure she was reading a Bible. Even though he was in a foreign land, he recognized the book in her lap. He made his way back up to the attic, wondering if she was a Christian.

Monday, March 20, 1944

Leyna was still fast asleep when Lieutenant Owen shook her awake. She was lying on the floor in her room, wrapped in two heavy blankets. She stared up at him groggily, not yet sure what was happening. The sun wasn't even up. There was only a faint ray of light coming through the window from outside. Lieutenant Owen beckoned urgently for her to follow him.

When they got up to the attic, she saw Lieutenant Kellam kneeling over Sergeant Wheeler. Leyna dropped to the floor on the other side of the mattress.

"He was calling for you," said Rand, looking at Leyna.

Leyna shook her head. She did not understand him.

"He's gone, Frank," said Rand a moment later, looking up at the bombardier.

Leyna touched him on the face and then looked up at the men. He was gone. Rand pulled the blanket over his head and turned away.

The first night they had spent in the attic, Rand lay awake, talking with Roy as he slipped in and out of reality. Though it was not Rand's habit to preach to anyone, he had felt the urgency to talk to the waist gunner about his soul. He had gently explained the simple message that he had heard all of his life.

He told Roy that Jesus died on the cross for the sins of every man and that it was possible by just believing and receiving his free gift of eternal life to settle his sin debt with God. He urged Roy to think about eternity, as it seemed nearer than they ever would have imagined only yesterday. Now Roy had stepped into eternity.

Leyna rose to her feet and walked over to the window. She pulled back the shade and stared out. The morning sky was splashed with pink, red, and yellow. *I hope he is with you, Lord,* she thought as a tear rolled down her cheek.

Leyna paced the floor in front of the window, wringing her hands, and then she stopped. Oh, how she wished she could communicate with the lieutenants. Now the only one who understood her was gone. What would they do with his body?

Leyna left the men upstairs, dressed, and went to milk the cow and to think. She set breakfast on the table for her mother and the Americans, and then she went to call the men downstairs. When she got to the top of the stairs in the attic, they were both standing at the window in a serious discussion. She looked down at Roy's body, and then she motioned for them to come downstairs.

No one ate much for breakfast. Afterward, both men went back upstairs. Her mother went to the front room, unaware of the miserable event that had taken place in her own home. Leyna grabbed her scarf and her coat and headed for the barn. She pulled her bicycle outside and rode down the driveway at a furious pace. As she got farther away from the house, the tears began to roll down her cheeks and into her scarf.

She did not know why, but she had liked Roy. Perhaps it was his little boy face. Perhaps she just imagined that he had a life that was precious to someone somewhere, and now it was gone.

She was greatly concerned. She knew that there was no way they could continue to live without a way to communicate with each other. The only thing that would come of it was frustration. She was also concerned because she and her mother had already been running low on food and supplies before the Americans had entered the equation. There was little chance that they would make it even another month on the food she had saved up. It was not even time to plant yet, and they wouldn't be getting any food out of a garden for months. Their only means of support, other than her occasional sewing project, had been her brother's army money that had suddenly stopped coming over a year ago.

Leyna rode straight for *Frau* Seiler's house in Engen. *Frau*

Seiler had mentioned something to Leyna the day before that Leyna had shrugged off. When she got to the outskirts of the town, Leyna noticed that the birds were singing sweetly, and the crisp air was beginning to calm her nerves. She set her bike against the brick wall in front of *Frau* Seiler's flower garden. She walked up the brick path to the front door, straightened her dress, and knocked lightly.

In a minute or so, a middle-aged woman with a kind face greeted Leyna and invited her inside.

"I'm sorry that I am here so early, *Frau* Seiler, but I have been thinking about what you said yesterday about my mother. She is quite alert this morning, and I thought that perhaps I might take you up on your offer to loan me some books for her to read."

Frau Seiler's face lit up with a smile. "Of course, Leyna. You may borrow all of the books you would like," she said, leading her into a room to the side of the house.

In the middle of the room, off of the main hallway, was a large, walnut desk. The desk was surrounded on three sides by several tall bookshelves. Leyna looked in wonder at all of the books.

"Heinrich collects these like they are candy. He can sit and read a book in a day. I like to take my time," she said with a good-natured chuckle. "Go ahead and look around. Take a few, and when you are done, you can return them and borrow some more."

"Thank you, *Frau* Seiler. I think that is such a good idea."

Frau Seiler excused herself, leaving Leyna plenty of time to peruse the collection. She felt a little guilty, as if she were only being half-honest with *Frau* Seiler. She knew that *Frau* Seiler had cousins who were in the United States. She used to talk about them all of the time and about corresponding with them. Leyna had seen a German-English dictionary in *Frau* Seiler's house less than a year ago. She searched the shelves for that book, picking up a book or two for her mother along the way.

She was making her way through the books rather quickly, not seeing the dictionary, and hoping she would not have to ask for it by name when she came to the last shelf. There, a particular book caught her attention. As she pulled it off of the shelf, she noticed that there were a couple of books stashed behind it. To her delight, one of the books was the German-English dictionary. Leyna sighed in relief. She placed the dictionary in the middle of the pile she had collected to borrow, and then she went to find *Frau* Seiler.

At first, she could not find her, but at last, Leyna found her in the kitchen.

"What did you choose for your mother?" asked *Frau* Seiler as she put a dishcloth down on the counter by the sink.

Leyna looked down at the pile of books she had cradled in her left arm and breathed in quickly. *Frau* Seiler was leaning close, wanting to take a look at the books. This was the last thing Leyna wanted.

Leyna handed her the thick book that was on top of the pile and shrugged. "Just a few very long books that I hope will keep her occupied," she responded at last.

"Mmm," said *Frau* Seiler, looking at the title of the first book. "And what else do you have there?"

Leyna hesitated just a moment, but it was long enough for *Herr* Seiler to interject.

"Where did you put my hat, Maria?" he asked as he rounded the corner from the hall into the kitchen. "Pardon me. I didn't know you had company."

Frau Seiler handed the thick book back to Leyna and stepped toward her husband, rolling her eyes. "Your hat is on the coat rack by the front door," she said a little impatiently. Then she let out a nervous laugh and turned back to Leyna. "This is what you have to look forward to some day, Leyna. These men can never seem to keep track of their things."

Leyna smiled and followed the Seilers out into the hall. Once *Frau* Seiler had located his hat for him, Leyna thanked *Frau* Seiler and left out the front door behind her husband.

Leyna was quite happy on her way home, with her basket

filled with books, especially the one book that she knew would help her wage her private war. She could hardly wait to show the lieutenants what she had borrowed.

Her excitement was tempered, however, as she got to the outskirts of town and noticed that someone in a car was following her at a distance. She pulled off to the side of the road, coasted to a stop, and put her feet on the ground. She was hoping that the car would pass her by and continue down the road. But, to her dismay, the car pulled over right in front of her and Captain Metzger got out. Leyna looked down at the stack of books in the basket hanging from her handlebars and swallowed hard.

"*Guten Morgen, Fräulein* Künzel," he said with a forced smile.

Leyna was so preoccupied trying to gather her thoughts that she did not even return the greeting.

Captain Metzger pulled his right arm behind his back and squinted into the morning sun. "You have been to Engen this morning?"

"Yes, sir," she replied.

Captain Metzger peered down into her basket.

"I have borrowed some books for my mother to read," she said, trying to steady her voice. "She was quite shaken by your visit on Saturday and I am hoping some reading will calm her nerves."

Captain Metzger shifted on his feet. "Yes, well, I am sorry for that, but it had to be done." He took in a big breath and then continued. "I happened to run into the sergeant who saw you by the Dornsberg River on Saturday. What were you doing in that area? Why were you collecting sticks?"

Leyna looked him straight in the eye. "I told you. I was delivering hay to *Herr* Hahn. Their barn burned."

"And the sticks?"

"If you hadn't noticed, our wood pile is getting quite low," she replied steadily.

Captain Metzger took a couple of steps to the side and then he returned to where he had been standing. He opened his mouth to say something, but then he closed it again. "Something is not right here. You were in the area where those men came down and three of them are still missing."

"Why do you think I have anything to do with this?" she asked suddenly.

"Someone is helping them!" The captain let out a sigh and looked away from her. "Forgive me for my frustration," he said softly. "We know that these enemy fugitives cannot survive on their own. We will find them." Then he turned his penetrating eyes to her. "In spite of what I might feel for you, I must carry out my duty. And therefore, I have to warn you. You have not seen the last of me."

Leyna was bewildered by his speech. She watched as he turned, went back to his car, got in, and drove off. She stood there a good minute before she put her foot back on the pedal and started on her way again. She was not sure whether he was frustrated because he could not find the men or whether he really thought she had anything to do with them. One thing he had succeeded in was rattling her, but she was determined not to let him know that. Now she was going to have to keep looking over her shoulder.

The first thing she did when she got home was to find her mother and hand her four books to read. Then she took the dictionary, looked up a couple of words, put the book under her arm, and climbed the steps to the attic. She found the two lieutenants lying on their beds, looking quite depressed.

"See what I have," she tried to say in English.

The two men sat up immediately and turned to her in surprise. Leyna smiled and held out the book for them to see. Lieutenant Owen stood up and took the dictionary from her hands.

"Paper and pencil?" he said eagerly. "Do you have a paper and pencil?"

Leyna shook her head, rather disappointed. She did not understand him. Rand snatched the dictionary from Lieutenant

Owen, paged through it, and then showed her *paper* and *pencil* in German.

Leyna smiled, turned quickly, and went downstairs. They had a lot of communicating to do, and although it would be slow with the dictionary method, Leyna was proud to have come up with a solution to a big problem.

When she returned with paper and pencil, the men began writing down questions with fury in broken German.

"Where are we?"

Leyna took the pencil back and drew them a map, showing Switzerland, Stuttgart, Engen, the Künzel farm, and last, but not least, Friedrichshafen. She knew now that they already knew where that town was. While she was in Engen, she had picked up a newspaper. On the front cover were pictures of the Saturday bombing. The headline read "10,000 Dead in Friedrichshafen." Leyna tossed the newspaper onto Lieutenant Owen's lap.

"Ten thousand dead," she said in German. Then she grabbed the dictionary to look up the word *dead* in English. All of Germany was furious. Both men looked away from Leyna in shame. Leyna laughed.

"There aren't ten thousand people in Friedrichshafen," she said in German. She tediously wrote the sentence in English. Lieutenant Kellam took an uncomfortable breath when he read it. Then Leyna wrote, "They lie." Lieutenant Owen relaxed a bit.

"What do we do with Roy?" was the next question.

Leyna responded by writing in broken English, "I think we have two options. I can take him closer to town and drop him by the road, where they will discover him. Second, we can bury him next to my grandfather up on the hill in the woods and pray that no one finds the new grave."

The two men discussed her ideas for a while, decided that the first option was too dangerous, and pointed to the second option.

"We can bury him tonight," she wrote.

The two men nodded.

"Will your mother tell the authorities?" was their next question.

Leyna moved her head from side to side. "My mother is not always sane," she wrote.

The two men looked at Leyna in shock.

"I told her you cannot speak. She accepted it."

"Where is your father?"

Leyna looked back at both men with curiosity. She had supposed that they had understood her the other day.

"He is in a concentration camp or he is dead."

"And your brother?"

"I believe he is dead also."

"Are we safe here?" came the next question.

Leyna nodded. "As safe as you can be in Germany."

"Is there any chance for us to get out?"

Leyna hesitated. This was a question that she had given thought to, but she always came up empty. She swallowed hard and took the dictionary back. After a long while, she handed them the paper with her response.

"I don't know of anyone to help you. I am working on your clothes in case you can escape. You would need passports and to know some German. I will write to my uncle in Zurich. By chance, he may know someone who can help."

Leyna watched their expressions as they read her note. To her surprise, they seemed satisfied reading it. She had expected the opposite. They must have seen her look of confusion.

"Please write your uncle," they responded. "We are thankful for your help."

Leyna looked up after reading the note. Her eyes were tearing. She was sure now that she had done the right thing on Saturday on the road to Engen. She took the dictionary back.

"It is not safe for you to be outside of the house except in darkness. There are no men your age left in this area. There are civilian patrols and eyes watching everywhere who will see you.

We have very little food and no sugar. I know you want that in your coffee."

Lieutenant Owen laughed as he read the last part of her note.

"The soldiers who came Saturday night, will they be back? Are they suspicious of you?"

Leyna took the pencil and paper. "They may come back."

"Why did they come?"

Leyna took the dictionary and the pencil back. "They were searching the whole area for you. Where do you come out of?"

Lieutenant Kellam looked at Lieutenant Owen. It had been drilled into them that if they were ever captured, according to the Geneva Convention, they were required to give only name, rank, and serial number. They were also cautioned that the Germans might use tricks to get other information out of them.

"I don't see the harm," said Rand to Frank Owen. "She has put her life on the line for us."

"Don't you think it would be better if she doesn't know anything about us, in case something happens?"

Leyna looked on with curiosity as they discussed her simple, innocent question. *Why don't they want to tell me where they are from?* she wondered.

"We don't want to tell you in case something happens," wrote Rand.

Leyna laughed nervously. "If they catch us, we will all be shot. Every night, I will burn our notes in the stove and pray to God that he will hide us."

Rand took the dictionary and the pencil. He drew a map of the United States and put a dot on Iowa. Frank Owen took the pencil and put an *x* on upstate New York.

Leyna took the pencil back. "Will you teach me English?"

"Yes," replied Rand out loud in English.

"Will you teach us German?" wrote Lieutenant Owen.

"Yes," replied Leyna in English.

They all laughed for a moment.

Having come to a better understanding of their situation, the men seemed to have lighter spirits. They left Roy's body in the attic and went downstairs with the box of dominoes in hand. Leyna set to work on dinner, and the men played dominoes in silence at the kitchen table.

After dark, once the cow was milked and Leyna's mom was tucked into bed, the lieutenants carried the sergeant's body, in the blankets Leyna had sewn together, out into the darkness of the night. Leyna carried two shovels and led the men up the hill behind the barn, through the trees and the snow, to a small clearing on the hillside.

Light from half a moon trickled through the branches as they set to work digging a grave next to the plot where Leyna's grandfather was buried. The ground was nearly frozen and hard. The digging was tedious and difficult, and soon both men had discarded their jackets. Leyna kept careful watch around the perimeter of the activity, hoping no one would come upon them. It was early morning before they had dug deep enough to bury the sergeant. In silence, they rolled his body into the grave. Leyna watched in tears as they piled the dirt on top.

It was too cold and too sad an occasion for any words. The weary funeral procession made its way down the hill in silence and was soon back in the house and fast asleep.

Wednesday, March 22, 1944

After the long night, no one was up early. It was well after eight o'clock before Leyna finished milking the cow. Her mother and both lieutenants were sitting in the kitchen, waiting for breakfast, when she came in from the barn.

She could see that her mother had begun to put breakfast on the table, but for some reason, her mother had gotten distracted and forgot what she was doing. Leyna made small talk with her mother while she boiled the eggs and finished fixing breakfast. Today, she would go into Engen with *Frau* Huber's new dress. After delivering the dress, she planned to go to the market. She was actually looking forward to the day.

When breakfast was all done, the two men went upstairs. Leyna followed them. She asked them on a piece of paper if they would move Sergeant Wheeler's mattress for her. Rand dragged the mattress down the stairs and back into her room for her. She took the linens off of the mattress to wash them. She was not sure how she was going to get the bloodstains out of the linens or the mattress.

After she had scrubbed the sheets as best she could and hung them in the back room to dry, Leyna sat down at the kitchen table with a pen and a piece of paper.

Dear Uncle Georg,

I hope that this letter finds you in good health. Mother and I are getting along as well as can be expected. Most days, Mother does not really know what is happening. She still asks for Father. We have not heard from Stefan in over a year. Thankfully, we have had food enough to make it through the winter. It will be time for planting soon.

I am writing because I need your help. You know how fond

I am of birds. The other day, I accidentally disturbed a nest of fliers by the barn. A couple of birds fell onto the ground. One of the birds died. The other birds need to get home, but I do not know how to accomplish this. I do not have any food to feed them. I don't know what kind of birds they are. I have never seen ones like these before around here. What should I do? I am thinking you will know. That is why I have written. If you can give me some advice, please write back soon.

Yours,

Leyna

Leyna read the letter back to herself, and then she folded it up. She was not sure if the authorities were reading mail that was going to Switzerland, but if they were, they would certainly know nothing from reading her letter.

She only hoped that her uncle would notice the oddities in her letter. She was not particularly fond of birds, and he knew that. She had never written such a strange letter to him before. She was hoping that if anyone would be able to read between the lines, he could. She slid the letter into an envelope and addressed it. After collecting *Frau* Huber's dress and her food stamps from a jar in the kitchen, Leyna headed out to the barn.

The day had started out sunny, but there were clouds gathering in the north. It was not quite cold enough for snow, but it looked as if it might rain a miserable, cold rain. Leyna glanced at the clouds as she brought her bicycle out of the barn. It did not make a difference to her. She had to go into Engen.

It was a chilly and windy journey into town. One thought kept her company all the way there. She kept hoping that she wouldn't run into Captain Metzger. The last thing she wanted was for him to see the buttons on the dress in her basket. Leyna went directly to *Frau* Huber's. *Frau* Huber invited her inside. She was especially chatty that morning. Each time Leyna would try to excuse herself, *Frau* Huber would say that Leyna should get going before the weather turned bad, and then she would go back to talking again.

It was a whole hour later before Leyna was headed for the center of town. Her next stop was to post the letter to Zurich. Tiny drops of rain began to fall as she made her way to the market. With her ration book, the little money she had from *Herr* Hahn and the small sum from *Frau* Huber, she purchased some much-needed staples and even spent a little too much on a pound of horsemeat.

On her way out of town, she turned onto Hegaustrasse and stopped at the bakery. A most delightful fragrance came wafting from the shop as she opened the front door. A short and somewhat round man stood up from behind the counter. He had a long, thin mustache that stretched out almost the entire length of his face.

"*Herr* Krueger," said Leyna with a smile. "How are you?"

"We are doing fine, Leyna. How is your mother?"

"She is no better," she responded. "How is *Frau* Krueger?"

"She has been, for this month, in Düsseldorf with her aunts. They are both terribly ill."

"I am sorry to hear that," replied Leyna.

"And Frieda is now at the hospital in Stuttgart."

Leyna smiled. "She always wanted to be a nurse, ever since we were little girls. Then who is helping you at the bakery?"

"There is only Klara and me. Klara is ten now," he said with a proud smile.

Leyna swung her head back and forth. "You must be beside yourself with work."

"It has been very hard with Frieda gone, and then my wife."

Leyna asked him for a dozen freshly baked rolls. While he was putting them into a paper sack, Leyna gained her courage. "If you need any help, *Herr* Krueger, I could try my hand at baking. You wouldn't have to pay me a thing, as long as you sent me home with some of this good bread," she said with a smile.

Herr Krueger smiled as he handed her purchase to her, and then his face turned serious.

"You should be careful what you offer, Leyna. I will think

about it. We are getting so many orders every day from the military headquarters in Mühlhausen. I cannot bake and deliver at the same time." *Herr* Krueger began to say something else but stopped abruptly as a couple of women came in the bakery door.

"*Heil* Hitler," he said in closing, and then he turned his attention to his other customers.

Leyna stepped out into the cold and dreary day. She pulled her coat up around her neck and drew her scarf around her head. So far she had not run into the Captain again and she was thankful for that. It was a long, wet ride back to the farm. By the time she got home, she was soaked.

Her mother met her at the back door. She had been worried that Leyna had gotten lost, and she complained that the men didn't seem to be doing much work. Leyna kissed her mother on the cheek.

"I got us some meat for dinner, Mother," she said, changing the subject.

"Good, dear," replied her mother, looking beyond Leyna toward the barn. "I do hope your father comes in before the weather turns bad. Did *Frau* Huber like her dress?"

"I think so," replied Leyna as she carried the food into the kitchen, marveling that her mother remembered where she had gone. "You know, it is not easy to please her." Then she chuckled to herself. *Frau* Huber would be horrified if she knew that the buttons on her new dress were taken from the uniform of an American airman.

"Do you know what has happened to the radio, dear?" asked her mother suddenly.

Leyna looked over at the radio. "What is wrong with it?"

"It doesn't work," stated her mother plainly.

Leyna shook her head and marched over to the radio. She flipped the switch, but nothing happened. She checked the cord to make sure it was plugged in. Leyna sighed. It would be a great loss to her not to have the radio. It was her contact with the outside world and her company when her mother was far away.

"Maybe he can fix it," said her mother, pointing to Lieutenant Owen.

Leyna turned her wet head and met the eyes of Lieutenant Owen. He was leaning against the kitchen door with his arms folded. He had been watching their whole conversation. He made his way slowly to the radio and unplugged it. He took it over to the kitchen table and motioned to Leyna for some tools.

It had been quite some time since she had used any of her father's tools, but she found his toolbox at last out in the barn. After she brought in the toolbox, she changed out of her soggy clothes and dried her hair with a towel.

By the time she had changed and returned to the kitchen, Lieutenant Owen had the radio plugged back in and working. He hobbled back upstairs before she could thank him.

Leyna's grandmother had passed down several recipes to her. As a little girl, Leyna had spent hours baking and cooking in the kitchen with her grandmother. Leyna had started one of her mother's favorite recipes the night before. Now she worked on finishing up the potato balls and plopped them in the water to boil as she pulled the horsemeat out of the oven. She dished up a bowlful of sour cream and put it on the table next to the horsemeat. Then she pulled the gravy off of the stove.

When they all sat down for dinner, Leyna's mother said a prayer, and then she looked up with confusion at Leyna. As the Americans were tasting the horsemeat and nearly spitting it out, Leyna's mother spoke up.

"Why are we serving such a nice, expensive meal to the workers, Leyna? They have hardly done any work all day."

Leyna looked at the men, whom she could tell by now were trying to politely eat what was set before them.

"Because we are celebrating, Mother," she replied cheerfully.

"What are we celebrating?" returned her mother, even more confused.

"It is your birthday," Leyna replied softly, and she got up and kissed her mother gently on the forehead. "Today, you are sixty years old."

Leyna's mother looked around the room and then got up and went to the window.

"What are you looking for, Mother?" asked Leyna as she went to look out the window to see what her mother was staring at. Leyna suddenly became concerned that perhaps someone was outside.

Leyna's mother returned to the table. "Aren't you going to set a place for your father and brother?" she asked. "I'm sure they will be in from the fields soon."

Leyna closed her eyes and swallowed hard, hesitated for only a moment, and then went to the cupboard for two more plates. She had learned over the last several months that it was much easier to go along with her mother's requests than to fight them.

The lieutenants looked at her nervously as she set two more places at the table and then went to the front room to find two more chairs. Her mother reached over and dished up a portion each for the missing men. Leyna tried to smile to reassure them as the lieutenants exchanged looks of distress.

When her mother had finished her potato dumpling, she got up out of her chair and wandered off to the front room. Leyna stood up and followed her to the door until she was sure she was safely in her chair, and then she returned to the table. She quickly took the two extra plates of food and dumped them onto the lieutenant's plates. In spite of the taste of the horsemeat, they ate up every last drop of food on their plates.

That evening, Leyna climbed down the three steps in the trap door in the kitchen floor to take better stock of what food she had left over from the canning she had done at the end of last summer. She sighed as she climbed back up to the kitchen. There wasn't much food left. They had a week more of food in the cellar box, maybe two if she could stretch it.

After her mother had gone to bed, she and the lieutenants wrote back and forth for a little while. They both told her they liked the potato dumplings. They did not comment on the horse-meat. Leyna already knew how they felt about that.

The lieutenants' uniforms were now black. Leyna had dried them out and, in the evenings, she worked on ripping out the collars and the hems. She planned to reshape the collars to make them look more like a German gentleman's coat. The men kept her company, playing dominoes while she worked.

Both of the lieutenants were getting tired of playing dominoes and being stuck in the little farmhouse, but neither complained. They carried on as if there were a rivalry between them, to see who could outlast the other. At night, when they could not sleep, they would talk about home, and then Rand would roll over toward the wall and close his eyes. There was an uncontrollable longing deep inside of him. He wanted to go home. Maybe he just wanted to set things straight. Maybe he just wanted to make a fresh start.

Monday, March 27, 1944

On a cloudy Monday afternoon, Leyna rode back from Engen after measuring *Frau* Lehmann for her new dress. In her coat pocket, she carried the return letter from her uncle. She had not opened it up in town because she did not want anyone to see her reaction. She hurried home as fast as she could, racing the wind. Soon, the weather would be warming up, the leaves would be growing on the trees, and the flowers would return. She was looking forward to spring. She was hoping it would somehow bring relief to her war-torn country.

Safe inside the kitchen, Leyna tore open the letter from her uncle. The lieutenants were at the kitchen table playing dominoes. She leaned on the wall by the kitchen window and read his letter by the light that the sun had left in the sky.

> Dearest Leyna,
>
> It was good to receive your letter and to hear from you. I hope you and your mother are doing well. Thankfully, I have been in good health and things in Switzerland are as good as can be expected. I will not bore you with the details of my day.
>
> Concerning your request for my help, I was wondering if you could give me some more specifics about the birds. What time of day was it when you disturbed their nest? Are they injured with a broken wing, or are they in good health? Can you distinguish any of their sounds? With the answers to these questions, I may be able to come up with a solution for you.
>
> Your Loving Uncle,
> Georg Hartmann

Leyna smiled broadly. He had understood her cryptic cry for help. He had asked her about the time of day because he wanted to know whether she was harboring Americans or British. She guessed that he also wanted to know if they had any injuries and if they spoke any German.

She turned around to the kitchen table, grabbed a piece of paper and a pen, and began to write.

> Dear Uncle Georg,
>
> I received your letter today as I went into Engen to visit *Frau* Lehmann. She is having me sew a dress for her also. Mother and I will be happy to have the few *Marks* she will pay me, as we are, along with everyone else, at the bottom of our barrel.
>
> I am grateful for any advice you can give me concerning the birds. I am very concerned for them, as they seem to be longing for home. It was afternoon when I disturbed their nest. Other than the fact that I have no food to feed them, they are in good health. I am also sorry to say that I do not understand any of their chirping, although they do not seem to be in any pain. I will do whatever you think is best, including releasing them, but their nest was completely destroyed.
>
> Yours,
>
> Leyna
>
> P.S. I am pretty sure that they are not Alpine swallows.

Leyna sealed up the letter in an envelope and grabbed the dictionary.

"I received a reply from my uncle. He asked me some questions that I have responded to. I am going to take my letter to town to post it."

The lieutenants, who seemed happy at the news, returned to their game. Leyna looked at the clock on the wall. If she hurried, she could get to the post office before it closed.

By the time she arrived at the post office, she was all out of breath. Two seconds after she opened the door to step inside she realized she had made a mistake. Directly in front of her stood Captain Metzger and one of his men. They were picking up a large sack of mail from the postman and making small talk with him.

Leyna stood as still and quiet as possible behind the men. She was hoping that when they turned to leave they wouldn't see her. She wondered for a moment if it would be safer for her to leave. She gripped the letter to her uncle and breathed in deeply. Their conversation with the postman was finished.

Leyna stepped forward as the captain turned with the sack of mail in his hand. She handed the letter to the postman without greeting him and then she held her breath. One second passed and then another. Then she heard the door to the post office close. Leyna breathed a silent sigh of relief and thanked the Lord for protecting her from another unpleasant encounter with the captain.

She paid the postmaster, and he put her letter on a pile to the left hand side of his counter. Leyna grabbed her bike and walked it most of the way to the edge of town. She was relieved to hear from her uncle and more relieved at the offer of help that she trusted would come from him. With Captain Metzger watching her, any help he could give would certainly not come too soon.

She already knew how her uncle felt about Adolph Hitler and the war. He had warned her father years ago about the mad-man. Leyna remembered how her father had resisted sending her and Stefan to the youth organizations. When it became harder, her father gave in, but not before sitting them both down and explaining what was going on. Leyna had not noticed then, but her father had some tough choices to make. How slowly the clouds of darkness had crept over Germany and then into their happy lives.

Leyna opened up the last jar of beets for dinner and set a small amount of cheese and bread on the table. Her mother ate very little. Leyna left the table still hungry. She would have to start praying for their daily bread now.

After the sun went down, Rand Kellam went out to milk the cow and to feed the animals without Leyna. Leyna had Lieutenant Owen standing up on a chair in the kitchen. She was working on raising the hem of his suit coat. After she had finished pinning the hem up, she went and got her gray dress with the buttons down the front. She was taking all of the buttons off of her dress when Lieutenant Kellam came in from outside with a pail of milk. Rand set the pail on the counter next to the sink. Then he watched her rip the rest of the buttons off of her dress. He guessed correctly that she was going to sew them onto their old uniforms.

Finally, Leyna motioned for him to get up on the chair, and then she helped him on with his coat. She tugged at the back seams. He had lost weight, and she would have to take a tuck in. She began pinning his hem up in the back. As she moved to his side, she looked up at his face. He was standing at attention on the chair, but was watching her out of the corner of his eye. He had a contemplative look in his eyes. She wondered what was going through his mind.

She looked over at Lieutenant Owen, who was sitting at the kitchen table, watching her work. She put in the last pin and stepped back to make sure she had the hem straight. Leyna smiled. She had taken their uniforms and nearly transformed them into suit coats. For their sake, she hoped no one would know the difference.

Lieutenant Owen took up the dictionary and started writing. He wanted to tell her that the coats looked great.

Saturday, April 1, 1944

The sun did not cut through the clouds on the first Saturday morning in April. The spirit inside the Künzel farmhouse was a little grim, perhaps due to the lack of sunshine. Leyna's mother was spending more and more of her days in bed, listening to the radio. This gave Leyna more time to practice German with the lieutenants and to learn a few words of English. Leyna could tell that their living situation was wearing on the men.

Later in the morning, the clouds began to break up, and the sun peaked through every now and then. Just after ten thirty, the lieutenants were sitting at the kitchen table playing dominoes. Leyna was sitting in the rocking chair, working on *Frau* Lehmann's new dress. Outside the farmhouse, a gradually rising humming sound began at a distance.

Lieutenant Owen looked at Lieutenant Kellam. All at once, and simultaneously, they left their game and ran to the kitchen window. In less than a minute, they began an excited conversation back and forth. Leyna set aside the dress and tried to get a glance out the window. Lieutenant Kellam turned to Leyna, forgetting which side of the war she was on.

"They're Liberators!" he exclaimed. "At least twelve of them."

Leyna looked at both men, who were gazing longingly upward. Suddenly, Lieutenant Owen made a move for the back door. Lieutenant Kellam reached out and grabbed him on the arm to stop him.

"Don't go out! You want someone to see you?"

Lieutenant Owen broke free but stopped short of the door to the back room, hung his head, and banged it several times against the door in frustration. Leyna looked out the window again and caught sight of one of the airplanes. She was not sure if it was a

German or an American plane, but she judged by the excitement of the lieutenants that the planes were American.

After the roar of the engines had subsided, Lieutenant Kellam sat back at the kitchen table but leaned his chair against the wall, looking quite defeated. Lieutenant Owen, who had recovered quite nicely from his sprained ankle, just paced back and forth on the kitchen floor.

Leyna looked from lieutenant to lieutenant. She did not understand war, but she had learned a lot about fighting men by watching the Americans. She had thought that they should be happy to sit the war out in a sleepy village in southern Germany, but she began to suspect that she had judged wrongly.

The day wore on, but the gloomy atmosphere never really subsided. Leyna made a thin soup for dinner, but no one ate much of it. Her mother retired to bed early that evening. After she had swept the kitchen floor, Leyna sat down in the rocking chair and opened her Bible. The lieutenants were at the kitchen table, playing dominoes and moping. Not a minute after she had opened her Bible, she heard a car coming up the driveway. It was not quite dark yet.

Leyna's heart stopped as she went to the window and saw who was coming. When she turned around, she met the questioning look of the lieutenants. Hastily, she opened the trap door by the cooler and motioned for the men to go in. In less than ten seconds, they had ducked into the crawl space. Leyna closed the door carefully. She stood up, straightened her dress, and then gathered the dominoes on the table, slid them into a bowl, and placed the bowl into the pantry. She tossed the dictionary and paper and pencil onto the top shelf, over the dishes. She took their scraps of paper containing their written conversations for the day, opened up the stove, and threw them inside. Then she waited for the knock.

Leyna tossed her hair back behind her shoulders and greeted Captain Metzger at the back door. He was immaculately dressed, as always, in his gray uniform, but this time he was alone. She looked down. His boots were polished to perfection. Leyna did not hesitate, but asked him to come in out of the cold. Instead of stopping in the back room, and to Leyna's horror, Captain Metzger proceeded into the kitchen. He removed his black leather gloves as he surveyed the kitchen. Then he turned to Leyna and smiled.

"Would it be too much trouble to ask for a cup of tea?"

Leyna hesitated only a moment.

"Of course not." She moved to the stove and took the kettle to the sink to fill it with water.

"I was just driving by and thought I would stop in for a little social visit," began the captain. There was a long pause. "Did you hear the bombers flying overhead this morning?"

Leyna turned her head away as she reached into the cupboard for the tea can. "Yes," she mumbled. "I—I did."

"Stupid Americans," replied the captain. Then he let out an evil laugh.

Leyna looked at him.

"They bombed Switzerland today!"

"*O nein!*" she replied.

"Yes, and that is how they expect to win the war?"

Leyna set out a cup for the tea, and as she did, she heard her mother's bedroom door open. It always made a distinctive groan when the door swung on its hinges. Leyna swallowed hard. Her mother soon appeared in the kitchen doorway.

"I thought I heard voices out here," said Leyna's mother. "Is that you, Hanke Metzger?"

The captain straightened up his shoulders and cleared his throat. "*Ja, Frau* Künzel. I hope that I am not interrupting your evening."

"Not at all, Hanke," replied her mother. "We have just finished our dinner. I believe the men are out in the barn right now, feeding the animals."

Leyna's heart stopped, and she suddenly turned to the stove to check on the water and to hide her pain. She closed her eyes and said a quick prayer that her mother would not say anything else.

The captain raised an eyebrow. "What men, *Frau* Künzel?"

Leyna held her breath and turned back to see her mother's reply and the captain's reaction.

"The men who are helping my husband with the harvest," she replied in a matter-of-fact way.

The captain glanced at Leyna, a bit confused. It was far from harvest time. Leyna shook her head back and forth slowly.

"The men my husband is teaching to farm," she went on. "They come from north of Hamburg. When we host the Olympics next year, they will not be able to come because they will be in Berlin competing in the races for Germany."

Leyna pressed her hands against the apron she was wearing, bit her tongue, and thanked the Lord for her mother's foggy memory. The captain still had a look of confusion on his face.

Leyna stepped forward and gently took her mother's arm.

"Would you like to go back to bed, Mother?"

"Not when we have company, dear," she replied rather soundly.

Leyna looked at the captain and then back at her mother. "Oh, I think the captain won't mind," she replied.

"Certainly not, *Frau* Künzel," responded the captain.

Her mother nodded, said goodnight, and began to turn around. Leyna walked with her to her room and tucked her back into bed. When Leyna returned to the kitchen, she pulled the kettle off of the stove and poured the captain a cup of tea.

"I am sorry, *Herr* Captain," began Leyna with a little wobble in her voice as she handed him the cup of tea. "Most days, my mother does not know what year we are living in."

The captain nodded his head. "I can see that plainly," he replied. "For a moment there, I thought that perhaps you ..." The captain stopped his sentence in midstream. Then he chuckled. He looked over at the Bible that was sitting in the rocking chair in the corner.

"Now, I have completely forgotten why I came by to see you," he said, turning his eyes to her in a longing way.

Leyna turned away for a moment. He always looked at her with such intensity. She could hardly stand it.

"Oh, yes," he said with a mischievous smile as he took a sip from the cup and stepped closer to where she was standing. "I have heard that you have been sewing for several of the ladies who will be attending the military dinner party in two weeks, and I thought you might be interested in attending the dinner yourself—perhaps as my guest?"

Leyna just stared at the captain, completely stunned by what he had just proposed. He was standing quite close to her now, cradling the cup of tea in both hands.

The captain raised an eyebrow and reached out and touched her on the arm. "Well?"

"I couldn't." She stumbled, looking away again. "I mean, I couldn't leave Mother here alone."

The captain was visibly displeased with her answer, but then his lips curved upward to form a confident smile. He took another sip of tea.

"So, you are living up to your reputation quite nicely, *Fräulein* Künzel," he said, stepping even closer to Leyna but looking out of the kitchen window. "Your dedication is both commendable and attractive at the same time." The captain paused, and then he cleared his throat and continued.

"Perhaps this time, I will let it slide by, *Liebchen*. But I hope you will think about it, as it is not in your best interest to turn me down." Captain Metzger turned his face directly next to Leyna's.

Leyna held her breath. Her mind was whirling. Had she understood what the captain was proposing? If she understood him correctly, she was in more trouble than she had ever thought. The last thing she needed was to attract the attention of a German officer.

At last, Captain Metzger set the cup down, slapped his leather gloves together into his left hand, turned on his feet, and paced toward the kitchen table with measured step. "Well, you will let me know when you change your mind, *Fräulein*?"

Leyna remained motionless in response to his question, unsure of what to say. Finally, after at least a minute had gone by in silence, the captain thanked her for the tea and bid her good night with a slight bow and click of his heels. Leyna followed him to the back door and shut it slowly behind him. Her heart was beating a mile a minute. She was sure that if the captain ever returned, it would be the death of her. She could feel the life draining from her head.

As soon as the captain's car was down the driveway, and as soon as she thought it was safe, Leyna opened up the trap door in the kitchen floor and let the men out of the hole. They proceeded cautiously to the kitchen table and asked for pencil and paper. Leyna took the dictionary down from the kitchen shelf and handed paper and a pencil to Lieutenant Owen.

"Who was that?" was their first question.

"Captain Metzger. He came on a social call."

The lieutenants looked at each other suspiciously. Leyna proceeded. "The Americans bombed Switzerland today," she wrote further.

Lieutenant Owen let out a curse. This news seemed to be the crown on a most miserable day. Lieutenant Owen picked up the pencil and wrote out a sentence for Leyna. Leyna stared in horror at the lieutenant's question. He had meant to ask her if the captain was her boyfriend, as they had watched the whole scene from between the boards in the floor, but he had mistakenly asked her if he was her lover.

"Please, sir," she replied softly in German, not bothering to write anything down. "Do not say such a thing."

Leyna placed the piece of paper back on the table and rose up wearily from her chair. Lieutenant Kellam caught her on the arm. Then he took the dictionary and wrote, "Are you all right?"

Leyna looked down into his concerned eyes. She nodded weakly and left for her room.

Rand waited until she had left the kitchen. "What did you

ask her?" asked Lieutenant Kellam, picking up the piece of paper and looking at his question.

Lieutenant Owen shrugged. "I just asked her if he was her boyfriend."

Lieutenant Kellam stared at the words in German, wondering why she seemed so disturbed by his question.

"That's the second time he has been here," he said to Lieutenant Owen. "Do you think we are in trouble?"

"There's no telling, Rand. But the way this day has gone, I would think he would have taken us outside and hung us if he knew we were here."

Rand rubbed the back of his neck with his hand. The strain of hiding was beginning to wear on him. He also saw it in Leyna's pale and weary face that evening. Something the German officer had said to her had frightened her. He knew her well enough by now to see that.

Wednesday, April 4, 1944

On a dreary April morning, Leyna made a trip into Engen. She returned to the farm without word from her uncle. She had hoped he would write back soon, but with the complexity of the situation, she knew that it might take time, if he were able to find her help at all. After she had stowed her bike in the barn, she went directly to her room and knelt down by her bed. She buried her head in her hands and began to pray.

On Sunday, Lieutenant Kellam had chopped the head off of one of the last of the chickens. They had eaten that chicken for three days. Her grandparents had made it through the Great War with four chickens and one cow. They were now down to three chickens and a cow. She knew she could not spare any more animals. Last night, they had finished her last jar of cabbage. She had nothing to serve them for dinner this evening. She didn't know what else to do, so she was on her knees.

The two lieutenants came down from the attic hungry, hoping there would be something on the table for dinner. When they found nothing on the table and did not see Leyna in the kitchen, Rand went to her bedroom. She had not completely shut her door, and Rand saw her through the crack in the door, on her knees.

Lieutenant Kellam turned respectfully back to the kitchen.

"She's on her knees again," he said quietly to Lieutenant Owen.

Lieutenant Owen shook his head. "I've never seen anyone so calm and confident as that girl," he mumbled.

They were not ignorant of the stresses she was under. They watched her mother, day in and day out, growing weaker and doing strange things. They knew—because Leyna had told them—that they were almost out of food. They knew, even if she did not tell them, that she was in danger every moment for harboring the enemy.

Rand peered out the kitchen window. He could hear his pastor reading from Isaiah: "In returning and rest shall ye be saved; in quietness and in confidence shall be your strength."

Rand closed his eyes and then took off with a start. "There's a car coming," he shouted. He and Lieutenant Owen dashed up the stairs to the attic, passing a dazed Leyna in the doorway of her bedroom on the way.

Leyna went quickly to the kitchen window and watched the car pull up in front of the barn. A short and round man exited the car with several items under his left arm. Leyna breathed a sigh of relief. She made her way quickly to the back door.

"*Herr* Krueger." She greeted the bakery owner before he had reached the back door. "What a pleasant surprise!"

Herr Krueger smiled broadly. "Good evening, Leyna. I am on my way to pick up Klara in Honstetten. She is at her cousin's house for a birthday, and I thought I would stop by with this bread left over from today."

Leyna could hardly believe her eyes as he handed her two loaves of bread and a couple of rolls.

The baker continued. "I have been thinking about your offer to help me, and I would like to ask if you could assist me first thing in the morning and stay until noon, perhaps six days a week. That would give me time to make the deliveries to the soldiers in Mühlhausen."

Leyna's mouth dropped open, and her lip began to quiver.

"I cannot pay you, but you are welcome to take home bread for your wages," he continued.

"What time shall I be there, *Herr* Krueger?" she asked, trying not to sound too desperate.

"Tomorrow morning at five," he replied.

"*Herr* Krueger, I will be there," she said with a smile as she grabbed his hand and shook it. "And thank you."

The baker wished her a good evening and then turned to leave. Leyna took the bread into the kitchen, bowed her head, and thanked the Lord for their daily bread. It was impossible, at this point, for her not to shed some tears, and once they started, they flowed freely down her cheeks. So great was her relief.

When she had wiped them all away with her apron, she sliced the bread and set the table with some butter and glasses full of milk. Then she went upstairs to call the men out of hiding.

The little miracle the Lord had sent that day was not lost on Rand Kellam. He had been watching Leyna carefully. He could count on her to read her Bible in the evenings, and he had seen her praying numerous times. He would always think of his mother when he saw her reading. His mother had the same kind and consistent character, steady in trouble and quick to help lift a burden.

And Doris? Rand thought of her less often now. He chalked it up to his captivity, but he couldn't see her face anymore when he closed his eyes.

Second Week of April 1944

By the next week, Leyna had already settled into a routine. She would leave the house at four thirty, before daybreak, and ride through the cool morning air to the bakery on Hegaustrasse. *Herr* Krueger put her right to work at the ovens. Every day was the same. After they had baked enough bread to fill the military base order, he would leave to make the delivery, and Leyna would tend the store.

Rand Kellam offered to milk the cow and feed the animals for her in the morning. He would get up and go out to the barn as Leyna was leaving. Lieutenant Owen confessed that he did not know anything about cows and asked to be excused from that duty. Because Leyna did not return to the farm until well after noon, and because they did not want to be seen by her mother, the lieutenants were basically confined to the attic or to the barn for most of the day. The best part of the day for them was when she came home with a basket of bread.

On one afternoon when she arrived home bringing bread into the kitchen, she found the trap door open and the legs of one of the lieutenants sticking out of the cooler. Leyna peered down curiously into the crawl space. The men were startled when they saw her. Lieutenant Kellam was down in the hole with a lantern from the barn. He handed a jar of honey, followed by a jar of tomatoes, to Lieutenant Owen, who was dangling down into the hole head first.

Leyna was surprised at their discovery. She had thought that all of the food was gone. When they came up from the crawl space, Lieutenant Kellam wrote on a piece of paper that he had bumped one of the jars the night they were hiding down there but that he hadn't remembered to look down there with a lantern until today. Leyna took the jar of honey and boiled it on the stove. She was going to use some of it for a bread pudding for supper.

Leyna took a letter from her pocket and set it down on the table between the men. Lieutenant Kellam picked up the envelope. It was from Georg Hartmann, Neumarkt 24, Zurich, Switzerland. Leyna took the pencil, a piece of paper, and the dictionary, and sat down to write the lieutenants an explanation of the letter. Rand pulled the letter out of the envelope and looked at the handwriting. It was written in old, German script.

My dear Leyna,

I hope this letter finds you well. Please give my greetings to your mother. I am sorry it has taken so long to respond to you. I am glad for your patience.

Concerning the Alpine swallows, I understand that this whole incident has caused you grief. To soothe your conscience, I would suggest that you should go to the *Minster* in Ulm next Friday, as you usually do. Take your father's Bible with you, and give your confession to the priest there, who will claim your father's favorite scripture. Do not be afraid to purge your conscience and tell him all. Perhaps then God will forgive this error to his little creatures.

Your affectionate uncle,
Georg Hartmann

Lieutenant Kellam sat down next to Lieutenant Owen to read Leyna's explanation of the letter. Leyna watched their faces closely. It was not always easy communicating with them using the dictionary. There were often tenses out of place and differences in translation, but it had been a better system than nothing. Leyna picked up her cup of coffee and took a sip.

She found it very curious that her uncle would recommend to her that she should go to confession, knowing that she had never been to confession in her life. She wondered how she would meet up with the man who would claim her father's favorite verse, and she wondered if she really could trust this man to help get the men back into Allied territory.

She spent the next couple of days trying to come up with a good reason to tell *Herr* Krueger why she would be going to Ulm on Friday. In the end, she decided not to lie but confidently told him that she had to take the train into Ulm and would not be able to work that day. To her surprise, he did not question her. Now all she had to do was find the money for the train trip.

One evening, as the lieutenants were engrossed in yet another game of dominoes, Leyna finished drying the dishes from supper. She put away the last cup, put down the dishcloth, and reached up for the jar on the top shelf.

She had always kept whatever money they had in the jar. She removed the lid slowly, knowing full well that there were only coins in the bottom. She peered hopefully into the jar. Then she caught the eye of Lieutenant Kellam. He looked away quickly and set a domino down on the table in front of Lieutenant Owen. Leyna set the lid back on the jar and replaced it on the shelf. She looked down at the floor as a look of despair crept over her face.

"Lord," she whispered quietly, "if you want me to go, you will have to make a way. I do not have the means."

By Thursday morning, Leyna was starting to doubt that she would be able to make the trip to Ulm at all. The sun was just beginning to rise as she rode into Engen that morning. Hohen-hewen Mountain looked as if it were on fire from the rays of the morning light. Leyna glanced up at the clock in the tower of St. Mary's Ascension as she passed by. She was one minute late.

Herr Krueger was not in the back of the bakery when she arrived. Leyna struggled to tie on her apron, and then she hurried to start the dough for the rye rolls. At a quarter past seven, *Herr* Krueger arrived with an armload of eggs and flour. She had been busy baking for two hours. He did a thorough inspection and inventory of the work in progress, and then he asked Leyna into the front of the store.

The baker went directly to where his coat was hanging on a hook behind the counter. Leyna followed him. She watched as he removed a small, white envelope from the inside pocket of his coat. Then he turned to her with a look of satisfaction.

"Leyna, you have been ... I cannot tell you ... such a wonderful help to me, and all without monetary compensation." *Herr* Krueger glanced down at the floor for a brief moment and then continued. "I feel it is only right to give you a small token of my appreciation. I may not be able to do this in the future, so I thought I should do so now." The baker extended his hand and the envelope to Leyna.

Leyna brushed her flour-covered hands on her apron and reached for the envelope in surprise.

"I ... thank you, sir!" she said as her voice quivered a bit.

"Now, we must get back to work, my good helper," said *Herr* Krueger awkwardly as he straightened the row of freshly baked bread on the counter.

Leyna turned toward the door to the back of the bakery and tucked the white envelope into her skirt pocket. She didn't even have time to peek in the envelope, but she was sure that this was manna from heaven, and she had no doubt that there was enough money in there for a train ticket to Ulm. Leyna breathed a sigh of relief and thanked the Lord. *This must be how the widow of Zarephath felt every time the Lord multiplied her oil,* thought Leyna.

Friday, April 21, 1944

The day for her trip to Ulm finally arrived. Leyna left the farmhouse in a rush, with her father's Bible in the basket on the front of her bike and her manna-from-heaven money in her coat pocket. The lieutenants seemed to be anxious for her.

At the train station, Leyna purchased her ticket and then boarded the train to Ulm. With the rush and anxiety of that part of the trip behind her, she settled down on the train next to an older woman who had propped her cane between the seat and the window. She was on her way to visit her sister in Ulm.

She was a small lady with white hair and round, gray eyes that were framed by delicate wrinkles when she smiled. The woman must have been quite lonely because she kept up a conversation with Leyna nearly the entire trip to Ulm. Leyna was thankful for the good companionship of this woman. Their conversation helped keep her mind off of the task for the day. The train moved slowly through the countryside, stopping every ten minutes for some unknown reason. The elderly woman seemed to blame it on the war, though she would not directly say so.

By eleven o'clock, the train was finally pulling into the main station in Ulm. The elderly woman was struggling to get her luggage down from the rack overhead. Leyna stood up, laid her father's Bible in a seat, and helped the lady with her suitcase. The older woman was shorter than Leyna, and her shoulders were hunched over from hard labor. She had worked all her life as a cook.

"May I carry this off of the train for you?" offered Leyna.

"That would be so kind of you, Leah," returned the older woman.

Leyna looked down at the woman's bowed and crippled hands. Leyna started to follow the lady down the aisle to exit the train. She had taken ten steps forward when she suddenly stopped and turned. She had left her father's Bible.

With her cherished possession now safely in arm and the woman's suitcase in hand, Leyna stepped off of the train and onto the platform. She looked up. The sun was trying to peek through the clouds.

"My sister lives five blocks from here, up by the minster," said the older woman to Leyna as she was getting a handkerchief out of her purse.

Leyna stood on the platform next to the lady. A slight breeze was blowing in from the north.

"I'm going that direction, ma'am," said Leyna. "Would you mind if I accompanied you?"

"Not at all," said the woman, drawing out each of her words.

With that settled, Leyna patiently walked beside the woman as she toddled along with her cane. Leyna felt a certain comfort in having a traveling companion. They waited in line as the soldiers checked the papers of each passenger, then they made their way out of the train station toward the street. Leyna was feeling a little nervous by now, imagining suspicious looks in the face of each person who passed by.

As they emerged from the train station, Leyna could see the tall spire of the church in the distance to the east. She had never been to Ulm, but she had heard that the cathedral was large and beautiful. She did not expect the sight before her eyes. The church tower rose all the way up to the clouds.

She followed the older woman for several blocks, and then the woman paused outside of an old apartment building and reached for her suitcase.

"You are so kind to help me with my luggage all this way, Leah," said the older woman, calling her by the wrong name again. "I wish you a pleasant stay in Ulm. Where did you say you are going?"

Leyna glanced down the street ahead of them. She was looking for the imposing spire of the Ulmer *Minster*. "To confession," she replied.

The lady nodded and hobbled her way into the building with her suitcase. Leyna turned and headed toward the end of the block. There was the Ulmer *Minster* and the Münsterplatz.

Leyna paused outside of the church before she went inside. There were a few people coming and going from the cathedral. She was struck by a rush of cold air as she stepped inside. On the main portal, she gazed at the work of art titled *Man of Sorrows*. Leyna walked up the center aisle, staring at the magnificent choir stalls and the light as it came through the stained glass windows. Two women in front of the altar were lighting candles. Every small sound echoed coldly off the walls.

Leyna looked over to the left. On the side were the confession booths. She turned into a pew on the left and sat down, putting the Bible on her lap. She swallowed hard. The confession booths looked empty. She did not know what to do next. Her heart began to grow faint. What was she doing there? She closed her eyes and began to hum a hymn.

When she opened her eyes, she smiled. If she had come all this way, at least she could pray. She bowed her head and asked God to help her. Her uncle had said to make her confession to the priest, who would claim her father's favorite verse. Leyna's eyes shot open. She turned in her father's Bible to Psalm 91. In the margin were copious notes her father had made over time. There were other such notes all over his Bible. Leyna smiled. She was thankful for the assurance that, no matter what happened, she would see her father again.

Out of the corner of her eye, Leyna saw a figure move into the pew in front of her and sit down. The man was wearing a black robe with a white collar. He was facing forward, but Leyna could see from the side that he was wearing glasses. He bowed his head as in prayer, and then he looked from side to side. Leyna closed her father's Bible. The man turned his head around slowly, glanced at the Bible in her lap, and smiled at Leyna. He drew in a breath, and then he whispered to her.

"Is that your Bible?" he asked without expression.

Leyna looked up in surprise. She gulped. "No. It is my father's," she whispered back.

The man turned his face forward for a second. He was a younger man, perhaps twenty years older than Leyna, but his hair was thinning on the top.

"Do you read it often?" he asked, turning his head again to her.

"Yes, I do," she replied.

"Do you like the book of Psalms?" he asked.

"Yes," she replied slowly as her heart began to pound.

"I would have to say my favorite is Psalm chapter 91. 'He that dwelleth in the secret place of the Most High shall abide under the shadow of the Almighty.'"

Leyna ran her hand across the cover of her father's Bible. He had just quoted her father's favorite verse. This must be the man about whom her uncle had written. She leaned forward slowly. "I have a confession to make," she whispered, her voice trembling a bit, "but I do not know how to do it."

The man glanced carefully around and then looked Leyna straight in the eyes. "I am here to take your confession, my child," he said, "but I do not think it is safe to talk in the booths. Wait here for five minutes, go light a candle, and then follow me up to the top of the tower."

The man in the black robe rose to his feet as soon as the last word had left his mouth, made his way to the center aisle, and then started for the back of the church without giving Leyna time to respond.

Since she did not have a watch, she guessed at the time and timidly made her way up the center aisle to the candles. After she had lit a candle, she wandered around until she found the doorway where she had seen the priest go as he left. She followed the hallway around until she came to the stairs for the tower.

The stairs went up and up and seemed to never end. After she had climbed over seven hundred sixty of them, she came out at the top of the Ulmer *Minster*. There, in a corner, stood the priest, gazing out at the fog and the clouds that hindered the breathtaking view of southern Germany. He turned around as he heard her steps.

"I am sorry to take you on such an arduous journey, but we cannot be too careful."

Leyna only nodded, as she was too out of breath to speak.

"On a clear day, one can see the Zugspitze," said the priest, pointing out into the clouds. Then he turned to Leyna. "I am confident we can speak freely here, but should anyone else come up, please do speak with me about the weather and tell me about your grandmother."

Leyna nodded her understanding.

"How many do you have?" he asked going directly to the point.

Leyna stared at him. She had gone to all of the trouble through her uncle to ask for help. She had sheltered them and fed them. She had used her hard-earned money to come all the way to Ulm, but she did not expect such a lump in her throat. She did not expect such a fierce hesitancy, such resistance to reveal her secret. She was afraid that she could not trust him, even though he was a priest. He must have sensed her uneasiness.

"You can trust me, *Fräulein*. I am here to hear your confession," he said gently. The wind was blowing his hair around the top of his head.

Leyna brushed her hair away from her eyes. "I have two," she finally said, looking up into his eyes.

"English or American?"

"American," she responded.

"They are in good health? No broken bones?"

Leyna nodded.

"Do they speak German?"

"No."

"What are their ranks?"

Leyna looked out at the clouds as a bird flew by. "They are both lieutenants, I think."

"Hmm. Officers," said the priest. He rubbed his hands together and turned around for a minute. "I don't know. I just don't know," he mumbled to himself.

"Is there any possibility to get them out?" she asked after a minute of silence.

The priest turned to her and sighed. "This would be a difficult feat, I fear. Not impossible, but difficult. It will take us some time to plan, but the sooner we can get them out the better. They are in a safe place now?"

"Yes," replied Leyna. "They are with me."

"Does anyone but you know about them?"

"Just my mother."

The priest drew his hair back from his forehead with his hands. He walked over to the door by the stairs and looked down nervously. Then he turned his eyes back to Leyna as if he were summing her up.

"You must go see the old man, with the cane, who sells fish in Singen at the market *am Schlossgarten*," he said at last.

Leyna stared back at the priest. "The market in Singen *am Schlossgarten?*"

"Yes. He should be there every week on Monday and Tuesday, beginning in May. If it is possible, he may be able to help you."

Leyna tried desperately not to look disappointed at what the priest had just said.

"This is going to take more effort than you thought?" asked the priest with a sympathetic look.

Leyna nodded.

"You must have patience, my child, and be brave," he said with a look of deadly seriousness. "Take an empty envelope with your address written on it. Tell the old man you want to purchase some eel and then give him the envelope. He will tell you what to do."

Leyna nodded slowly.

"Give me a ten-minute start, and then you can go," said the priest as he turned toward the stairs.

Leyna reached out and caught him on the arm. "Aren't you forgetting something?" she asked with a twinkle in her eye.

At first he looked confused, and then he smiled.

"It is not that I need the blessing, sir. My sins are forgiven. I have settled my account with God, but I thought we should make this meeting official."

A slight smile lit the corner of the priest's lips, and then he crossed her in a most ceremonial way. "God bless you, my child, and may he give you courage and protection and light for your pathway." With that, he turned toward the stairs.

"Thank you," she called after him.

He waved a hand to let her know he had heard her, but he did not turn back again. Leyna breathed in deeply and looked out at the countryside. She could see pieces of green mixed with white as the clouds swept by.

She waited for quite a while, and then she began the long journey down the stairs. About halfway down, she met a man on the way up. When she reached the bottom, she looked around, but she did not see the priest anywhere, so she made her way out of the *Minster* into the fresh air.

A strange feeling entered her heart as she walked back to the train station. She had somehow hoped that she would get the Americans the help they needed. But she had secured nothing for them by going all the way to Ulm—nothing but a referral to a man who sold fish at the market in Singen.

It was five minutes past noon as Leyna walked on the street bordering the railroad tracks. If it were not for the harsh, commanding voices that pierced the air, she would never have stopped to notice the boxcar sitting on the tracks beyond the bushes that separated the sidewalk from the rail yard.

Leyna peered through the fence, between a gap in the bushes, and watched the commotion taking place in a boxcar that sat on the other side of the rail yard. She could see that the car was stuffed full of agitated men. An impatient guard was standing on the ground, barking at the men inside. A few seconds later, she saw two guards in the boxcar kick and then roll a limp body out of the boxcar.

Leyna swallowed hard as one of the prisoners in the boxcar seemed to look directly at her. He had a sick and hopeless look in his eyes. A second later, one of the guards slammed the boxcar door shut. Leyna watched helplessly as the boxcar moved slowly out of sight. The body that now lay between the tracks never moved. The hopeless look of the prisoner hung like a picture in her mind.

Leyna took a step back, and then she turned toward the train station with an uneasy feeling in her stomach. She was not exactly sure what she had just witnessed, but she thought that the men in the boxcar looked like Americans. The priest had told her to be brave. Be brave she must.

Once Leyna had passed the soldiers on the platform and was on the train and in her seat, she cradled her father's Bible in her arms, leaned her head against the window, and tried to go to sleep. The train snaked its way out into the countryside. In between Ulm and Engen, a soldier came through the cars, checking everyone's identification. Leyna was startled out of her sleep by the soldier. He asked her for her papers twice. She reached into her coat pocket for her identification. The people in the seats across from her were staring at her now. Leyna looked up into the soldier's cold eyes. He tossed her papers back into her lap and moved on to the seats behind Leyna.

First Week of May 1944

Spring had finally come to southern Germany. The days were getting warmer, and the trees were in full bloom. After washing the laundry, Leyna hung her and her mother's clothes outside on the line that stretched between the house and the barn. She closed her eyes for a moment to soak in the warm sunshine. This time of year held many good memories for her.

Leyna breathed in deeply. Could she dare to hope that the war would end soon, and that her world would return to how it was before? Though she tried never to think about it, she missed her father and her brother with an ache that never really went away.

Leyna's thoughts were interrupted by the sound of the back door. Her mother stood in the doorway with an impatient look on her face. "Why do you always hang the men's clothes in the back room to dry, when you could put them outside?" asked her mother innocently. "Their dripping clothes always make such a mess on the floor."

Leyna tried to smile as she walked toward her. "Because I don't want anyone to see them, Mother," she replied honestly. "I'll mop up the floor."

Her mother shrugged as Leyna put her arm around her waist and closed the back door.

"Do you like the flowers I picked for you, Mother?" asked Leyna, changing the subject.

"Your brother brought me those flowers," she insisted.

"Aren't they beautiful?" Leyna responded after a sigh.

Leyna's mother sat down at the kitchen table and picked up the newspaper Leyna had brought home from town. Leyna glanced impatiently at the calendar on the wall in the kitchen. Tomorrow was the first Monday in May.

"Mother, I'm going to go to Singen tomorrow after work. I won't be home until late."

Her mother looked up from the newspaper with a blank stare. "Be careful, dear," she said.

Leyna looked closely at her mother's face. For a moment, she almost thought that her mother knew the reason for her trip into Singen.

Leyna left the bakery just after twelve thirty in the afternoon. She pedaled quickly through the streets, past the medieval fountains and under the colorful flower boxes that adorned the second-story windows in that part of town. Instead of heading east to the farm, she took the road to the south. The hour-and-a-half journey to Singen was relatively easy. The hard pedaling would be on the trip back.

Leyna wound her way around the roads on the outskirts of Singen until she found the way to the *Schlossgarten*. She could see several tables and tents in the market as she hopped off her bike and parked it next to the other bikes on the gravel. She took her bag out of her basket and headed toward the market.

There were two soldiers smoking and standing guard at the wrought-iron-gated entrance to the marketplace. Leyna put her head down as she passed them and reached into her bag, under the bread, to make sure the envelope with her address was still in there. She wandered with purpose from stand to stand, searching for the old man with the cane. Toward the middle of the market, there was a fish stand manned solely by an older woman. Leyna stood for a moment, looking at the fish, but when the woman asked what she wanted to buy, Leyna backed away, gently shaking her head.

After she had gone the entire length of the market and back again, she sat down on an empty bench. The old man selling fish was not there. Leyna played the words of the priest in her memory. Had she mistook his instructions to her? Certainly she had not traveled all the way to Singen to return home empty handed. Leyna watched the people passing by for nearly twenty minutes before she rose to her feet. She decided to take another look at all of the merchants and then to stop again at the only fish table.

By the time Leyna made her turn at the end of the market, the wind had picked up and the clouds were blocking the sunshine. Several other customers were in front of Leyna at the fish table. The tall, skinny woman at the head of the line was arguing with the fish lady. Leyna looked up to see the two soldiers walking her way. She turned her eyes quickly in the other direction.

Leyna had intended to ask the fish lady if she had any eel on the chance that she was somehow connected with the old man who sold fish, but she was losing her nerve. Leyna stepped aside as the soldiers passed the fish table. She needed to start home before too long. Her mother and the lieutenants would have nothing to eat until she got home with the bread that was in her bag.

Her spirits were very low as she pedaled up the hills toward Engen. Even the wind seemed against her. She had done the best that she could to find a way to get them out of Germany, but she had nothing to show for it. About a half hour after she left Singen, Leyna began to pray. Her lungs were burning, her legs were aching, and her heart was in turmoil.

All along, she had supposed that she was doing the right thing. Now it had come to this. She was helpless to find them a way out, and she was not convinced there was anything else she could do. Twenty minutes from home, Leyna was startled out of her dismal thoughts as the front tire blew on her bicycle.

An hour before the sun set that evening, Lieutenant Kellam glanced out the window by the barn door and down the empty driveway for the hundredth time since noon. He turned back to the stool by the cow stall and answered Lieutenant Owen's inquisitive look with a negative nod.

"What's happened to her?" asked Lieutenant Owen as he shook his head. "What if she's been caught?"

Rand let out a sigh and looked out the window again. He and Lieutenant Owen had both noticed a somberness in her since her trip to Ulm a week and a half earlier. Though they had pressed her, she told them little of the details of her encounter with the priest, and, in the end, she admitted only that there were further contacts she had to make.

The lieutenants had pondered for hours why Leyna had not come home after noon as she always did and what that meant to their fate. As the moments ticked slowly away, they grew hungrier, and the explanations in their minds for her absence grew graver.

All of a sudden, Rand ducked away from the window. Frank Owen, in a hunched-over fashion, made a dash to Rand's side.

"There's that man again with his dog," said Rand in a whisper as they both sneaked a peek out of the corner of the window.

"He's going around the other side of the house now," said Lieutenant Owen. "What do you suppose he's looking for?"

"I hope not us," replied Lieutenant Kellam.

"If he comes back around," continued Lieutenant Owen with determination, "I'm going up into the loft to hide."

"And I'll be right behind you," replied Rand slowly, craning his neck around to catch another glimpse of the man and his dog.

Five seconds later, the man emerged from the back of the house, took a long look toward the barn, and then headed off across the field, away from the barn and the house with the large brown-and-black dog following at his heels.

The two lieutenants let out a simultaneous sigh of relief. Lieutenant Owen sauntered back to the milking stool, shaking his head as he went.

"I don't like this one bit, Rand," he mumbled. "They must have got her, and we're next."

Rand gazed out the window at the white clouds with a forlorn look in his eyes. He hadn't quite decided yet if he would rather be where he was, in a prisoner-of-war camp, or dead.

"Frank! I think that's her," said Rand quietly after a good twenty minutes of silence. "She's back, but it looks like something's wrong with her bike."

Rand Kellam bit his lip as he watched her coming up the driveway toward the barn. The relief he felt on seeing her was tainted with a little bit of shame. It had suddenly occurred to him that he had been afraid for their lives all afternoon long but had given next to no thought to the trouble Leyna might be in.

Leyna rolled her crippled bicycle up the driveway of the Künzel farm as the sun sank low behind the trees. With the last of her strength, she led the bike to the back door of the house and let it fall down to the ground. She picked up her bag with the bread, swung the back door open, and lifted her weary feet into the house.

There was no one in the kitchen when she set the bread on the counter. She found her mother slumped over in the chair in her bedroom.

"I'm back, Mother," she said wearily. "I brought some bread. Are you hungry?"

"Thank you. I've already had dinner," said her mother happily.

Leyna sighed quietly. She knew full well there was no food in the house. "Can I make you some tea?"

"No, dear. I'm going to bed now," she said as she rose from the chair and shuffled slowly toward the bedroom.

As Leyna tucked her mother into bed, she heard the back door open and shut. The lieutenants were waiting for her, poised in their usual spot at the table, when she entered the kitchen. As a result of the failure she had experienced that day, Leyna could not look them in the eyes. She fumbled with the bread as she put a couple of rolls on two plates and placed them down in front of the hungry men.

She could feel their piercing stares as she put a pot of coffee on the stove. She grabbed a roll for herself and sat down at the table. With her hands folded in front of her, she mumbled a quick prayer. When she had finished, she looked up into the baffled and concerned eyes of the lieutenants, who, instead of tearing into their meal, clearly wanted her to write them some kind of explanation.

Leyna gently pushed the dictionary to the center of the table and took a bite of her roll. She was too tired to write, and what made her even more upset was that she had nothing to tell.

When the coffee was ready, Leyna poured two cups for the lieutenants. After she had placed the coffee in front of the men, she left the kitchen and went straight to her room. Two minutes later, she was sound asleep on her bed.

Lieutenant Kellam finished his cup of coffee at the same time as Lieutenant Owen. They both went straight to the hallway, where they saw that Leyna's bedroom door was shut. After exchanging looks of confusion, Lieutenant Owen pointed toward the back door. Rand nodded affirmatively, and they headed out into the darkness. Rand picked up Leyna's bike and wheeled it in the back door of the barn. The front tire was flat.

"What are we going to do now? We don't have anything to fix her tire with," said Lieutenant Owen.

Though she had intended to get up earlier, Leyna awoke at her usual time. As soon as she was awake enough to realize that she would have to walk all the way to the bakery, she took off with a start. She threw her dress on, ran a brush through her hair, and shot out the back door, still struggling to put on her coat. The stars in the sky were just beginning to fade as she stumbled down the driveway.

By the time her eyes had adjusted to the darkness, her right shoelace began to flop around. Leyna sighed and stooped down to retie her shoe. She was going to be very late getting to the bakery, but there was nothing she could do about it.

Leyna whipped her head around as she heard the sound of someone coming toward her from the farmhouse. She stood up straight and squinted into the darkness.

She was not sure if it was an angel or one of the lieutenants, but a figure rode up on her bike, shoved the handle bars into her hands, and took off running back toward the farm without saying a word. Leyna reached down and felt the front tire. It was fully inflated. She wasted no time. Leyna hopped on the bike and ped-aled as hard as she could toward town.

Several times that morning, Leyna had to shoo away the dogs from the back door of the bakery. Several times that morning, she put the wrong amount of flour or salt into her dough. Several times, she wondered how they had fixed her tire. After yesterday's disastrous events, she had decided to give up on trying to find the Americans a way out of Germany. But having her transportation restored to her gave her a tiny bit of hope.

Leyna served customers at the bakery until well beyond one in the afternoon. She had been glancing anxiously at the clock behind the counter since noon, when *Herr* Krueger should have been back from his deliveries. At ten past one, *Herr* Krueger came bursting in the back door of the bakery. Leyna left the front counter to see if he was all right.

"I am sorry for the long delay, Leyna," he said with an exas-perated look in his eyes and a pant. "I have been arguing this whole hour with the quartermaster. Can you believe it? He wants to pay me only half of what he owes me."

Leyna shook her head. "What are you going to do?"

"What can I do," he said with a shrug, "but hope that his payroll comes in soon? I explained to him that I cannot purchase the supplies that I need to make the bread on his promises that I will be paid soon." *Herr* Krueger shook his head. "But I do not need to bother you with these problems. Thank you for watching the store for me."

"It was no problem, *Herr* Krueger," replied Leyna with a smile as she ducked out of her apron.

"Then I will see you tomorrow morning early," said *Herr* Krueger as he reached for his apron and left for the front room.

Leyna grabbed her bag with the bread for the day and went as quickly as she could to her bike in the alleyway. She rode around the Catholic church, passed the fountains, and then turned onto the road to Singen, all the while with hope that she would find the old man at the fish market growing brighter in her heart.

She could not get the image of the American prisoner on the boxcar in Ulm out of her mind. She had already determined to do everything in her power to keep the lieutenants from falling into German hands, but with each passing day, the mission to find them a way out of Germany became more urgent to her.

The ride to Singen seemed a little shorter this time. The same two guards were posted at the entrance to the market. At first, Leyna saw the same vendors as she had seen the day before. But as she made her way to the last tables, she noticed two extra tents. A fancy, hand-carved cane, lodged between a tent peg and the table at the last tent, caught her eye.

She tried to still her heart as she saw an assortment of fish laid out on the table in front of her. She glanced behind a pile of wooden crates and saw the figure of a white-bearded man seated toward the back of the tent. Leyna swallowed hard.

"Eh, what can I get for you, *Fräulein?*" asked the man as he rose from his rickety folding chair.

Leyna looked him in the eyes and tried to smile. The man was of medium height and build and was dressed in a heavily weaved sweater. He had a square face that was framed by a very white beard and light brown eyes.

"I would like some eel," Leyna said softly.

The old man twisted his head toward her.

"Eh?"

"I would like some eel," she repeated a little louder than before.

The old man wrinkled his nose. "I haven't got any eel," he said. "Can I interest you in some nice whitefish or this delicate perch?"

Leyna looked blankly at the fish before her. Then she reached into her bag to try to locate the envelope with her address on it.

"I came to get some eel," she said boldly. Leyna saw the old man's right eye twitch, and then he took a pipe out of his shirt pocket and stuck it in his mouth.

"I'll be with you in a moment, *Fräulein*," he said between his teeth as he turned to a rather heavy-set woman who had approached the fish table to the right. Leyna stepped away, pretending to look at the other fish the old man had on display. She waited patiently as the old man sold some blue carp to the other woman. Then the old man put the pipe back in his mouth, crossed his arms, and waited until his other customer was out of earshot.

"If you'd like, *Fräulein,* I can let you know when I have some eel in," he said with half a smile.

Leyna dug deeper into her bag and pulled out the envelope she had prepared.

"I would like that very much," she said, pretending along as she handed him the envelope. "This is where I can be reached."

The old man took her envelope and quickly slid it under his sweater and into a pocket as his eyes were scanning their surroundings. "I would like to show you some of my fish, *Fräulein*," he said softly, leaning toward her. "Try to say as little as possible."

Leyna followed him to the very end of his table and feigned interest in what he was showing her.

"You have two Americans?"

Leyna nodded.

"How tall are they?"

Leyna put her teeth together. She had not expected this

kind of question. "One is about your height and the other is a bit taller."

"Do they have their photos?"

Leyna looked back at him with a blank stare. "I don't know," she said.

"Do they have clothes, civilian clothes?"

"Yes," she replied proudly. "I have seen to that."

"Good," he responded. "You are in town or in the countryside?"

"On a farm," she said.

"And your nearest neighbor?"

"The nearest neighbor is two kilometers away, but they cannot see our farm."

"Security in the area?"

Leyna drew a blank. She was not sure what he meant. "There is the military base in Mühlhausen. We have civil patrols, and they are quite dedicated," she finally said.

The old man smiled at Leyna and gestured to another box of fish.

"It will be about a week or two, but have them ready to go at any time."

Leyna's heart leapt at the serious tone the old man had suddenly taken.

"You should wait for a visit from an aunt or an uncle," he said cryptically.

Leyna lowered her eyebrow and leaned forward. "From whom?"

"An aunt or an uncle will pay you a visit as soon as everything is arranged, and they will take the men."

Leyna looked away and then back at the old man. "Who will come? What are their names?"

The bearded man sighed. "In this business, it is best for us not to know the names of those involved. That way, if one is caught, they do not know the identity or involvement of the others. It is a deadly business, and that is how we must operate."

The old man drew back for a moment and looked around. "Now, give me a smile and point to the fish that you want."

Leyna smiled and then gave the old man a look of confusion. The old man reached behind a box for a piece of a newspaper.

"Do you know how to cook perch, *Fräulein?*"

Leyna shook her head as the old man wrapped up two fish for her.

"They are best fried in a heavy pan with butter and a little milk. Don't overcook them," he said in his regular speaking voice.

"I can't pay you," said Leyna softly.

"You won't be disappointed with this fish, *Fräulein,*" he said as he handed her the fish wrapped in the newspaper.

"Ah, *Frau* Neuheim!" said the old man, turning to his next customer. "It has been so long since I saw you last. How is the family?"

Leyna turned quickly away from the fish table and strolled at a reasonable pace to the market entrance, where she had left her bike. Her heart seemed light for the first time in a long time. She had not imagined that she would find anyone in Germany who would help her get the Americans home. Now at least she had hope.

A little before dark, Leyna set the two fish and a pile of bread on the table for dinner. She did not expect the Lord to multiply the meal. She simply thanked him for his provision and her prosperous trip. As her mother and the lieutenants were eating, Leyna pushed her plate away, grabbed the dictionary and a piece of paper, and began to write at a furious pace.

"What are you doing, Leyna?"

"I'm writing a letter, Mother."

"Aren't you going to eat?"

"Yes. I just want to finish this letter," replied Leyna as she was turning to another word in the dictionary. She had such good news to tell the lieutenants that she could wait to eat her fish. It took her fifteen minutes to write out a one-page explanation of everything that had happened. She stuck the paper in the dictionary and set the book on the floor. She would have to wait until her mother was out of sight to pass the note to the lieutenants. Leyna reached for her plate and took a bite of the perch. The old man was right. She wasn't disappointed.

Friday and Saturday, May 5–6, 1944

It was early Friday afternoon as Leyna rode up the driveway with a basket full of bread and a short letter from someone Leyna did not know, informing Leyna that she was coming on the one o'clock train for a visit on Wednesday. It was signed "*Tante Zelma*," or Aunt Zelma.

She found the lieutenants in the barn. Leyna climbed up into the hayloft. With all of her efforts to find the lieutenants a way out of Germany, she had neglected to start to prepare the ground to lay seed. If she was going to have any food for the coming winter, she had to get started soon. Last fall, she had stored bags of barley and wheat seed for planting, just as her father always did.

Leyna sighed. She was not looking forward to the work that lay ahead of her. She was no farmer. She had helped her father and brother on occasion, but she had had to struggle through plowing, planting, and harvest alone for two years now. Deep inside, she felt that she did not have the strength to do it all again, especially not while she was working at the bakery.

Leyna pulled out a wooden box from between the seed bags and opened it up. Inside were the dried seeds for their garden. Leyna looked over at the ladder. Lieutenant Kellam was making his way up to the loft.

"Seeds," he said, pointing to her box. "It's planting time."

Leyna just looked at Lieutenant Kellam and swallowed hard. She wasn't sure what he had said. "I am loath to begin this all over again," she confessed.

Lieutenant Kellam stared back at her and then he smiled. "Follow me," he said, beckoning her toward the ladder.

Leyna followed him down the ladder and over to the corner, where Lieutenant Owen was busy working on the gang plow.

Leyna stooped down and surveyed her newly sharpened plow blades. She stood back up slowly and smiled.

"How did you know?" she asked, by now, not expecting an answer. Leyna was a little surprised. She knew that it normally took her father hours to sharpen all of the blades. She had never done that job. He must have been working on this for days.

Leyna looked from lieutenant to lieutenant. It was just about time for a visit from *Tante* Zelma, and they would be gone. For a moment, she was sad at the thought. She had grown accustomed to their presence in her house. She had gotten used to putting her thoughts into writing using the dictionary, and she had enjoyed having sane company while she sat and sewed in the kitchen.

Leyna turned away suddenly and walked over to the window by the back door. She wanted to hide the tears that were forming in her eyes.

"Is something wrong?" said Lieutenant Owen to Rand.

Rand shook his head. "I don't know," he replied with a puzzled look.

Leyna wiped away a tear or two and then turned back to the men.

"Thank you," she said in English.

The day *Tante* Zelma was to arrive, Leyna awoke before four o'clock in the morning to the noise of commotion by the back door. When she got to the back room, she found Lieutenant Kellam guarding the back door and Lieutenant Owen determined to leave the house dressed in the uniform she had modified for him. Leyna stepped back into the doorway, out of sight.

"Don't do it!" said Lieutenant Kellam. "We're almost there."

"I can't stay here another day," said the bombardier out of desperation. "I'm going mad."

"Leyna said they would come for us, and they'll come. You don't stand a chance out there alone."

"Anything is better than being cooped up in this house for another day," said Lieutenant Owen with a sigh. "Out of my way!"

"Frank, Leyna said that the woman is coming today. You can make it one more day," said Lieutenant Kellam with the voice of reason.

Leyna peeked around the corner, but she did not step back fast enough. Lieutenant Kellam caught a glimpse of her.

"Now you've got Leyna up, and she's worried about you. If you go out there, you're going to ruin everything she's done to get us out of here alive and put her in danger too!"

Lieutenant Owen looked back toward the hall and saw Leyna's concerned face. She turned and went into the kitchen. Leyna returned a minute later and held up a piece of paper.

"What is wrong?" she had written.

The bombardier looked at the navigator, who was still standing with arms folded, blocking the back door. Lieutenant Owen breathed in deeply.

"All right," he said at last. "One more day."

Lieutenant Owen slid past Leyna in a huff and went up the stairs to the attic. Leyna stood, wide-eyed, staring at Rand, still holding her piece of paper. Rand Kellam ran his hand through the side of his hair. How was he going to explain this to Leyna without upsetting her?

Rand stepped closer to Leyna, took the piece of paper from her hands, folded it in half, and headed for the attic stairs, having decided not to say anything.

That afternoon, Leyna left the bakery and went straight to the train station. She waited a long hour for the one o'clock train to arrive. Leyna brought her hand over her eyebrows to shield her eyes from the glaring sun as the passengers embarked from the train. Then she saw a dark-haired woman step down from the last car with a carpetbag in hand. She was wearing a black hat, just as she had noted in her letter, but she was younger than Leyna had expected. Leyna stepped forward with a smile to greet her.

"*Tante* Zelma," she said, half with a question in her voice.

The woman reached out and hugged her halfheartedly. "Leyna, so good to see you," she said, giving Leyna a kiss on each cheek. "I am glad to see you after so long." She grabbed Leyna by the arm and started toward the train depot. "Tell me how you have been."

Leyna hesitated a moment. She was not used to making personal conversation with a complete stranger who was supposed to be a relative of hers.

"I am doing all right, *Tante*," she finally said, "but Mother is not."

Once they were outside of the train station, Leyna collected her bike, and the two ladies headed down the street toward the outskirts of town. Soon, they were out in the country. *Tante* Zelma peppered her with a lot of questions about Leyna's family and about their situation. Leyna did not ask any questions in return. She remembered what the old man at the market had said about this deadly business.

By two o'clock, they were walking up the driveway of the farm. As they started up the driveway, *Tante* Zelma turned to Leyna.

"I want to see the men and talk with them. We have a plan to work out, but I have to see exactly what we have to work with here. Your neighbors are far away, I can see. That is good."

Leyna put her bike against the barn and opened the barn door to see if the men were inside. She called their names, and they both popped up from behind the wagon. Leyna motioned for *Tante* Zelma to follow her into the barn. After she had closed the door behind them, she turned to see the lieutenants staring at *Tante* Zelma.

"This is Lieutenant Frank Owen, and this is Lieutenant Rand Kellam," said Leyna, introducing *Tante* Zelma to the men.

Tante Zelma stepped forward and shook hands with both men.

"I am Aunt Zelma," she said in English with a thick, German accent. "I have come to try to help you get out of Germany."

Leyna did not understand what *Tante* Zelma was saying, but she could see the relief in the faces of the lieutenants.

Tante Zelma sat down on the edge of the wagon and talked with the lieutenants for over an hour. Leyna stood patiently by. Both of the lieutenants handed over their escape photos to *Tante* Zelma and listened with riveted attention to everything she said. They asked her questions in return, and soon they seemed comfortable with what she was telling them. Finally, *Tante* Zelma turned to Leyna.

"We will return within the week to take the men. They should be ready to go when we arrive. We will most likely come right before evening, after daylight."

Leyna's mouth hung open for a minute, and then she closed it. She didn't know what to say. She wanted to ask questions, but she knew that it was best for her not to know. *Tante* Zelma turned to talk with the men; then she faced Leyna with serious eyes.

"They have told me everything you have done to save their lives and to feed them. They want you to know that they are thankful."

Leyna bit her lip and looked at the lieutenants.

"You are a brave girl, Leyna. The German Resistance will be proud to hear your story."

Leyna brought her eyes quickly to *Tante* Zelma's. "German Resistance?" she said. Leyna did not know that there was such a movement.

"Yes," replied *Tante* Zelma coolly. "You are surprised to learn that not everyone in Germany is a fan of Adolph Hitler?"

Leyna nodded.

Tante Zelma put her hand on Leyna's shoulder. "I must get back to the train station. Will you accompany me at least until we get to Engen?"

"Certainly," replied Leyna.

Tante Zelma said a few more words to the men, then she grabbed her carpetbag and Leyna's arm and left the barn.

"Tell me, Leyna," said *Tante* Zelma with much thought as they went down the road, "why did you help the Americans? You have taken a great risk."

Leyna looked away from the woman and focused on the road ahead. She was lost in thought for a minute, not quite sure *Tante* Zelma would understand. Finally, Leyna cleared her throat.

"My father fought in the Great War," began Leyna. "For the most part, he did not talk about this time in his life, except for one experience. He would sometimes tell us about Montfaucon and how the Germans were overtaken there by the Americans. He would always tell us how indebted he felt to the American soldiers who spared him and to the American doctor who saved his life. When I saw the American hanging in the tree, and then the other two who came out of the woods, I felt that I could not repay the kindness the Americans had showed to my father so long ago by turning them in."

The two women walked along in silence for a moment.

"And you, *Tante* Zelma? Why are you in this business of helping them?" asked Leyna boldly.

Tante Zelma glanced at Leyna, and then she sighed.

"My husband, my late husband, was born in Paris," she said, her voice trailing off at the end. "He resisted the German occupiers, until one day, the last day of his life …" *Tante* Zelma said no more, and Leyna thought she saw her eyes tearing up.

When Leyna got back to the farm, she found the men still working on the farm equipment in the barn. They seemed to be in high spirits, like little boys at Christmastime. There were so many things she wanted to ask them, so many things about them that she did not know and wondered about. It was all she could do not to ask *Tante* Zelma how she was going to get them out of Germany.

Leyna went into the house to change her clothes. Then she returned to the barn, took the hand plow, and went to till the garden soil. She decided to tackle the garden planting before she would start on the fields. At least the government would not take any of the food from her garden.

She worked in the garden until night fell. That evening, after supper, she took the lining out of her winter coat and stretched it out on the kitchen table. She had one more project to work on before the men were ready to go.

Tuesday, May 8, 1944

Leyna's mother was fast asleep. Leyna was washing up the supper plates and listening to the radio as the lieutenants played dominoes at the kitchen table when she heard a car coming up the driveway. The lieutenants gathered up their dominoes in the wooden box and ran upstairs without saying a word. Leyna dried her hands on her apron and braced herself for another visit from the captain.

She went slowly to the back door and opened it enough to see *Tante* Zelma and a very short man emerging from their car. Leyna ran out to greet them.

"Leyna, this is *Onkel* Klaus," she said, introducing the short man. Even in the dark, Leyna could see that the man walked with a limp.

"Would it be possible to park the car in your barn?" asked *Onkel* Klaus with an unusually high-pitched voice.

"Certainly," replied Leyna. "I'll open the doors, and you can pull it in."

Tante Zelma reached in and snatched her carpetbag out of the back seat. *Onkel* Klaus started the engine and pulled the car around while Leyna opened the barn doors for him. Then she made her way with the hobbling *Onkel* Klaus to the back door, where *Tante* Zelma was waiting for them.

"The bugs are bad this evening," said *Tante* Zelma, swatting the air as they stepped inside.

Leyna shut the back door and led the way into the kitchen.

"My mother is in bed, so we are safe to talk," she said as she offered them a seat at the kitchen table. "Can I get you some coffee?"

Onkel Klaus responded immediately in his high-pitched voice. "I would love a cup with some hot milk to go along, if possible."

Leyna looked at *Tante* Zelma. This was an unusual request coming from a German man. Leyna shrugged and filled the coffee pot with water.

"Where are the lieutenants?" asked *Tante* Zelma at last.

Leyna breathed in deeply. "Oh, I should go and get them out from under their beds." She had completely forgotten about them. After nearly two months of hiding them, she had gotten into the habit of pretending that they did not exist at times. Leyna went upstairs in a hurry and returned with the lieutenants after a few moments. *Tante* Zelma introduced the men to *Onkel* Klaus while Leyna heated up some milk on the stove. The lieutenants sat down at the table, and the four of them began a hushed but intense discussion.

Leyna poured a cup of coffee for *Tante* Zelma and *Onkel* Klaus and brought him a warm cup of milk. He thanked her. From their tone of voice, Leyna could sense that there was a problem, and she wondered what was being discussed in English. Lieutenant Kellam glanced over at Leyna, who was leaning against the kitchen sink. *Tante* Zelma got up from her chair and came over to Leyna.

"Unfortunately, we can only take one man at a time. So they have decided to let the one with the wife and son go first."

Leyna looked over at the lieutenants, a little surprised. She did not know which one that was.

"We'll be taking Lieutenant Owen as soon as he can get dressed," continued *Tante* Zelma. "If all goes well, we will be back in a week or two for Lieutenant Kellam."

Leyna looked back at *Tante* Zelma. She had thought they would both go at once. Suddenly, Leyna remembered the project she had been working on. She excused herself from the kitchen and went to her bedroom. She returned to the kitchen carrying two pressed, white shirts and two silk ties. She handed one shirt to Lieutenant Owen and the other to Lieutenant Kellam.

Onkel Klaus reached out and ran his hands along the sleeve of

Lieutenant Owen's shirt and looked up at Leyna with an envious look.

"Where did you get these shirts?" asked *Onkel* Klaus.

"I made them from our linen," replied Leyna.

Tante Zelma sent Lieutenant Owen upstairs to get dressed immediately.

Lieutenant Kellam was looking at the tie she had made. *So that was what she had done with the lining of her winter coat.*

It was not long before Lieutenant Owen was back downstairs, dressed in his modified uniform with his new white shirt and blue tie. Leyna looked proudly at the embroidery she had sewn onto the collar of his coat. Except that she knew otherwise, he looked like a proper German gentleman.

"We must leave now," said *Tante* Zelma when she saw that Lieutenant Owen was ready. Then she spoke to the lieutenants in English.

Onkel Klaus thanked Leyna for the coffee and the hot milk, and then he wobbled toward the back door. *Tante* Zelma patted Lieutenant Kellam on the arm and followed *Onkel* Klaus to the back door. Lieutenant Owen began to follow them, but then he turned back to Leyna.

He reached out with his left hand, took her hand and squeezed it. "I can't thank you enough, Leyna," he said in English.

Leyna just smiled and took in a deep breath.

"God bless you, Frank Owen," she said in German.

Lieutenant Owen stepped back and gave Lieutenant Kellam a nod. Then he waved good-bye to both of them and stepped out into the night.

In the barn, *Tante* Zelma and *Onkel* Klaus hid Lieutenant Owen in a tight space under the backseat of the car. Then Leyna and Lieutenant Kellam opened the barn doors. *Onkel* Klaus backed the car out of the barn and started down the driveway before he turned on the headlights. The frogs were singing in the distance. Leyna and Rand stood there in the dark until they could see the taillights no more.

Wednesday, May 9, 1944

Leyna did not sleep very well that night, and four o'clock came quickly. Lieutenant Kellam went out to the barn when Leyna went to get her bike. She imagined that he was wondering how Lieutenant Owen had faired in his midnight journey, just as she was. Lieutenant Kellam was milking the cow when she left for town.

The day dragged on for Leyna at the bakery. *Herr* Krueger was not his usual, jovial self, and Leyna knew that she had to start plowing when she got home from work. The sun was especially hot as she rode home that afternoon. She prayed that God would keep Lieutenant Owen safe, all the way home.

When she got to the farm, Leyna went straight inside and changed her clothes. After she had braided her hair, she grabbed a hat, and then she opened the door to her mother's room. Her mother was lying in bed, happily listening to the radio and knitting a scarf.

Leyna pulled up a chair and spent a few minutes telling her mother about her day at the bakery. Her mother seemed to enjoy her company for a while, but she tired quickly. Leyna turned the radio back on for her mother, put on her boots, and headed out the back door. She rolled up her shirtsleeves as she walked toward the barn.

She found Lieutenant Kellam in the barn, tinkering with some of her father's old equipment. He seemed happy to see her.

"I'm going to get the plow out," she said in German. By this time, she did not care if he did not understand her. She was going to talk anyway. "*Es ist Zeit zu pflügen.*" She added, "My favorite thing to do in life." She opened the barn doors all the way and pulled down the harnesses for the horses. She led four horses, one by one, outside and put them into the harnesses. Then she began to thread all of the lines to the gangplow.

This was the part of the operation where she always needed help and never had it. Leyna stood beside the plow and pulled the lines from the first horse through the O-ring; then she tried to thread the lines from the second horse, but they had already gotten twisted with the lines from the third horse. Now the horses were getting antsy.

Lieutenant Kellam watched as Leyna struggled to hook the horses to the plow. Then he stepped forward. This seemed like the perfect situation to put his grandfather's good instruction to the test. Rand came up quietly behind Leyna, slipped his right arm around her right side and his left arm around her left side, and took the twisted reins from her hands.

In just a moment, he had threaded the eight lines neatly through the ring. Leyna watched him carefully. When he had finished the task, to her surprise, he did not step back away from her. Leyna turned halfway in his arms and looked up at him. He was looking down at her with his pretty eyes. Leyna blushed.

Lieutenant Kellam stepped back suddenly when he saw her blush. He swallowed hard. He was surprised at himself. He shook the thought he had out of his mind and turned back to his prior project. Leyna watched him leave, and then she directed the horses and the plow out to the field.

Rand watched her from inside the barn. *What a strange turn of events the war has caused, that a beautiful young girl is forced to toil out in a dusty field, doing the work of a man.* Slowly, a thought entered his mind as he watched Leyna riding the gangplow. He thought about telling Leyna, but then he decided that she would probably be against it.

It was almost dark by the time Rand and Leyna came into the house. Her mother was sitting at the kitchen table, eating bread and cheese. Leyna poured her a glass of fresh milk. She tried to make conversation with her mother, but her mother was quite weak that evening and was not much interested in talking. She soon got up and went to her room.

One good thing about Lieutenant Owen's departure was that there was now an additional portion of bread to eat. Leyna split his portion with Lieutenant Kellam. She took the dictionary down from the shelf and started writing as she finished the last roll.

"I wonder where he is," she wrote.

"They didn't say where they were taking him—to France or Switzerland—but I think they were going to take him over a lake," wrote the lieutenant back.

Leyna raised her eyebrow. "Maybe they are taking him over Lake Constance into Switzerland. That is probably the best route."

Lieutenant Kellam changed the subject. "How much plowing is left?"

"Lots," she responded.

"Where is your property line?" he asked next.

Leyna took the pencil back and drew him a detailed map of the farm, complete with illustrations of the two large trees on the eastern border. Lieutenant Kellam downed the last piece of cheese and finished up his glass of milk.

"Will you play dominoes with me?" he wrote next.

Leyna smiled. Now that his game-playing partner was gone, she figured she would have to learn to play. The evening sped away. By the time she caught on to the game, it was an hour past her bedtime.

Thursday, May 10, 1944

When Leyna left the bakery after midday on Thursday, she was close to exhausted. She was not looking forward to going home and doing more plowing. However, it was not the plowing that was on her mind all the way home. She was thinking about Captain Metzger. It had been over a month since she had seen him. She hoped that meant that he had given up on her.

Leyna slowed her bike as she approached the back door of the farmhouse. As she was leaning the bike against the house, the bread spilled out of the basket onto the grass. She stooped down and picked up the rolls one by one.

There was no one in the kitchen when she set the rolls on the counter. She found her mother half-asleep on her bed. Leyna climbed the stairs to the attic to call Lieutenant Kellam to eat, but he was not there. She went out to the barn fully expecting to find him there, but after a thorough search, including the loft, she began to panic. The lieutenant was missing.

She ran back into the house to check the front room again, in case she had overlooked him. This time she started calling his name. Had the captain been out to the farm while she was at the bakery? Had her mother turned in the lieutenant?

Leyna searched the house again and then went into her mother's room and woke her. "Mother, do you know where the farm help is?"

"I think they are out in the field with Stefan," she replied groggily.

"Did someone come out to visit this morning? Was Captain Metzger here?"

"No. What is the matter?"

"Nothing, Mother. I am sorry to wake you."

Leyna left her mother's room in a hurry. She wasn't sure if her mother was telling her what really happened or not. He had to be in the barn. Maybe she had just missed him. She went outside to check again.

This time she noticed that the horses were missing. The gangplow was gone. She swung the barn door open and ran out onto the gravel. She scanned the horizon until her eyes lit upon a figure in the distance beyond the farmhouse, in the east field. A cloud of dust was trailing behind it. Someone was clearly plowing her field.

If that was him, he was taking a big chance. If anyone saw him plowing, that would be the end of it all. Everyone knew there were no men left at the Künzel farm.

Leyna took off to the east field as fast as she could go. As she got closer to the gangplow, it made a wide turn and stopped at the end of a row. The person who was plowing her field stepped off of the seat and turned to Leyna. Leyna squinted at the figure before her. It looked like a woman. She was dressed in a raggedy, old skirt and a checkered shirt. Her thick legs were protruding from the boots on her feet. Leyna looked up at her head. From underneath the hat on her head flowed long, straight, thick, black hair.

From the shadow of the hat, Leyna could not see her face, but as she got closer Leyna broke out laughing. She laughed so hard, in fact, that she fell down onto the newly plowed earth. The face in the shadow of the hat was Lieutenant Kellam's. For a moment, he had fooled even her.

Lieutenant Kellam came and stood over her. He was dusty and sweaty and did not look amused at her laughing. Leyna pulled herself up out of the dirt and tried to compose herself. He had taken two of her aprons and tied one on in the front, the other in the back. Leyna looked over at the horses' tails. They were all missing half of their hair. The other half of their hair was spilling down from the hat on the lieutenant's head.

Leyna walked all the way around him. He had made a good disguise. She looked out at the field. He must have been plowing since she had left that morning. He had made quite a big dent in the east field.

Leyna looked back at Lieutenant Kellam. "Why don't you come in for something to eat and give the horses a rest," she said, motioning with her hands for him to follow her.

Lieutenant Kellam climbed back onto the gangplow and brought the horses back to the barn. He happily removed the hat with the horsehair and came into the kitchen for something to eat. Leyna wanted to be angry with him for leaving the house, but he had come up with such a good disguise and had made such good progress that she found it impossible to scold him.

That evening, after the cow had been milked, Rand brought the milk pail into the kitchen and set it in the sink. When he turned the kitchen light out to go upstairs, he noticed a light coming through the shade at the east window. He went over to the window and lifted the shade up slowly. There, piercing the dark, he saw a giant, full moon slipping up over the horizon on its way to the top of the sky. The light it gave out that night was so bright that it lit up the forest and the fields around the farmhouse almost like daylight. Rand stared out at the beautiful countryside and the deep shadows cast by the moonlight for almost half an hour. It was such a beautiful evening that he forgot for a moment that he was a fugitive in a hostile land.

Third Week of May, 1944

Leyna awoke early Sunday morning to the gentle tapping of rain on her bedroom window. She looked out of the window at the fields. Between Lieutenant Kellam's plowing in the morning and her plowing in the afternoon, they had almost finished all the fields. The rain would soften the ground for planting, which she hoped to start on Tuesday. Leyna looked up at the drips coming off of the eaves on the farmhouse. She wasn't going to make it to church that morning.

After breakfast, Leyna sat down with her mother and Lieutenant Kellam in the front room. Leyna read a couple of chapters from the Gospel of John out loud, and then she and her mother sang a couple of songs. Lieutenant Kellam sat respectfully through their little church service without saying a word.

Her mother returned to bed when they were finished, and Leyna brought the radio into her room to keep her company. When Leyna returned to the kitchen, she saw that Lieutenant Kellam was sitting at the table with the dictionary and her German Bible. Leyna sat down in the rocking chair, waiting for him to pass her the paper with a question on it, but he never did. After a long while, he folded the paper, put it in his pocket, and reached for the dominoes box. Then he looked up at Leyna as if to ask her if she wanted to play.

By evening, the rain had stopped. After the sun had gone down, Leyna went out with Lieutenant Kellam to milk the cow and to feed the animals. She found herself singing her favorite hymn, and the soft sound of her voice echoed off the roof of the barn. Leyna got to the second stanza, and she suddenly stopped. Then she started it again. Rand Kellam was humming along with her from the next stall. Leyna smiled. When she finished the song, there was only the sound of the milk filling the pail. She wondered if Lieutenant Owen was still safely on his way home.

Lieutenant Kellam had finished plowing the fields by the time Leyna got home Monday afternoon. He carried the seed bags down to the seeder for her, and Leyna went out that afternoon to begin planting.

Tante Zelma's return was always at the back of Leyna's mind. On Tuesday afternoon, she and Lieutenant Kellam were in the barn. Leyna was hitching the horses to the seeder, and Lieutenant Kellam had climbed the ladder to the loft to bring down another bag of seed when a car drove up. Before Leyna could make it to the barn door, Captain Metzger stepped inside with his imposing presence and a smooth smile.

Leyna was visibly startled to see him. Rand froze in position in the loft, trying desperately not to disturb the stray strands of straw at his feet. He peered cautiously through the opening in the floor where the ladder stood. He had a good view of the captain's back from above. Rand could feel his heart pounding in his chest.

"Well, my darling," began the captain, "I can see that you have been hard at work in the fields."

Leyna pulled her hair back behind her ears. She looked past the captain and saw that he had brought his two men with him. She swallowed hard and prayed that over the last few days no one had seen the lieutenant out in the field and turned her in.

The captain walked up close to Leyna and grinned. "I have come to see if you have changed your mind about me, *Fräulein* Künzel," he said confidently.

Leyna looked down at his boots. He was terribly close to her. Before she could step away, the captain slid his arm around her waist and kissed her on the neck. Leyna cleared her throat and tried to push him away.

"*Herr* Captain," she began, looking up into his eyes, "you— you are an important man with a bright future ahead of you. I—I am a poor peasant girl. Why do you want to have me hanging over your head for the rest of your career? Your men are already laughing at you behind your back."

The captain turned halfway around. His men were smoking, laughing, and carrying on at his car. After seeing this, the captain turned back around with rising fire in his nostrils. His piercing, brown eyes turned cold and hard. He raised his right hand with lightning speed and slapped her on the left cheek with the back of his hand, as hard as he could. This happened so quickly that Leyna did not anticipate the blow, and her hair went flying across her face.

Rand was squatting on the floor of the loft watching the whole scene from above and trying not to make any sound or movement, but when he saw the captain hit Leyna, he instinctively reached back and pulled the gun that Lieutenant Owen had left him from his belt. He cocked the hammer and pointed it directly at the captain. He had been at the top of his class in marksmanship, and he had no doubt that he could finish him off with one shot. The consequences of this action, should he proceed, were immaterial to him at that moment.

Leyna held the side of her face with her hand and peered out at the captain in confusion. She swallowed her next words and breathed in deeply. The captain pointed straight at her with fury in his brow.

"Don't you ever speak to an officer like that again," he shouted through clenched teeth, "or it'll cost you your life!"

The captain turned on his heels and exited the barn, all the while in Rand's gun sight. He and his men got into the car and left a cloud of dust behind them as they sped down the driveway. Leyna stood there in the barn door, still stunned at the whole scene. Now she was shaking.

Lieutenant Kellam lowered the hammer of Lieutenant Owen's gun, emerged cautiously down the ladder, and closed the barn doors slowly. Then he went to Leyna. He tilted her head back gently and looked at the side of her face, where she had received the blow.

"I don't know what you said to him," said Rand softly, "but he sure didn't like it."

Leyna closed her eyes, fell forward slowly onto his chest, and rested there in his arms for a moment. She was still shaking.

The lieutenant had grown weary of the German officer's visits. His calls had been a frequent topic of conversation between him and Lieutenant Owen. They both had several theories as to why he kept showing up. They even referred to him as the general.

This was the first time Rand had had a good look at the man. It was clear to him that the German officer had no good intentions when it came to Leyna. All Rand could do now was hope that this was the last visit the officer would make.

That evening, as she was reading her Bible, Rand came over and looked over her shoulder. Then he handed her a piece of paper.

"What did you read to us on Sunday?"

Leyna put her Bible down and went to the table. She picked up the dictionary and the pencil.

"John, chapter fourteen through chapter sixteen."

Lieutenant Kellam nodded his head and took back the pencil. "Do you believe it?" he wrote simply.

Leyna looked over at Lieutenant Kellam. "Yes, I do. Without God, I have no hope for eternal life. Without him, I would have nothing."

Lieutenant Kellam read her words carefully and then looked down. Leyna took the pencil and wrote further.

"Have you trusted him with your life?"

Lieutenant Kellam reached over and took her Bible in his hands. He was surprised that, even with a German Bible, he was able to make out the books. He turned to the book of First John, and he wrote out a verse in German for her, hoping that his memory would serve him well.

"Believe on the Lord Jesus Christ and thou shalt be saved," he wrote. "He that hath the Son hath life," and then he wrote, "I am a believer."

Leyna smiled as she read his words. "Then I can be confident that when you leave here I will see you again," she wrote.

Lieutenant Kellam nodded. "My life is in his hands," wrote the lieutenant slowly.

Leyna opened her Bible to the book of Psalms.

"Do you know this chapter?" she wrote.

Lieutenant Kellam looked down at her Bible. She began to read chapter twenty-three in German. Lieutenant Kellam began to recite it from memory in English.

Rand paused after he said, "Thou preparest a table before me in the presence of mine enemies," and a tear formed in his eye.

Leyna read on to the end alone.

Rand put his head in his hands and sighed. All of the time he had been in hiding, he had needed the truth in those verses applied like a salve to his heart. He needed the comfort that they gave. He was so hungry for any sign of hope. It was getting harder and harder not to fall headlong into despair.

Leyna closed her Bible and rose from the chair. It was time for her to go to bed. After a moment, she said good night and left him there in the kitchen. She did not know what to say to him. She could tell that he was familiar with the passage, but she had not expected the words to touch him so. She understood also that it was probable that there were some thoughts and some feelings that were impossible to translate between a German girl and an American airman.

Lieutenant Kellam sat there a while longer before turning out the light and climbing the stairs to the attic. The fourth verse of Psalm 23 was ringing in his heart: "Yea, though I walk through the valley of the shadow of death, I will fear no evil, for thou art with me."

Friday, May 19, 1944

Two months and a day from when his plane was shot down, Lieutenant Kellam awoke in the attic of the farmhouse. He went with Leyna out to the barn to milk the cow before the sun came up. As she did every day but Sunday, she took her bicycle and rode into town to the bakery. He was getting used to the hunger pains in the morning. Now he just ignored them.

As the sun rose, he loaded the last of the wheat onto the planter, hooked up the horses, put on his hat with the horsehair, gathered up his skirt, and made his way out to the east field. If he did not run into any difficulties, he would have the rest of the field planted by the time she got back from town.

By midmorning, Lieutenant Kellam had tossed his horsehair-laden hat aside and was lying on the dirt underneath the planter. A lever had broken on the seeder mechanism, and he was trying to figure out how to fix it. He finally decided he would have to pull the planter into the barn and see what he could find there to repair it. What he really needed was a welding machine, but he knew there wasn't one in the barn.

When Leyna rode up on her bicycle, a little after noon, Rand was on his back under the planter in the barn. The barn door was wide open. Leyna leaned inside the door and saw his legs sticking out from under the planter. She tapped him firmly on the foot. After a moment, he slid out from underneath the machine.

Leyna smiled at him and handed him a pastry. He wasted no time consuming it, and then he slid back under the planter. He was almost finished rigging up a temporary lever with some bailing string and a piece of scrap wood. Leyna stood back while he finished the project. She was contemplating how she would have done the plowing and planting all alone without his help.

It was not long before Lieutenant Kellam crawled back out,

hooked up the horses, and tossed his ridiculous hat back on his head. Leyna did not argue with him as he headed back out to the field. He seemed determined to finish the job.

When Rand returned to the barn from the field, hot and dusty, Leyna was waiting for him with a bucket of cold water she had just drawn from the well. Rand drank almost the whole thing. Never had water been so clear and tasted so sweet to him.

Not ten minutes after Lieutenant Kellam had returned to the barn with the planter, after finishing the last field, Leyna heard a car coming slowly up the driveway. She went cautiously to the barn door as Lieutenant Kellam ducked into a cow stall, removed his skirt, and rolled down his pant legs. Leyna recognized the car right away. She swallowed hard. It felt like a rock went straight to her stomach. It was time to say good-bye.

"It's *Tante* Zelma," she said to Rand in a feeble voice. Leyna opened the left barn door and motioned for *Onkel* Klaus to pull into the barn.

When he turned off the engine, *Tante* Zelma opened the passenger door and stepped out. She greeted Leyna with a kiss on each check.

"Did Lieutenant Owen make it?" Leyna asked immediately.

Tante Zelma nodded. "We know he at least made it to the first point," she replied.

Leyna let out a sigh of relief.

"Where is Lieutenant Kellam?" asked *Onkel* Klaus, emerging from his car.

Leyna turned around, and Lieutenant Kellam peeked up over the cow stall. Leyna stood there, motionless. In just a few hours, he would be on his way to freedom, and if the Lord saw him safely through, he would soon be back in America with family and friends. Leyna closed her eyes for a moment, and then she glanced back at Lieutenant Kellam. He turned away from her gaze.

"Can we go inside the house, Leyna?" asked *Tante* Zelma, breaking the awkward silence.

"Certainly," said Leyna as she moved toward the barn doors and began to close them.

"We'll want to leave just after dark," piped up *Onkel* Klaus.

Leyna nodded in return, and they all headed for the house.

Leyna's mother met the whole entourage at the back door as they came in. Leyna struggled to introduce the visitors.

"Mother, this is Zelma and Klaus. Uh, they are friends of the farm help," she said, stumbling over her words. *Tante* Zelma reached out and shook her mother's hand.

Her mother smiled and welcomed them. Leyna noticed that she was in rare form that day. Her mother sat them down at the kitchen table and began to slice up the bread Leyna had brought home from the bakery to serve them. Leyna put the coffee pot and some milk on the stove for *Onkel* Klaus.

Soon, they were all sitting around the table, eating. Her mother was telling them all about her father, how proud she was of how hard he always worked. *Tante* Zelma and *Onkel* Klaus listened politely. It did not take her mother long to tire out, and when she did, she excused herself, wrapped her shawl around her shoulders, and went to the front room to sit in her chair.

Leyna cleared the plates and began to wash them up. They were waiting for night to fall. Leyna looked at the clock. They would be leaving in about an hour.

Tante Zelma and *Onkel* Klaus talked quietly with Lieutenant Kellam for a little while, and then he went upstairs to change out of his farm clothes. Leyna offered *Onkel* Klaus another cup of coffee and some more warm milk, which he gladly accepted.

"We thought it would take much longer to get here than it did," said *Tante* Zelma, trying to find something to fill the silence.

"Will I know if they make it home safely?" asked Leyna, almost in a whisper.

Onkel Klaus shook his head.

"That is highly unlikely, Leyna," responded *Tante* Zelma, with sympathy in her voice.

Lieutenant Kellam came slowly into the kitchen, wearing his civilian clothes. Leyna looked at his outfit and smiled proudly. Then she looked down at his feet.

"Your shoes," she said to him. "Give me your shoes."

Tante Zelma translated for Rand. Lieutenant Kellam sat down at the kitchen table and unlaced his shoes. Leyna took them to the back door and dug through the wardrobe in the back room for her father's shoe polish and his old rag. Once she found them, she went back to the kitchen, sat down in the rocking chair, and started polishing.

Lieutenant Kellam paced the kitchen floor nervously in his socks until Leyna was done shining her brother's old pair of shoes. She looked out the window. It was almost dark.

Tante Zelma rose from her chair and spoke to Lieutenant Kellam. He looked over at Leyna and then looked down at his shoes.

Onkel Klaus got up and took his coffee cup to the kitchen sink. Then he extended his hand to Leyna. "*Auf Wiedersehen,*" he said with a smile and a peculiar bow.

"*Auf Wiedersehen,*" she replied.

Tante Zelma came over to Leyna and touched her on the arm. "Your job is done," she said. "Wish us luck."

Leyna tried to smile. Lieutenant Kellam followed *Tante* Zelma and *Onkel* Klaus out to the barn. Leyna was not far behind. While *Tante* Zelma was opening the hidden compartment in the backseat, *Onkel* Klaus slid behind the wheel and turned the key to crank the engine.

Leyna looked up at Rand with concern as the engine turned over and over but did not start. *Onkel* Klaus stepped out of the car, threw his hands up, and cursed. "We must be there on time. It is very important that we are there on time!" he said with clenched teeth.

Rand made his way quickly to the hood of the car and released the latch. Leyna perched herself on the top rung of a stall and watched him work under the hood. *Onkel* Klaus paced nervously between the engine and the driver's compartment. *Tante* Zelma stood on the passenger's side, leaning against the door, looking quite concerned. For several minutes, there was tension in the barn, and then Rand backed out from underneath the hood.

"Crank her up," he said, and then he turned with a serious look and glanced at Leyna.

Onkel Klaus scampered into the driver's seat and turned the engine over. To everyone's relief, it started on the second try. Not wanting to waste any more time, *Tante* Zelma motioned for Lieutenant Kellam to climb into the hiding place in the backseat. Leyna climbed down from her perch and tossed him a rag so he could wipe his hands off. Time was slipping away.

She wanted to thank him for all he had done for her. She wanted to tell him she would miss him and would be praying that he would make it safely home, but all that she could do was bite her tongue to try to keep the tears from coming. Rand handed the rag back to Leyna and gave her a peculiar look as if he wished to say something.

Onkel Klaus was anxious to leave, and *Tante* Zelma was pulling on Lieutenant Kellam's sleeve. Rand turned and ducked into the backseat of the car. Leyna watched as they tried to fit Lieutenant Kellam into the hidden space under the backseat. Before *Tante* Zelma closed up the secret compartment, Leyna saw Rand Kellam wave good-bye with a smile and a wink.

Leyna opened up the barn doors, and *Onkel* Klaus backed the car out into the night. This time, Leyna watched alone as *Tante* Zelma waved good-bye and the car rolled slowly down the driveway.

Friday Evening, May 19, 1944

Lieutenant Kellam took shallow breaths in his cramped hiding spot under the backseat of the car. It seemed that he felt every bump in the road as they sped toward an unknown destination. He was anxious to be on his way out of Germany. He had tried not to think about it until that moment. Now, he could picture himself returning to the States, seeing Doris, his parents, and his brother and sisters again.

He opened his eyes to the darkness as he remembered that afternoon in the belly of the doomed B-24, when he had made his promise to God. *It is a little early to tell,* he thought, *but it looks as if God is going to give me a chance to keep that promise.*

It was a long time before the car came to a complete stop. Rand listened carefully. He could feel the car still at an idle, but they were not moving. Maybe they had finally arrived at their destination.

"Be as still as possible," Rand heard *Tante* Zelma say. "We are at a checkpoint."

Rand felt his heart leap in his chest. The fear that suddenly swept over him prevented him from moving even an inch. Now he could hardly breathe.

A young soldier with a shiny new gun strapped across his chest approached the driver's side of the car with his flashlight and motioned for *Onkel* Klaus to roll the window down.

"Your papers, sir?" demanded the private coolly.

Onkel Klaus reached for his identification, and as he did the soldier began with the questions.

"What is your destination?"

Tante Zelma leaned over so that she could look the private in the eyes. "We are going to visit my cousin in Konstanz," she replied with an air of importance.

The private squinted and pointed his flashlight directly and purposefully into her eyes. "You are not permitted to be out at this time of the evening in this area, just driving around, no matter whom it is that you are going to visit," he stated quite firmly. "Who is your cousin, and where is her residence?"

"He is the son of the late Baron Von Zollach," replied *Tante* Zelma. "He lives off of Wendelgardweg in Konstanz; and were it not for the fact that my husband cannot keep this contraption masking itself as an automobile in good running condition, we would have been there by sundown and not subject to your scorn, Private."

"Cannot keep this contraption in good running condition?" retorted *Onkel* Klaus in a gasp, turning to *Tante* Zelma with a red face. "We are late, indeed, because you and your mother have mouths that were running nonstop until the sun set."

"That is nothing compared to the time it took you to fix the automobile so that we could start down the road, Klaus, and you know it!" responded *Tante* Zelma definitively.

Rand lay paralyzed in the hiding compartment, listening to the voices in the front seat increase in a heated argument until a deeper and less coherent voice silenced them.

"Stop! You are both arguing like little children, and this will not improve your situation!" shouted the private at last. "Out of the car!" he commanded *Onkel* Klaus. "I must see into your trunk."

Onkel Klaus opened the door slowly and rose to his feet. He hobbled to the back of the car and lifted the trunk lid for the private. On his way to the back of the car, the private looked thoroughly into the backseat. Then the soldier ran his flashlight carefully across the inside of the trunk.

Rand felt the hair on the back of his neck stand up as a flicker of light from the flashlight beam entered his hiding space through a crack somewhere. He had come too far to be caught now. He closed his eyes and said a prayer.

The sound of the trunk lid closing startled him, but he did

not move. "You should not be on the road at this hour. Go directly to your cousin's house, and be careful in the future not to be out at night," said the private with finality.

"Thank you, Private," said *Onkel* Klaus meekly as he got back into the car.

In a moment, they were rolling slowly down the road, and less than fifteen minutes later, the engine shut off. Rand heard the back door open, and he heard *Onkel* Klaus and *Tante* Zelma as they worked to remove the seat above his head. He climbed stiffly out of the hidden compartment into the cool, night air. It was just as dark outside as it had been in the compartment.

Tante Zelma took him by the hand, and they followed *Onkel* Klaus, who held a small flashlight, down a dirt path. He was still wiping sweat off his brow. Rand could hear the chorus of frogs, and he smelled must in the air. Before long, they were at the edge of water. Rand hesitated a moment, bent over, and removed his shoes and socks. Then he rolled up his pant legs. Leyna had gone to all the trouble to polish his shoes, and he wasn't about to get them all muddy.

With shoes in hand, he followed *Onkel* Klaus slowly through the mud and reeds into the water. Hidden inside a bunch of tall, thick reeds was a small fishing boat with two gray oars. A thin man wearing a dark shirt and a fisherman's cap was sitting in the boat, waiting for them.

"Thank God you waited for us," whispered *Onkel* Klaus to the man. "We were stopped at a checkpoint."

"I was just about to leave," replied the man in a hushed tone.

Onkel Klaus helped Lieutenant Kellam climb into the boat. The thin man motioned for him to lie down longwise underneath the rowing seats. Rand complied, and when he had stretched out almost the entire length of the boat, the thin man covered him with a thick tarp. At last, *Onkel* Klaus handed Lieutenant Kellam a packet.

"This is your identification. There is money inside for them to purchase for you a train ticket to Bern," he whispered hurriedly. "You will have to switch trains in Zurich." Rand took the packet and shoved it inside his coat.

Onkel Klaus exchanged a few more hushed words with the man, and then he thrust the boat out into a small channel. The thin man took the oars and began rowing with all of his might. From the bottom of the boat, Lieutenant Kellam did not see the darkness into which they were gliding, but he felt every tug that the thin man gave on the oars.

At one point in time, not long after they had left shore, Rand smelled cigarette smoke and thought he heard some laughter in the distance. The thin man slowed his rowing a bit and then continued on as quietly as he could.

For two hours, the man rowed. Every ten strokes, he would turn his head and look over his right shoulder to make sure they were headed for the tiny light on the opposite shore. The rowboat left only a small wake as it made its way slowly across Lake Constance toward the small town of Bottighofen in Switzerland. At midnight, the thin man directed his boat into a dimly lit boathouse.

He scrambled out of the boat and onto a dock, securing the boat to a post with a rope. He looked around cautiously and then rolled the tarp off of the lieutenant. "We were lucky," he said in German in a whisper. "Not one patrol tonight."

Rand pulled himself up off the floor of the boat and stepped onto the dock with the help of the thin man. After Rand had replaced his shoes on his feet, the two men headed up the dock and out the side door of the boathouse. Lieutenant Kellam had no idea where he was or where he was going. As a navigator, this bothered him. Rand and the thin man stumbled up a dark path that ran next to a large hotel and across a road to a small house on the side of a gentle hill just above the hotel.

As they stepped inside the door of the house, the thin man removed his cap and hung it on a rung by the door. Then he lit a lamp and showed Lieutenant Kellam over to a bed on the opposite wall. A door on the other end of the room popped open, and a boy about twelve years of age peeked out at the lieutenant. Rand smiled at the boy. A large woman with a round face came to the door and pulled the boy back into the room.

The thin man disappeared into the room where the woman was, taking the light with him. Lieutenant Kellam was left in the dark. He took his shoes off, removed his coat, tie, and shirt, and tried to stretch out on the bed he was sitting on. He pulled the blanket over his head and closed his eyes. He knew he was on his way home, so what did it matter to him if he had no idea where he was or where he was going?

End of May 1944

Lieutenant Kellam awoke before the sun came up. By now, he was used to getting up early to milk the cow. He had not slept very well. He was stiff from the car ride and then from being cramped up in the bottom of the boat. It wasn't long before the thin man's wife was up and getting some food on the table for breakfast.

The boy and his father joined them at the table for a meager breakfast of bread, cheese, and jam. The boy stared at the lieutenant the whole time. Lieutenant Kellam counted two words that were spoken that morning. When he tried to thank the woman for breakfast, she responded with a slight smile. They must not have spoken any English.

As Rand was finishing his cup of coffee, the thin man got a piece of paper from a desk in the corner and began to draw a picture for the lieutenant. He marked an *x* and drew a straight line where he scribbled the word *Zurich*. In between the *x* and *Zurich*, he marked a series of lines, clearly indicating stops.

"*In einen anderen Zug umsteigen,*" said the thin man in German.

Lieutenant Kellam nodded. He remembered what *Onkel* Klaus had told him the night before. The thin man then drew a straight line and wrote the word *Bern*.

Rand looked up at his host. "I understand," he said with a nod.

The man turned to the boy and spoke some words. Rand reached into his coat pocket and pulled out the packet *Onkel* Klaus had given him. The man nodded as Rand took out the money for the train ticket. He reached over the table, took the money from Rand, and counted it out for his son. The boy folded up the money and put it in the front pocket of his trousers. Then the thin man looked at his pocket watch and said something to his son. The boy came and tugged at Lieutenant Kellam's arm.

Rand stood up, put on his coat, and followed the boy out of the house.

The air that morning was crisp and clean. The sun was shining over the treetops, and there was a chorus of birds singing as the boy led the lieutenant down a gentle path, through some bushes, to a road that wound its way past the hotel. As they made their way beyond the hotel, Lieutenant Kellam could see the shore of Lake Constance. It was a clear day, the water was a deep blue, and he could see all the way back into Germany.

As they passed people on the road, the boy would greet them. Lieutenant Kellam tried not to let the fear he had inside show on his face. He was desperately hoping no one would speak to him. *Tante* Zelma had warned the men that they would not be out of harm's way and should not let their guard down until they were safely back in England. Although Switzerland was considered a neutral territory, in actuality, they were, at times, very cooperative with the German government.

The boy led him to a rack of bicycles. He picked out a bike for Lieutenant Kellam and then took one for himself. Lieutenant Kellam followed the boy down the road. In less than half an hour, they rode up to a train station. The boy left his bicycle at the rack and headed straight for the train depot. Lieutenant Kellam followed him at a distance.

The boy stood in line impatiently at the ticket window. Lieutenant Kellam posted himself in front of a bulletin board and pretended to read the train schedule until he saw the stationmaster hand the boy a ticket. He followed the boy through the doors to the platform. There were several people already there, waiting for a train. To Lieutenant Kellam's relief, no one seemed to notice him as being out of place. He reached up and adjusted the dog tags underneath his shirt.

Lieutenant Kellam and the boy with the knee-length trousers sat down on a bench and waited ten minutes. The boy's legs were dangling underneath the bench. At last, a train came puffing slowly up to the platform. The boy got up and ran to one of the cars. He read the destination card in the train window carefully, and then he beckoned for the lieutenant to board.

Rand shook the boy's hand and patted him on the head. Then he boarded the train. He made his way into a car and sat down in the first vacant seat he could find. He reached up and nervously patted his chest. He wanted to make sure his train ticket and his identification were still in his coat pocket.

At last, the train pulled away from the station, and Rand looked back out the window to see the boy waving at the train. Soon, the train was wandering through some of the most beautiful countryside that Lieutenant Kellam had ever seen. The mountains climbed all the way up to the blue sky, and their tops were still a snowy white. Rand looked around the car. It was not even half full.

Not long after they had pulled out of the next station, a conductor came through the car. Rand pulled out his ticket and his identification for the man. The conductor seemed to look a long time at the identification. Rand looked out the window, pretending not to care.

The conductor called to a Swiss soldier who had just entered the car from the other end. The Swiss soldier came over to where the conductor was standing. Lieutenant Kellam looked him straight in the eyes, and then he turned his gaze back out the window.

"His identification has the expired approval stamp," said the conductor to the soldier in German.

Lieutenant Kellam looked up at the men, pretending to understand their conversation.

The Swiss soldier took Lieutenant Kellam's identification in his left hand and peered down at the lieutenant for a moment. He looked at the lieutenant from head to shoes. Then he let out a grunt. "His shoes are polished, Gerhardt. They probably just used the wrong stamp. We have to finish the rest of the cars by the next stop. Let's move on."

The Swiss soldier handed Rand his identification back, and

the conductor punched his ticket. Lieutenant Kellam sat back in his seat, unaware of what was said but aware that he had just had a close call. He stared at his fake identification. It looked authentic to him.

Lieutenant Kellam breathed in deeply and then looked out the window again. He was swaying to the *clickety-clack* of the car going down the tracks. Now all he had to do was make it to Bern.

Lieutenant Kellam watched every stop carefully until he arrived in Zurich. He exited the train and followed the others to the train depot. He wandered around until he saw a train schedule posted on the wall. Next to it was another schedule. He was not sure which one to follow. Rand took a step back and looked over his shoulder at the platforms.

"*Entschuldigen Sie,*" said a porter as he ran directly into the back of the lieutenant with the edge of one of the suitcases he was carrying.

Lieutenant Kellam stepped quickly out of the porter's path and nodded graciously. "Bern?" asked the lieutenant immediately before the porter was completely out of earshot.

"*Gleis drei,*" replied the porter without turning back.

"*Danke,*" replied the lieutenant. He looked up at the platform numbers and headed directly toward platform three. Now he could have hugged Leyna. She had at least taught them to count to ten.

In under an hour, he was on the train to Bern. Though he was plenty tired, he dared not fall asleep for fear he would miss his stop, but there was beautiful scenery to keep the lieutenant awake. He had plenty of time to think about life, and what he was going to do with his once he got home.

It was early afternoon as the train from Zurich pulled into Bern. Lieutenant Kellam was tired and hungry as he stepped down off of the train. He looked both ways down the platform, not sure where he was supposed to go next. He searched his memory. No one had told him what to do once he got to Bern.

He followed the other passengers toward the train depot, but he stopped as he got to an empty bench. He sat down for a moment and retied one of his shoes. *Perhaps someone is supposed to meet me here,* he thought.

A middle-aged woman sat down on the bench next to Lieutenant Kellam.

"Lieutenant?" she said in a southern American accent.

Rand looked at the woman and she smiled.

"Come on," she said.

The woman took his arm, and the two of them strolled out to the streets of Bern. They walked in silence for several blocks, and then the woman opened a gate and beckoned for Lieutenant Kellam to enter.

They walked through a garden and into the back door of a large, white building. Once they were inside, the woman welcomed Lieutenant Kellam to the American embassy. She led him to a spacious room at the end of a long hall. There, sitting on a plush, brown couch, reading a newspaper, sat Lieutenant Owen.

"Frank!" said Rand with some surprise. "I thought you would be halfway home by now."

Lieutenant Owen put his newspaper down on his lap. "I had to wait here for you," he said, a little impatiently.

"Make yourself comfortable, Lieutenant," said the woman. "But you won't be here very long. You've got to catch the two-thirty train. I'll tell Mr. Aspling that you've arrived and see if I can find y'all something to eat."

Rand watched the woman disappear down the hallway; then he wandered over to the couch and sat down next to Lieutenant Owen.

"Where do we go from here?" Rand asked.

Lieutenant Owen took up his newspaper again. "I'm not sure, but Mr. Aspling will let us know."

Rand looked around the room. There was a phonograph in the far corner by a built-in bookcase that held a mixture of old, classic books and glass artifacts. He noticed the elaborate woodwork on the ceiling and all of the walls. The windows behind him and to the left were long and large and were flanked on each side by heavy sets of burgundy, paisley drapes.

Rand listened to the ticking of the grandfather clock by the doorway. Over on the right, on a table in the corner, was a small picture frame in front of the lamp. Rand stared at the picture of the American flag on top of a flagpole, flowing in a breeze. He turned his gaze out the window.

It had been a long time since he had seen the flag, but he did not expect the wave of patriotism that washed over his heart at that moment. Would he really see home again? Rand looked down at his shiny shoes. They were resting on a very expensive-looking, light-shaded rug that covered a highly polished, wooden floor.

Lieutenant Owen and Lieutenant Kellam both looked up toward the doorway as they heard the faint sound of footsteps in the hallway. In a moment, the woman who had brought him to the embassy entered the room, carrying a tray with a teapot and a plate of sandwiches. She was followed by a stately, older gentleman of medium height and build, who looked just as a diplomat should. He wore small, wire-rimmed glasses that sat precariously on his nose, and when he smiled, he had a golden tooth that glistened in the light. He was fashionably attired in a pinstriped suit and was wearing a vest underneath his coat.

"Lieutenant Kellam," said the man, extending his hand stiffly. "I am Henry Aspling, general secretary to the ambassador."

Lieutenant Kellam rose to his feet. "A pleasure to meet you, sir," he said with a friendly smile. "I am glad to be here."

"Well, we are glad you are here. However, you should not consider yourself to be out of danger just yet," he replied. "Please have a seat and get started on the sandwiches, gentlemen."

The general secretary's face twisted in disapproval as he looked from Lieutenant Kellam to Lieutenant Owen. "I can see that you both had the same tailor. We do not have time to fix this now," said Mr. Aspling, rubbing his eyes underneath his glasses.

"Perhaps it will suffice to change out one tie. Evelyn, see if you can find me another tie. I may have a spare one in my office on the back of the door." The woman who had met him at the train station handed Rand a cup of tea, and then she left the room in a hurry.

"I must give my apology for the ambassador," continued Mr. Aspling. "He would normally attend to these matters himself, but we have been somewhat inundated with a most delicate situation with the Swiss government since the unfortunate and accidental bombing of Schaffhausen. I need not go into more details, but our relationship with the Swiss is quite strained at the moment."

Mr. Aspling caught his breath and then continued. "Listen to me carefully, gentlemen. We have no time to waste," he said, leaving his diplomatic voice behind and taking on a tone of urgency. "Shortly, we will send you both out with a ticket for the two-thirty train to Lausanne. Which one of you can remember the way to the train station?"

Lieutenant Owen looked at Lieutenant Kellam and shook his head. "I have no idea where I am, Mr. Aspling. But Lieutenant Kellam here is a navigator."

"Very well," continued the secretary. "We will send you, Lieutenant Kellam, out the servants' entrance. You, Lieutenant Owen, will leave from the garden door. You will go out the garden gate and make a right-hand turn, where you will see Lieutenant Kellam, who will already be half a block on his way back to the train station. Try to maintain as much distance between yourselves as possible. There is always the possibility that someone will be watching you or following you from this building."

Rand and Lieutenant Owen glanced quickly at each other. Somewhere in the last two sentences, the secretary had lost his smile.

"Lieutenant Kellam, do not go directly to the train station. If you can, take a small detour. Go around a block if you must. But be careful not to lose your friend. He should be the only one following you.

"When you get to the station, do not speak with each other. You must act as if you are complete strangers. Board the train for Lausanne, but do not sit in the same car. If possible, sit so that you can see one another, but do not let anyone suspect you know each other." The secretary looked from Lieutenant Kellam to Lieutenant Owen.

"At all costs, you must keep your mouths shut. Now, on the other end, you will be met by a man in a white hat. The network has been informed of your coming, but I must warn you. It may be a long time before you are back in Allied territory. The couriers will wait until it is safe to move you. You must both be patient." Mr. Aspling paused and looked out the window for a moment.

"Should anything go wrong, gentlemen," he began again, turning to them, "your best bet would be to try to make it to the coast of unoccupied France."

Rand swallowed hard. Perhaps the hardest part was not getting out of Germany after all.

Before the general secretary could go on, the woman returned with a tie in hand. Mr. Aspling handed it directly to Lieutenant Owen. "I'll trade you, Lieutenant. We don't want you two looking like twins," he said with his gold tooth sparkling underneath a forced smile.

Lieutenant Owen removed the tie Leyna had made for him and replaced it with Mr. Aspling's shorter, green tie.

"Now," said the secretary with a slap on his knee and rising to his feet. "You must go. Good luck, gentlemen." He reached out and gave them both a solid handshake.

"Evelyn will show you, Lieutenant Kellam, out the servants' entrance, and I will take you, Lieutenant Owen, to the garden door. Oh, and I almost forgot," he added, reaching into his vest pocket. "Here are your tickets to freedom."

The lieutenants thanked him for his help, and then they parted as planned. Two minutes later, when Lieutenant Owen turned the corner by the garden gate, he could see Lieutenant Kellam a half a block ahead of him, just as the secretary had said.

At twenty-seven minutes past two, Rand Kellam took a seat in the second car back from the engine as Frank Owen made himself comfortable in the third car. At half past the hour, the train to Lausanne made a slow lurch forward out of the station.

Halfway through their journey to Lake Geneva, when Rand had just nodded off, the conductor came by and tapped him on the knee. Lieutenant Kellam came to attention and reached in his coat for his identification and his ticket. This conductor took the same long look at his identification as the previous conductor had, and, for a moment, Rand thought there would be trouble. But then the man punched his ticket, gave him his identification back, and moved on to the next car.

Out of the corner of his eye, Rand watched as the conductor took Lieutenant Owen's identification and ticket. He held his breath until the ticket was punched, and the conductor gave Frank his identification back without incident.

The train carrying the Army Air Corps officers pulled into Lausanne late that evening. As soon as they got off of the train, a thick man wearing a white hat tapped Rand on the shoulder, startling him almost out of his skin. Lieutenant Kellam looked straight into the tough man's face. He motioned for the lieutenant to follow him. Lieutenant Kellam's heart sank. The man looked like a Gestapo agent. Rand looked behind him. Lieutenant Owen was following them at a distance.

Even though Mr. Aspling had told them to look for a man in white hat, they were not entirely sure that they were out of danger until the man led them down a steep ravine to the edge of Lake Geneva and put them on a boat toward France.

By ten o'clock that night, the lieutenants were in a small boat on their way across Lake Geneva and almost back to freedom. The spray from the boat occasionally doused the lieutenants. When they reached the other side of the lake, Rand followed the guide and Lieutenant Owen up to a cabin. They stepped inside a room with a warm stove in one corner and a large bed in the other. It took Rand less than a minute to go to sleep that evening. The excitement and tension of the day had drained him dry.

Over the course of the next three weeks, the lieutenants were shuttled through an elaborate network of the French underground to a port city in Spain. Finally, two days after D-day, they were loaded onto a cargo ship with some very expensive wine.

As Rand sat on the floor of the cramped compartment space next to the coal-burning engine room, he watched Lieutenant Owen's face turn several different shades of color. The swaying of the ship on the sea was causing them both to feel squeamish.

They had not exchanged a single word since the ship had left port, but Rand figured Lieutenant Owen was thinking the same thing he was. If, by some miracle, the ship was able to pass by the German naval vessels that patrolled the coastline of France without a thorough inspection, and if they were not sunk by a German U-boat in the open seas, they would soon be back in England.

Rand could not decide if he preferred eight hours of fear and the unknown completing missions in a heavy bomber or the feeling of being hunted like a fugitive every moment of the day and night. At any rate, he figured, his fugitive days were drawing shortly to a close.

Lieutenant Kellam swallowed hard and took in a shallow breath. He was starting to feel sick. The pistons inside the engine in the room next door were stroking at equal intervals as Rand turned his attention to more cumbersome thoughts. Now that he was almost back to safety, he was struggling deep inside. There were questions that kept haunting him. *Why was our copilot shot and not me? Why did he have to go down with the plane? Did the others make it to the ground safely? Were they alive or in a dark prison camp? Why did God have mercy on me?* He thought of nothing else but these questions all the way back to England.

Rand lifted his eyes to check on Lieutenant Owen. He was curled up against the wall by the compartment door. It did not matter how many times he heard the engine turn over or how sick he felt inside; he always came to the same conclusion: he had no answers to his questions. He knew that if he just dismissed the questions from his mind, they would follow him the rest of his life.

He also knew he may never have the answers to his questions. He knew enough about God to know that he had a plan for his creation and that he sometimes worked in ways that men cannot understand. At that moment, Rand looked down at the palm of his left hand. He made a fist, turned it upside down, and stretched his fingers all the way out. Then he settled the issue for good. He decided to trust the one who had spared his life. He decided not to ask him why anymore.

One day later, a weary Lieutenant Kellam and a seasick Lieutenant Owen staggered off of the cargo ship and onto a crowded dock in Brighton, England. They were collected at the dispatch shack by a staff sergeant, who whisked them by truck to Stone in Kent, where they were met by an intelligence officer and processed back into the Army Air Corps. The next morning, Rand got what he desperately wanted: a hot shower, a good shave, a haircut, and a full American breakfast.

June 1944

One full week after D-day, amid the chaos that surrounded them, Lieutenant Kellam and Lieutenant Owen sat in endless sessions of mind-numbing interrogations and debriefings. At the end of the second week, sometime after lunch, Lieutenant Kellam sat at a metal table in a small, dimly lit room, waiting to complete his last interrogation session. A major and a lieutenant colonel entered the room. Lieutenant Kellam stood at attention.

"At ease, Lieutenant," said the lieutenant colonel. "Please, have a seat."

The lieutenant colonel had a nicely rounded face adorned with piercing, brown eyes. He had a handsome head of hair and carried himself with distinction. The major was a man of slight build. He wore round, wire-rimmed glasses, and he had a mole just above his lip. Rand had not seen these two men the entire two weeks he had been in Stone.

The men took turns repeating questions he had already answered about his final mission. Who made it out of the plane? How many parachutes did he see? Where were they when they bailed out? The major was taking careful notes of everything he said. Lieutenant Kellam answered their questions again, as best he could. Then they asked him to tell them how it was that he managed to escape out of Germany.

Lieutenant Kellam looked from the colonel to the major and back to the colonel. They had posed the question to him in a tone that indicated disbelief.

Lieutenant Kellam cleared his throat and began to tell them how Leyna had found them; how she had hid them; and, finally, how she had found a way for them to get out of Germany. The major and the colonel were familiar with the particulars of his escape once he crossed into Switzerland. The thin man at Lake

Constance had phoned a man who lived across the street from the American embassy. He walked over to the embassy and told them that Lieutenant Kellam was on his way. The embassy then phoned the man in the white hat, who had made arrangements for their transport across Lake Geneva, into the hands of the French Underground, and then on to Spain.

For over three hours, the interrogators asked him detailed questions about his two months in Germany. Was Leyna working alone? Did she leave the house regularly? Was she in contact with any German authorities? Why did she help them? What information did she try to get out of them? Did she ask him for anything in return for hiding them? Did they have to pay her with any favors?

There was an endless stream of questions. Lieutenant Kellam answered them all, except for the last question. Rand understood clearly, from the tone of his voice, what the major was insinuating. Rand stood straight up out of his chair, knocking the chair, he was sitting on over on to the floor. Then he took in a deep breath.

"No, Major," said Lieutenant Kellam, trying to remain calm. "Leyna is not that kind of girl."

The lieutenant colonel got up from his seat, walked over, and picked up Lieutenant Kellam's chair.

"Sit down, Lieutenant," he said calmly. Then he leaned against the table a short distance away from Rand and folded his arms.

"We are on your side, Lieutenant," said the colonel. "Look. We are just trying to figure out how you and Lieutenant Owen got out of Germany. During this whole bleak war, not one airman has evaded capture behind German lines with the help of a German citizen. We are just trying to understand what happened."

"We need the information to help other airmen, to help our ground forces," continued the major. "We are trying to determine what our men will face when they get into Germany. Will the German people welcome them, or will they face fierce hostility?"

Lieutenant Kellam sighed. "I can tell you how this happened, Major," said Rand at last, "but you're not going to like my explanation."

"Try me," shot back the colonel.

Lieutenant Kellam looked the colonel straight in the eyes. "God had mercy on us, and that is the only reason we made it out alive," he said boldly.

The lieutenant colonel nodded his head up and down. "You're probably right, Lieutenant. You're probably right." The lieutenant colonel brought his hand down from his chin and crossed his arms. "Major, we've got a briefing in fifteen minutes."

The major shuffled some papers around and then handed Lieutenant Kellam several sheets of paper.

"You probably want to notify your parents or your wife or your girlfriend that you're alive. Fill these out, and I'll make sure they get off to the right people. If we wait for the war department to find their addresses, they won't find out you've been found until after you get home."

Lieutenant Kellam let out a chuckle.

"You've earned yourself a two-week pass, Lieutenant, and a desk job stateside."

Lieutenant Kellam looked up from the paperwork. He hadn't expected to hear that and he didn't much like the sound of a desk job in the states.

The major must have seen the discomfort on his face. He continued.

"But there is still a war going on, Lieutenant. Should you be so inclined to volunteer, we could sure use someone with your knowledge and experience here in the European Theatre in flight ops. You wouldn't have to fly missions."

Lieutenant Kellam looked back down at the paperwork.

"Let the post officer know what you'd like to do tomorrow when you pick up your leave papers, Lieutenant. He'll be reassigning you," said the lieutenant colonel as he got up to leave.

Lieutenant Kellam stood up and gave both men a smart salute.

"Welcome back, Lieutenant, and congratulations on your escape," said the colonel just before he left the room.

Rand sat back down, filled out his parent's address on the telegram form, and handed it back to the major. He sat there, listening to the echo of the major's footstep down the hall, and then he slid down in his chair and rested his head on the back. If it weren't for Leyna's help and God's mercy, he would either be dead or rotting in a miserable prisoner-of-war camp somewhere in Germany, and he knew it.

The next morning after breakfast, Lieutenant Kellam and Lieutenant Owen reported to the post officer on duty at the base. The post officer was a gruff-looking man with green eyes and a very short haircut. Rand stood behind Frank Owen as the officer processed Frank's leave papers and gave him his new assignment. Frank smiled at Rand with his leave papers in hand and stepped out into the hall to wait for him.

"Lieutenant Kellam," said the post officer without looking up, "you will have a two-week pass once you arrive back in the States."

"Sir?" said Lieutenant Kellam as the officer paused for a moment. "Forgive me for interrupting you, sir, but the interrogation officer mentioned to me that if I was not interested in returning to the States just yet that I could volunteer to remain here?"

The post officer raised his eyes slowly to Rand's.

"What do you have in mind, Lieutenant?"

"Well, sir," began Rand with a hard swallow. He straightened his shoulders and leveled his chin. "I am willing to go back to my unit, to be reassigned, and to fly as a navigator with a new crew, sir."

The post officer tried unsuccessfully to hide a smile. "Son, I can't reassign you to combat duty after you have been behind enemy lines. No regulation in the Army Air Corps will allow for that."

Rand looked down at the post officer, hoping the relief he felt in his heart was not showing all over his face. He had no desire to return to navigating, but he could not stand the thought of returning to the comfort of the States while there was still a war to be fought in Europe. He had seen the face of the enemy up close. He had felt the oppression, and he simply could not turn his back and go home. He had decided that while floating in the middle of the Atlantic.

"However," continued the post officer, without hesitating, "since you have indicated to me your desire to stay here, I am sure there are plenty of places we can find for your reassignment, Lieutenant." The post officer reached up and took back Rand's leave papers.

"Come back and see me tomorrow, Lieutenant, and I will have your new assignment and see that you get a pass to London for some R and R."

Rand managed a smile. "Thank you, sir," he responded, and he turned to leave empty-handed.

When he stepped out into the hall, Lieutenant Owen gave him an inquisitive look.

"What took you so long, Rand? Where are your papers?"

On a blustery June afternoon, when Lieutenant Kellam should have been leaving for the States, he stood on the platform of the train station in Stone to send Lieutenant Owen off.

"You're sure about this, Rand?" asked Lieutenant Owen with a look of disbelief.

Rand nodded.

Lieutenant Owen shook his head. "You're crazier than I thought," said Lieutenant Owen, reaching out and taking a hold of his shoulder. "You've got my address, Rand. If you are ever in New York, you better come and see us," he said, pointing a finger at Rand.

Rand smiled and reached out to shake his friend's hand. "I will," he said confidently.

Rand watched as Lieutenant Owen boarded the train to the coast. In three more weeks, he would be back home. Rand caught a ride back to the base. In his pocket was a two-week pass to London and his new orders to report to High Wycombe at the end of June. Now all he had to do was write a letter to Doris and to his parents, explaining the past three months. He had no idea how he would do this without his entire letter being blacklined by the Army censors.

It wasn't really until his third night in London that Rand started to feel like his old self again. He was staying at the Red Cross Club near Oxford Circus with men on leave from several air bases near Wendling. They were mainly B-17 crewmen, but they took Rand in as one of their own once they learned he was a Wendling veteran.

Rand, not wanting to be left alone in his room, was persuaded by the other officers at his hotel to go with them to the Friday night dance put on at the Columbia Red Cross Club. After a long walk across town, they all finally arrived at the club. As they got to the middle of the block, Rand saw dozens of Army airmen filtering in and out of the building. They were laughing, drinking, and generally trying to forget the more important issues of life. Once he entered the building, the music from the dance hall hit Rand directly in the face. The officers he had come with went right in to find dance partners, but Rand could not bring himself to go into the hall.

During his stay in Germany, he had grown accustomed to

the peaceful sounds of the birds singing. He had learned to face head-on the gravity of war. It was almost too much of a shock for him to see his fellow men carrying on in such a reckless manner instead of maintaining their dignity when, for some of them, death lay straight ahead.

Rand found his way out of the building and stepped into the street. The daylight was fading quickly, and London was falling into its mandatory darkness. Lieutenant Kellam wandered around the streets in a daze. Three long blocks away, he wandered into a church and sat down in the last pew. It was now almost dark outside, and he was alone. Only a faint glow remained in the stained glass windows above the altar in front of the church.

Rand rubbed his eyes with his hand. He had felt it most keenly that evening on the way to the dance. No one knew how tied up he felt inside. No one for miles around understood what he had been through in the past three months. He would never be the same.

Before he had left for London, he had written to his parents and tried his best to explain what had happened and what he had decided to do now that he was back to England. He had also written to Doris to let her know that he was alive, but it wasn't Doris who had occupied a good bit of his thoughts lately. Rand breathed in deeply and let out a sigh. He wanted nothing more than to do the right thing now, but he wasn't quite sure what that was.

Night fell heavily on Rand as he sat in the darkness. On his first two days in London, he had seen the destruction the German bombs had wreaked on the city. There were whole blocks of ghostly rubble, followed by whole blocks of buildings that were unscathed. But the sight that resonated the most with Rand was the missing building in the middle of an otherwise untouched block. That was exactly how Rand felt deep inside.

At last, Rand stood. It was getting late, and he decided that he had better find his way back to his friends at the dance. After only one wrong turn in the dark, Rand arrived back at the door of the Columbia RC Club. He stepped inside the hall and stood against the wall next to a plant for a moment until his eyes adjusted to the light.

Lieutenant Kellam scanned the room for sight of his friends, but instead, his eyes fell almost immediately upon a familiar figure. She was standing sideways, twenty feet from where Rand was standing, wearing a slender, red dress. She was smiling as she was engaged in flirtatious conversation with a tall Army major, who had a full head of dark, red hair. Rand blinked his eyes and stared at her. He thought for sure that he was dreaming until she turned and looked his way.

Rand smiled nervously as she made her way through the crowd to where he was standing. What was Doris doing in London?

"Hello, Rand," came her voice clearly as she stepped closer to him.

Lieutenant Kellam swallowed his greeting. "Doris? Sweetheart? What are you doing here?" he asked in disbelief.

A large smile lit up her lipstick-laden lips as she glanced back at the red-headed major. "Rand! This is quite a surprise. I mean, I never expected to see you here."

Rand narrowed his eyes and she glanced back at the major again. "What are you doing here?" he tried again.

"I, uh, joined the Red Cross effort after you left for England, and then, when I stopped getting your letters, I figured you had a new girlfriend or you were dead, so I applied to come to London so I could be closer to Herb," she replied carelessly.

By this time, Rand could see the major making his way to where they were standing. Rand was now looking straight into the eyes of a jealous man. Lieutenant Kellam felt his heart drop to the floor.

"Herb, this is an old friend from college," began Doris nervously. "Rand Kellam." Her smile faded away.

The red-headed major looked at Lieutenant Kellam, and then he turned firmly to Doris without saying anything to Rand. "Let's dance, Doris. We're running out of time."

"Okay, Herb," she responded, trying to appease him. "Just give me a minute to say good-bye."

Rand was trying desperately to process what Doris had just told him when she reached out and patted him twice on the cheek. "Good-bye, Rand," she said with a flare of finality as the major dragged her away from him and back to the dance floor.

Rand leaned back against the wall and closed his eyes. Had she really just introduced him as "an old friend from college?" They had made plans together, serious plans. He had opened his heart to her, and she had brought some excitement into his otherwise dull life. He had written her every day while he was in England. Even before he was safely back, she had moved on to someone else. Rand breathed in deeply and turned to leave the hall. He wasn't feeling well.

The part of him that had wandered away from God had enjoyed life with Doris and the excitement of going off to war. He had made plans, that the part of him that wanted to do right, knew would never work out. Now it seemed that he was free of those commitments, and the part of him that wanted to be all of him the rest of his life was actually not unhappy at what had just happened.

"Hey, Rand," called one of his friends. "Where have you been? We're just about to head back to the hotel. Henry went back inside looking for you."

Rand went slowly over to his friend, who was standing near the front door.

"What's the matter, Rand? I didn't see you dancing."

Rand reached up and scratched the back of his head. Doris had left him speechless. Rand looked back toward the hall, as a flood of people seemed to be making their way out of the building. In the middle of the throng, he saw the red-headed major coming, with Doris clinging to his arm. Rand stood at attention, but he did not say a word. She did not even look at him as they passed by.

Rand was unprepared for it to come to an end like this, but

he did nothing to stop her. Maybe it was a good thing they didn't marry before he was shipped off to England. He knew all along that Doris was not the kind of girl who would have taken life and the trials and struggles of it well, but she had been fun. Now he was free to serve his country, live the way he knew he should, and pursue the hope that had been in his heart for some time.

England, Summer 1944-
Spring 1945

Lieutenant Kellam reported for duty at the Eighth Air Force headquarters at the Wycombe Abbey School for Girls in Buckinghamshire, England, on June 27. His commanding officer immediately put him to work, coordinating bombing run plans for the Second Air Division and arranging support for the ground troops, who were struggling to make headway out of Normandy.

In the next couple of months, in addition to his other duties, Rand traveled across England to many of the air bases, updating the green heavy bomber crews on what to expect in case of bail out, as he was one of only a handful of men in the Army Air Corps who was not a prisoner of war, who had experienced this firsthand.

As the weeks rolled by, Rand gained a good reputation at his new assignment, and his responsibilities increased. He worked long and grueling hours, getting up before the sun rose. He was often still at his desk in the evening as the RAF heavy bombers took off, heading to Germany to drop their bombs. Every time he heard them overhead, he would pause and ask God to keep Leyna safe.

Summer gave way to fall. Fall soon withered away into winter. Lieutenant Kellam eyed the strategy board, marked with the current location of the Army's ground troops. They were making slow progress toward the Rhine River, but he had somehow hoped the progress would be faster.

Spring came slowly to England, and with it also came a commendation for his work and a promotion to first lieutenant from none other than Lieutenant General James Doolittle. Now the ground troops were moving past the Rhine River into the heart of Germany.

At the end of April, American soldiers began liberating the prisoner-of-war and concentration camps inside Germany. On April 25, 1945, Lieutenant Kellam dispatched the final bombing run orders. Five days later, they all received word that Hitler was dead. Rand was at his desk when news of the German surrender came over the wire. The events of the rest of that day suddenly became a happy blur.

In the wake of the end of hostilities in the European Theatre, the men at the Eighth Air Force Headquarters were given the daunting task of retrieving and transporting home the tens of thousands of American prisoners of war. Lieutenant Kellam worked nearly around the clock for weeks on end to assist in accomplishing this mission.

Every time an updated list of evacuees would come in from Camp Lucky Strike in France, Rand was one of the first ones in line to check it for the names of his former crewmembers. Rumors and bits of information about the prisoner-of-war experiences were also flowing into headquarters. The more Rand heard the more he realized that God had spared him the suffering, starvation, and death marches that his fellow crew members had to endure.

He found the pilot, Lieutenant Peterson's name, on a list of the initial round of evacuees. By the end of May, the only two names he had not seen on the lists were their copilot, Lieutenant Camistro, and the waist gunner, Sergeant Lidgard. Seven out of ten of them had made it through the war.

In the early evening on the last Sunday in May, Lieutenant Kellam sat on a wooden chair next to an open window in his living quarters. A light breeze was playing with the leaves on the trees outside. He had a pencil in his hand and a piece of paper in his lap. He had been waiting for enough time to pass before sending the letter he was now composing to an address he had memorized over a year ago.

Herr Georg Hartmann
Neumarkt 24
Zurich, Switzerland

Dear *Herr* Hartmann,
    My name is Lieutenant Randall Kellam. I am one of the men that Leyna helped over a year ago and consequently one whom, although we have never met, I understand you also helped. Before I go on, I want to thank you.
    Now that the war is at an end for us in Europe, I am wondering every day whether Leyna made it safely through. Do you know how she is and where I can find her? Any information you can give me I will receive with great appreciation.

Sincerely,
Randall Kellam

Rand folded the piece of paper in half and stuck it in an envelope. He hoped the letter would reach Leyna's uncle and that, by now, the initial chaos and confusion in Germany would be cleared enough for her uncle to have received word from Leyna.

A week passed and then two, but there was no response from her uncle. Lieutenant Kellam began to wonder if the old man had moved or had died. One afternoon, when he returned to his desk from a meeting, he saw a small, white envelope on the corner of his desk. He recognized the old, German lettering on the address. Without hesitation, he snatched the letter up and tore open the envelope.
    The letter was written in English, but the old, German let-

tering was difficult for him to decipher. Lieutenant Kellam choked back the tears as he read the letter slowly. When he had finished reading it, he folded the letter carefully and headed for the stairs.

Once he was outside, he sat down on the back steps and read the letter again slowly. His heart was breaking now. The news from her uncle was not what he had hoped to hear, nor what he had expected.

Germany, Summer-Fall 1944

Leyna watched the car carrying Lieutenant Kellam until she could see the taillights no longer. She dried her tears as she made her way back to the farmhouse. In all of the excitement of the past two months, she had not noticed how terribly tired she was. Now the weight of the war and the dreariness of it all came back with a force.

She was late getting to the bakery on Saturday morning. She had taken too long to milk the cow. *Herr* Krueger was kind enough not to ask her why her eyes were puffy and swollen, and he did not scold her for being late. She took home too much bread that afternoon, out of habit, but she wasn't very hungry, and her mother was barely eating enough to keep herself alive.

That evening, while Leyna was out in the barn milking the cow, her mother fell in the kitchen. Leyna found her in pain on the floor as she came in with a pail of milk. With great effort, she helped her mother up and into her bed and tried to make sure there were no broken bones. Leyna pleaded with her mother to let her call the doctor, but her mother insisted she was just bruised.

In the days to follow, her mother did not leave her bed. Leyna felt torn between keeping food on the table and staying with her mother. She also began the futile task of keeping weeds out of the fields. As the days grew longer and hotter, the task became more grueling for her.

Leyna was out in the field one evening when she noticed a car driving up to the farmhouse. She made her way back to the house as quickly as she could. As she got closer to the car, she recognized it immediately. *Tante* Zelma emerged from the driver's side and greeted Leyna with a kiss.

"Is everything all right?" asked Leyna cautiously.

"Yes," replied *Tante* Zelma with a mysterious look in her eyes. Then she paused for a long time and looked back at the car.

"I have come to ask you for a favor, Leyna," she began at last, taking Leyna by the arm. "I have two girls and a little boy with me who need a place to stay until we can get them out of Germany. Will you take them for a week or two?"

Leyna stared at *Tante* Zelma and shifted nervously on her feet. This was the last thing she had expected of *Tante* Zelma.

"They are Jewish?" asked Leyna perceptively.

Tante Zelma finally nodded, a tenseness rising in her face.

"Don't worry, *Tante* Zelma," said Leyna. "I will hide them."

Leyna walked with *Tante* Zelma to the car and opened the back door. Two girls, ages ten and eight, got out of the backseat cautiously. Leyna took the younger one by the hand and hurried her into the farmhouse. The older girl carried the five-year-old boy inside, followed by *Tante* Zelma.

When they were all safe in the house, Leyna closed the door behind *Tante* Zelma.

"Do they have any belongings?" asked Leyna, as *Tante* Zelma fussed with the collar on the boy's shirt.

Tante Zelma shook her head from side to side. Leyna swallowed hard.

"I must leave before anyone sees me, Leyna. I will be back in a week or two," said *Tante* Zelma as she reached for the doorknob nervously. She turned her head quickly. "Thank you, Leyna."

Tante Zelma wasted no time. Before Leyna could reply, she was out the door and halfway to the car.

Leyna looked at the children, who were all looking up at her. The girls had long, beautiful, black hair, and the boy had big, brown eyes. Leyna smiled.

"What are your names?" she asked sweetly, trying to imagine how she would feel if she were just deposited in a stranger's house.

"I'm Martha," said the oldest girl softly, without a smile. "This is Maria," she continued, putting her arm around her sister, "and Johann."

Leyna stooped down and looked the little boy straight in the eyes. "Well, you are all welcome at my house. I am Leyna, and we shall make the very best of your stay as we can," she said, looking back to the girls.

Leyna tried not to stare at the tattered, yellow Star of David that was prominently sewn on the front of each of their shirts. *At least these new guests can speak German,* she thought with a smile.

"The first thing I would like to know is if you would like some bread to eat and some milk to drink," said Leyna after a moment.

All three heads nodded in unison. Leyna led them into the kitchen and poured three glasses of milk for them. Then she cut up a loaf of bread and set it on the table. While they were busy eating in silence, Leyna stood by the kitchen sink, wondering where their parents were and wondering when the insanity of the war would be over.

After they had eaten, Leyna led them up the stairs into the attic and pulled out a box of toys from under one of the eaves. The boy clung to his older sister for a while, but then he became curious and started to pull items from the box. Leyna told the girls about her mother. Leyna told them that she would be gone to town until well in the afternoon every day, and she told them plainly that they should not leave the house. They seemed to understand.

During the next two weeks, Leyna never saw the children smile. She worked, one by one, at removing the yellow Star of David from their shirts. She figured if they were caught they would most likely be sent to a concentration camp, with or without the star. Such was the sorry state of affairs in Germany.

The children were well-behaved and quiet. Leyna took them

out to the barn with her every night to milk the cow. Maria was the only one who tried her hand at milking. She seemed to love animals. Johann would run around the barn and get into all sorts of things while Martha followed him around like a shadow.

Tante Zelma did not return as promised until three weeks later. Leyna had begun to worry that something had happened to her. A part of her would not have minded if the children had to stay longer, but for their sake, she hoped they could make it safely out of Germany. *Tante* Zelma told Leyna that they were having trouble making arrangements for the children on the other end, but that someone had finally agreed to take them. Once again, the house was empty.

Leyna prayed daily for rain as she watched the barley and the wheat crops grow. By the end of September, Leyna had finished up the harvest and was working on gathering up straw for the winter months. *Herr* Krueger's wife had returned from Düsseldorf, and Leyna no longer went into the bakery every morning.

On the second of October, Leyna sat beside her mother's bed. She had not eaten in weeks and would take very little to drink. She no longer recognized Leyna. Leyna read her several chapters from the book of Psalms, and then she closed her Bible and put it aside.

She pulled a piece of paper from the front of her Bible and opened it carefully. It was a letter, written in broken German, pieced together by a *Terrorflieger* using a German-English dictionary, but Leyna's heart clung to every ill-formed sentence.

> Leyna,
>   You are kind and beautiful. I will never forget what you have done for me and will never be able to thank you. God will reward the cup of cold water you have given.
>   I am sorry to think that there are hard days ahead. But

God will be with you. Remember what Isaiah wrote. "Do not be afraid, for I have redeemed you; I have called you by name: you are mine. When you pass through the waters, I will be with you; and through the rivers, they will not overflow you: when you walk through the fire, you will not be consumed. You are mine. You are precious in my sight."

No matter what happens, I will meet you again.

RJK

Leyna folded the letter and put it back in her Bible. Then she got up from her chair and shifted her mother in her bed. She had painful bedsores by now. Leyna had long ago spent the rest of the money from *Herr* Krueger to pay for two doctor's visits, but the doctor said there was nothing further he could do for her. Finally, Leyna kissed her mother goodnight and turned out the light.

A part of Leyna's life ended that evening. In the morning, she found her mother sleeping peacefully. She had gone home to heaven sometime during the night. A strange feeling crept slowly over Leyna. She felt totally alone, and yet, by some grace, she felt that God was with her. Through the tears that she shed, she found that she was actually relieved that her mother was free from the pain and confusion and in the presence of her Lord.

Leyna sent word immediately to Uncle Georg and called the *Bergermeister*. Two days later, on a gray day, Leyna stood at the cemetery in Engen next to a freshly dug grave. Her mother's casket was resting at the bottom of the hole. *Frau* Seiler and *Herr* Krueger were the only ones who were willing to brave the scorn of others to come to the burial of the wife of the disgraced minister who was taken away by the Gestapo. Leyna did not know why, but Uncle Georg never arrived.

That evening, as Leyna was leaving the barn with a pail of milk, *Tante* Zelma drove up in her car. An older man with a crooked nose got out of the passenger's side of the car. He extended his hand and introduced himself as *Onkel* Klaus.

Leyna gave the man a puzzled look. Perhaps all of the men

in the German Underground had the name *Onkel* Klaus. Leyna turned to *Tante* Zelma and explained that they had just buried her mother. *Tante* Zelma took her by the arm and led her inside the house.

After several kind words of sympathy from *Tante* Zelma, *Onkel* Klaus came in the back door, followed by a Catholic priest. Leyna looked from the man to *Tante* Zelma.

"I would not ask you now," began *Tante* Zelma, "now that I know what all you have been through, but I have no one else to turn to." *Tante* Zelma breathed in deeply.

Leyna closed her eyes and buried her head in her hands on the kitchen table. She somehow knew what was coming next. "This will have to be the last one, *Tante* Zelma," said Leyna, raising her head. "I can't do this anymore."

Tante Zelma reached over and patted her on the arm. "I understand, dear. *Onkel* Klaus will be back in a week or more for our priest."

Leyna nodded numbly. *Tante* Zelma and *Onkel* Klaus said their good-byes and left Leyna in the kitchen with the priest. She offered him a chair at the table and then rose to put a pot of coffee on.

She found that the priest was not a good conversationalist and that he did not know the Bible very well. Leyna handed him a cup of coffee and a piece of bread.

"You're not a priest, are you?" she asked boldly, fairly sure of his response.

The man turned his gaze to his cup of coffee. "No, I am not," he said softly. "And I'm not a very good Jew either."

Leyna raised an eyebrow and sat down at the kitchen table. "The Bible says that there is none righteous, so at least you are not alone."

"I don't believe in a God who would turn his back on his people," said the man quickly, with a bitter edge.

Leyna drew her hair back from her eyes. "God has not turned his back on his people. His people have turned their backs on him," she said tenderly. "That is the way it always is. We are all sheep that have gone astray."

The man grunted in response and scratched the back of his head. Leyna studied his face. He looked like he was forty years old, but she could tell that it had been a hard forty years. In his thin, beady eyes, there was distrust and hatred. She wondered silently if he had been in hiding all of this time and how he had come to *Tante* Zelma for help.

For some reason, Leyna was quite uncomfortable with the man in her house, though she did want to help him. On the fourth day since his arrival, she left him alone in the front room and rode into town to go to market. When she got back, the priest was nowhere to be found. By nightfall, he had not returned.

Leyna was somewhat relieved that he was gone. This relief lasted only until midmorning the next day, when Captain Metzger pounded on her back door and arrested her.

Leyna was not sure what was going on until evening, when she was sitting in an interrogation room at Mühlhausen and a hefty, mean-looking major entered the room, demanding that Leyna tell him how she knew the man known as *Herr* Zimmer. Before the door shut behind the major, she caught a glimpse of the priest as he was being dragged through the hall.

Leyna swallowed hard. So, he had gotten himself caught, and now she was going to have to pay. The major was losing patience. Leyna looked down at the floor.

"He needed a place to stay for a couple of days," she heard herself say.

"*Fräulein!* Look at me when you speak!" demanded the major.

Leyna looked up into his angry eyes. "Do you know that he is a Jew?" asked the major with a look of disgust.

"I don't know that for sure. Is he?" asked Leyna innocently. "He told me he was a priest."

The major lifted one of his feet onto the empty chair next to Leyna and leaned forward with his elbow on his knee.

"You are in a lot of trouble, *Fräulein* Künzel. It is forbidden for the people of Germany, the master race, to assist these swine in any way. You have insulted the *Führer*, and you are a disgrace to your people," he said with his teeth clenched tightly together.

Leyna looked down at the floor. "Look at me, *Fräulein!*" said the major. "Tell me who brought *Herr* Zimmer to you. Who asked you to keep him? Who is your contact?"

Leyna shook her head and said a prayer. She had been taught, all of her life, not to lie. For a moment, she wished that she could.

"*Herr* Major, I don't know her real name," said Leyna at last, looking him straight in the eyes.

"What do you mean you don't know her real name?" asked the major in disbelief.

"I don't know her name. I don't know where she lives. I don't know anything about her," said Leyna honestly.

The major let out a mocking laugh and paced a little around the room.

"You want me to believe that someone—you don't know her name—asked you to help this Jew, someone that you don't know anything about, and you just did it?" The major ended his sentence with a dramatic shrug.

"Yes," replied Leyna. "I could make up a name for you, but I would not be telling you the truth."

The major searched her eyes, and then he slapped her hard across the face.

The major asked her the same questions over and over again, until Leyna was tired of giving the same answers. Then he left the room in a big show of rage.

Leyna sat still in her chair, stunned at what was happening. Then she heard the major and the familiar voice of Captain Metzger mumbling outside of the room. She got up and slowly crept over to the door.

"Her father was arrested for defying the orders of the *Füh-*

rer. Someone should have been watching her," said the major in disgust.

"*Herr* Major," said Captain Metzger timidly, "I have been watching her house. I have gone there no fewer than five times and inspected."

"She won't tell me who her contacts are," said the major. "She tells me she doesn't know who they are. For some reason, I am inclined to believe her."

"She is a deeply religious girl, *Herr* Major. It is expressly forbidden for her to lie."

"This 'deeply religious girl' is going to face the firing squad tomorrow, Captain," said the major.

Leyna covered her mouth to keep the scream that rose up in her throat from escaping.

"Begging your pardon, *Herr* Major," interrupted Captain Metzger with an evil tone in his voice, "but may I suggest that sending her to a place such as Dachau with *Herr* Zimmer would be much more of a punishment than the firing squad for her acts?"

There was a long pause, and Leyna leaned up against the wall, as she felt that she was going to faint.

"That is an appropriate suggestion, Captain. You may make those arrangements," said the major at last. "She can rot there with the rest of the swine."

Leyna listened to their footsteps as the two men proceeded down the hall, away from the interrogation room.

Leyna sat down on the floor and pulled out the letter Lieutenant Kellam had written to her from her skirt pocket. She folded it up into a small square, curled it inside the fingers on her left hand and held it to her heart. So she had gone through the floods, and now she was to be sent into the fire.

June 1945

Leyna's uncle had carefully written to Lieutenant Kellam all the
details of which he was aware relating to Leyna. He wrote that
he was unable to attend the funeral of his sister, Leyna's mother,
because he was stopped at the border of Switzerland and Germany by German guards who had refused him entry.

Then he had received word from a *Frau* Seiler in Engen, who
had told him that Leyna had been arrested for helping a Jew and
that she was sent by railcar to the concentration camp at Dachau.
All of his attempts to find out what had transpired with his niece
since then had been met with silence.

He had hoped to receive word from her by now, as he had
heard that American forces had liberated the concentration camp
over a month ago, but he had, to date, heard nothing from her.
Leyna's uncle promised that he would write if he received any
news about her, but he told Lieutenant Kellam that he remained
doubtful that would ever happen.

Rand sat on the back stairs of the Eighth Army Air Force
Headquarters building, frozen in place, for over half an hour.
When he closed his eyes, he could see her face. He could see her
face that afternoon in the barn, the first time he really looked into
her eyes. He could see the concern in her eyes as she removed the
lead from his forehead. He could see the smile on her face as she
came up to the attic with the dictionary; he could see the tears
when they had buried Roy. He remembered the painful look as
the captain came back to haunt her, how sweetly she had blushed
in the barn, and how beautiful she looked asleep in the rocking
chair in the kitchen.

Finally, Rand folded up the letter and put it back in the envelope. He got up and walked slowly down the path toward the

front gate. He walked for several blocks, not really paying attention to where he was going.

Her mother's death, while certainly not a surprise, must have been a sore blow to her. He knew from the way that Leyna cared for her mother that Leyna loved her deeply. She had been caught helping a Jew; that certainly sounded like Leyna. But she had been so careful with them, even down to the last detail of polishing his escape shoes. He wondered what had gone wrong. He had heard, and now the world was hearing, of the horrible discoveries at the concentration camps.

He shuttered to even think of what she must have encountered there. He had been through the valley of the shadow of death several times, but he was a soldier. He never would have dreamed that he would make it through the war, but she would not.

Soon, his work in the European Theatre would be drawing to a close, and he would board a ship back to the States. Without Leyna, his world seemed like an empty and cold place. He had been hoping and praying for over a year now that he would be able to see her again, to tell her how he felt about her, to ask her a very important question.

Lieutenant Kellam made his way back to headquarters. On his way, he poured out his heart to the Lord. He told the Lord that he was having a hard time, but that he was going to trust him all the way. He had no intention of returning to his old way of living, apart from his rock and his fortress. Leyna had taught him much in such a short amount of time, without even saying a word.

On June 22, when most of the combat wings of the Second Air Division had shipped or were shipping back to the States, Lieutenant Kellam requested a four-day pass to go to Zurich. A few days earlier, he had received a short letter from Leyna's uncle stating that Leyna was alive and with him in Zurich. Lieutenant Kellam quickly boarded a transport plane to Paris.

Once Rand was on the ground in Paris, he rushed to get to the train station, and late that evening, he boarded a train for Zurich. In the early hours of the morning, the train passed through Bern, Switzerland. Lieutenant Kellam peered out the window at the familiar sight of the snowcapped Alps and mused over how different the world was now that the war in Europe was over. A year ago, as he had passed this way, he was running, scared, and hungry. Now he didn't care where he was. All he knew was that he was on his way to see Leyna.

His train arrived in Zurich on platform three at ten o'clock in the morning. After several attempts to get directions to Neumarkt, a kind old man finally drew a map on the back of an envelope for Rand.

By eleven o'clock, he had arrived in front of an apartment building on a quaint, cobblestone street. The mailbox on the outside gave apartment number six for *Herr* Hartmann. Rand went inside and took the stairs two at a time. He found apartment number six on the third floor and knocked quickly on the door. He waited outside the door for five minutes, knocking several times. After a while, Rand made his way slowly back down the stairs.

He had fully anticipated that he would find Leyna there without much trouble. Was he in the right place? He walked to the end of the block and read the street sign again; then he returned to number twenty-four. He sat down on the stairs that led up to the front door, sure that he was in the right place.

While he waited, he began to get quite nervous. He wondered if she would be as happy to see him as he was to see her. He wondered what damage the concentration camp had done to her. He wondered what he was going to say when he saw her.

For a whole half hour, Lieutenant Kellam waited and wondered. Then, he saw three people round the corner of the block. First, he saw a shorter, older gentleman with a petite, white beard, immaculately dressed in a coat and hat, followed by a young man, handsome in face and appearance. On the arm of the young man was the frail figure of a woman who was wearing a scarf around her head. Lieutenant Kellam's heart jumped when he recognized her face. It was Leyna.

His countenance fell quickly as he saw her leaning affectionately on the young man and laughing as they walked. Did her heart already belong to someone else? Maybe he shouldn't have come. Rand swallowed hard, rose to his feet, and stood up tall and straight. A sober look came across his face.

Leyna was tired by the end of their morning walk. She felt as if she was getting stronger, but it did not take her long to tire out. She was looking forward to a nice cup of coffee and a good rest before dinner as she rounded the corner to her uncle's apartment. Her uncle was on her left. He had his walking cane in his right hand. She was leaning heavily on her joy and pride and the answer to her many prayers.

Suddenly, Leyna's eyes met the big, blue eyes of Lieutenant Kellam, who seemed to be standing at attention in front of her uncle's apartment building. Leyna stopped abruptly. She could hardly believe what she was seeing. The handsome young man at her side and her Uncle Georg both looked at her, wondering why she had stopped all of a sudden.

Leyna's face moved slowly from disbelief to happiness. Then, as quickly as her feet would move, she made her way into Lieutenant Kellam's arms. He received her gladly as the old man and the young man looked on, both of them perplexed. Leyna clung to the lieutenant for a long while and let the tears roll down her cheeks. He rocked her back and forth gently and then pulled her away so that he could look into her eyes.

She gave him a beautiful smile. "You made it. We made it! What are you doing here?" she asked in German.

His smile slowly faded away, as he did not understand what she had said.

Leyna laughed. She had forgotten how difficult it had been to communicate. Leyna turned around. *"Das ist mein Onkel,"* she said, trying to make introductions, "Georg Hartmann. *Onkel Georg, das ist* Lieutenant Rand Kellam. He is one of the men who ..."

Lieutenant Kellam extended his hand to her uncle.

"Ah, yes," said her uncle. "We have been corresponding," he said in German, interrupting Leyna.

"It is an honor to meet you, Lieutenant," said her uncle, in English.

Lieutenant Kellam's face lit up, as he realized that her uncle spoke English. He had not known whether the letters he had received from her uncle had been written by him or translated by someone else.

Leyna turned next to the young man. "*Und das ist mein Bruder, Stefan,*" she said proudly.

Rand extended his hand to her brother with somewhat of a confused look on his face. He had understood that both her father and her brother were dead. Her brother did not shake his hand and returned the greeting with a glare. Leyna looked down at the ground. Uncle Georg cleared his throat.

"Shall we all go inside?" he suggested to Leyna and Stefan. Leyna took her brother's arm, and Uncle Georg motioned for Lieutenant Kellam to follow them up the stairs.

Once they were inside the apartment, Leyna took the lieutenant's coat and hung it up by the door. She noticed immediately that he was wearing the blue, silk tie she had made for him.

"Won't you please sit down, Lieutenant," said Uncle Georg, motioning for Rand to sit in a chair by the window. The late-morning sun was casting its sunbeams through the window and onto the floor in the living room. Lieutenant Kellam took the seat he was offered. Uncle Georg sat across from the lieutenant. Stefan wandered over to the seat farthest away from Rand, sat down, and continued to glare at him.

Leyna removed her sweater and hung it by the door. Then she reached up timidly to take her scarf off. As she did, her eyes met Rand's. Leyna turned away and pulled the scarf off of her head. It was then that he saw that she had no more than half an inch of hair on her head.

"Lieutenant," began Uncle Georg in a soft tone, "she is quite, how do you say, embarrassed about her hair."

Lieutenant Kellam faced her uncle. "She shouldn't be," he said.

Leyna came over and sat between her uncle and her brother, and looked down at the floor.

"This is quite a surprise, Lieutenant, to meet you."

"I came as soon as I got your letter."

Uncle Georg nodded and sat back in his seat, looking over at Leyna's brother.

"As you can see, I am here with two miracles, Lieutenant: Leyna and Stefan."

"I had understood that her brother was dead," returned Rand.

"We all thought so. No one had heard from him for years. He was captured by American troops in Africa and spent over two years in a prisoner-of-war camp."

Lieutenant Kellam nodded. That would account for the glare he was receiving from her brother.

"Tell him, please, that I am glad he made it."

Leyna's uncle paused, and Rand thought for a moment that he was not going to translate, but then he finally did.

Rand watched Stefan's face, but it did not alter after hearing Lieutenant Kellam's good wishes. There was no response at all.

"You will have to ignore him, Lieutenant," returned Uncle Georg in English. "He was, I believe, a little mistreated by the Americans there. It will take him a while to sort through his pains and to come out on the other end, thankful to be alive."

Lieutenant Kellam nodded his understanding.

"Now, Lieutenant, why have you come so far?" asked Uncle Georg with a telling smile underneath his beard.

Lieutenant Kellam looked at Leyna. She was sitting patiently, waiting for something to be translated into German for her.

"First of all, I owe you thanks for helping to save my life. I do not have a full understanding of what you did, but I know that you had a hand in helping me escape from Germany. I am grateful," began the lieutenant.

Uncle Georg smiled. "It was a very, very small part, young man. I simply went up to Bern to your American embassy, and they gave me the telephone number of a man here in Zurich, who arranged for everything else."

"And," continued the lieutenant bravely, "I am here—" Lieutenant Kellam paused to take in a deep breath. He straightened his shoulders. "I am here to ask for permission to marry Leyna," he said at last.

Uncle Georg blinked his eyes a couple of times, and then he chuckled softly. Rand looked at Leyna and then at Stefan. To his relief, neither one of them seemed to understand what he had just said.

At the temporary pause in conversation, Leyna turned to her uncle. "What are you talking about?" she asked him.

Uncle Georg reached over and patted her on the arm. "This is, how do you say, quite a surprise, Lieutenant. Why, may I ask, do you want to marry her?"

Lieutenant Kellam cleared his throat. "I have given this a lot of thought and a lot of prayer, *Herr* Hartmann. There are girls in the United States, I know, but there is no one there like Leyna."

"What do you even know of her?" asked Uncle Georg skeptically.

Lieutenant Kellam folded his hands together in his lap. "I know that she is smart and beautiful, kind and selfless. I know that she gave up her bed for a dying enemy airman while she slept on the floor. I know that she fed us with the last food she had and when she had no more food, she went out and got work at a bakery so that she could bring bread home to keep us alive. I know that she loved her mother and cared for her in spite of all of the hardships in the world. I know that she took the lining out of her winter coat to make this tie for me. And I know that she has faith in God like no one I have ever met."

Uncle Georg raised one of his eyebrows. He had not anticipated such a detailed response.

"I won't say anything to her, sir, unless I have permission to ask her," continued Rand. "I know this is sudden, but I am leaving for the States shortly, and if I am to marry her, I am told that there are all sorts of paperwork and applications I must put in now. It will take months." Rand paused for a moment, and his brow dipped in serious thought. "If you say no, I will go back to the States and I will probably eventually marry." Rand glanced over at Leyna. "But I will always wonder where she is and who it is who had the privilege of loving her the rest of her life."

After a long time, Uncle Georg turned his eyes from the window to the lieutenant.

"I have been wondering now for days, Lieutenant, what their future will be. I cannot support the three of us. Leyna cannot work in her condition. She is weak and needs rest." Uncle Georg pointed to Stefan and continued. "There are no jobs for a young man such as Stefan and likely will be none for quite some time, so Stefan cannot support her. I tell you this not to make it seem as if I am eager to rid myself of her, but you have impressed me, Lieutenant. What have you to offer her?"

Lieutenant Kellam looked blankly at Uncle Georg. "I—I can offer her a home with my family. I do not pretend that it would be easy for her in America, but I will be there to help her and to love her. She deserves much more than that, but I can do my best."

Uncle Georg smiled. "I would like to think about it for a while, but you will most likely have the most resistance from her brother, not me, and I do not think from Leyna," he said with a playful smile. "I will talk with Stefan, and we will see if his youthful foolishness will prevent him from doing what is best for her."

"*Onkel!*" said Leyna, at last exasperated at the long bits of conversation that were nothing but foreign to her ears.

"You are going to have to learn English, Leyna," said her uncle in German.

"Why?" asked Stefan stoically. "What is this American doing here? How do you know him?"

"I found him on the road to Engen," replied Leyna quickly.

Uncle Georg turned his brow seriously. "Stefan, he is our guest, and you must set aside your differences this once."

"What have you been discussing?" asked Leyna curiously.

Uncle Georg turned back to Rand, ignoring her question. "How long can you stay with us, Lieutenant?"

"I must return to England on Monday, *Herr* Hartmann."

Uncle Georg nodded. "He will be here until Monday, Leyna," he said in German. "Now, tell me what you want to talk about with him, and I will translate."

"Why has he come?" asked Leyna.

"He has come to see you, Leyna," replied her uncle, without asking the lieutenant. Stefan sighed loudly. Leyna turned to scold him.

"I want to know how he got out of Germany," she said at last.

Uncle Georg listened as Lieutenant Kellam told her what had happened after he had left the farm, and then he translated it all for Leyna and Stefan. Leyna listened with wide eyes. When Uncle Georg was through, Rand asked her what had happened to her after he had left and how the crop had turned out.

Leyna got up and went into the only bedroom in the apartment. When she returned a moment later, she handed the lieutenant a tattered and stained piece of paper folded in half. Lieutenant Kellam opened it up. The edges had been ripped or worn away, but in the center, he could see the faded ink of his own handwriting.

He looked up at Leyna. She had tears in her eyes. "This verse got me through the worst days of my life," she said slowly.

Uncle Georg translated for the lieutenant, but he somehow already guessed what she had said. Rand handed the piece of paper back to her, and then he ran his hand down the length of his silk tie.

His reunion with Leyna had not been what he had thought it

would be. There was a mixture of joy and pain that was still fresh in both of them, yet he was thankful. Three weeks ago, he had been faced with the thought that she had not made it through the war. Now, it seemed that their only obstacle was time—time to heal.

Leyna looked a good thirty pounds lighter than she had been a year earlier. Her head had been shaved, and she was frail and weak. Still, he loved her. If only he could somehow turn the bitter heart of her brother, perhaps he would be able to go back to the States with the promise that she would marry him.

Uncle Georg translated for them back and forth until they had exhausted their questions. Stefan, in the meantime, sat in the corner with a look of death on his face. Before Leyna got up to prepare their dinner, she went over to her brother, sat on the arm of his chair, wrapped her arms around him, and kissed him on the forehead.

In the afternoon, Uncle Georg took Stefan on an errand with him, and Leyna and Lieutenant Kellam sat at the table with a set of dominoes. Leyna brought him a piece of paper and a pencil on which to keep score. He wrote her name and his own name at the top, and then he wrote a number under each name. He had remembered their last game at the farmhouse, and he had remembered the score. Leyna glanced at the paper and then looked up at Rand.

"*O nein,*" she said. "How can you remember that?"

Rand looked at her and nodded, insisting the previous score was correct. Leyna had been ahead. Leyna took the pencil and zeroed out the old total.

Lieutenant Kellam smiled. He was ready to make a fresh start too. He played dominoes with Leyna all afternoon, nervously waiting for her uncle and brother to return and praying that her uncle was able to convince her brother to let him marry her. Most of all, he was enjoying her company once again.

Uncle Georg and Stefan returned with some food from the

market before five o'clock. Leyna went to the small kitchen just off of the living room to start preparations for supper.

Uncle Georg sat in the chair by the window and read the evening newspaper. On one occasion, as he turned the page, he winked at Lieutenant Kellam. Rand looked over at Stefan, who was sitting in the chair clear across the room, looking contemplatively out the window. He wondered what was going on in Stefan's mind.

After supper, Leyna did as her uncle suggested and made up a bed for the lieutenant on the floor in her uncle's bedroom. Leyna lay awake in the dark on the couch that night in the living area. Stefan had been silent the entire evening. She was torn between the feeling of happiness at seeing the lieutenant and sadness because she knew her brother was displeased that the American had come to see her.

Leyna rolled over onto her side. Stefan was lying on the floor next to the couch, but he was not asleep. He had both of his arms up over his head, and his hands were under his head.

"Stefan," she said almost in a whisper, "will you tell me what is on your mind? I have been so long without you. I don't want there to be anything between us."

Leyna listened patiently for his response, but all she heard was a sigh. Finally, it came.

"What do you expect me to think, Leyna?" he began louder than a whisper. "This American shows up here today, and I find out for the first time that you took the enemy into our house, fed them all of our food, and put your life and Mother's at risk for them. If you do not want there to be anything between us, tell me why you did this!"

Leyna took in a deep breath and propped her head up on her hand. She knew that this conversation would have to happen sooner or later. "It was a quick decision, Stefan, when I saw them scared in the forest. I could not stand the thought of them being in the hands of the men who took you and father away. I know Father would have done the same."

"Would he, Leyna?" shot back Stefan.

"Yes, he would have," she replied confidently.

"Would he have starved Mother to feed the enemy?"

Leyna swallowed hard at his accusation. "Mother had all of the food she could eat, Stefan. I did not starve her to feed the Americans." Leyna sniffed back a tear. "I took good care of Mother all the way to the last."

Stefan sat up on the floor and turned toward Leyna. "Mother and Father are gone. Because of your heroics, we don't even have the farm to go back to," he said with a crackle in his voice. Leyna took a deep breath.

"What does it matter, Stefan?" she began with tenderness in her voice. "The Germany father loved and the Germany that you and I knew as children has been gone a long time and will never return."

"What is the meaning of all of this, to make it through these nightmares and then to have no future?"

Leyna hesitated a moment. "By some grace of God, we are alive, Stefan. We are alive! That is more than hundreds of thousands of people can say after all of this. We have our whole lives in front of us. The Lord will be our shepherd, and he will help us. Do you remember? That is the last thing father said to us. That is our future."

Stefan lay back down on the floor. Leyna waited for a response from him, but it never came. She wished that she did not know the torment that he felt inside after all that he had been through. She wished that she did not have her own nightmares. In time, she hoped God would wipe away the tears.

It wasn't until the next afternoon, as Leyna was resting, when the three men went out to market that Rand had an opportunity to find out how her brother felt about his proposition. Uncle Georg explained to Lieutenant Kellam that he had talked with Stefan and that Stefan was reluctant to let her go.

He explained to Rand that Stefan was only seventeen when their father had been arrested and when Stefan was forced into the army. He explained that Stefan had struggled to keep his faith, but that, at last, the death and evil had seemed to overcome him. He was released from prison camp only to find out that his father was most likely dead, his mother had died, and his only living sister was imprisoned at Dachau. They had both made their ways separately to Zurich but had arrived within a day of each other.

The three men were walking along a beautiful river, bordered on each side by white row houses with colorful flower boxes in their windows. Lieutenant Kellam stopped abruptly.

"Would you please tell Stefan that I understand and that I will not proceed without his blessing," asked Rand.

Uncle Georg, seemingly pleased by the lieutenant's mature decision, turned to Stefan and translated.

To Rand's surprise, Stefan replied back. Rand waited for the translation. Uncle Georg turned to the lieutenant. "He says that she is the only thing he has left in this world."

Lieutenant Kellam shook his head. Stefan walked a couple of steps and then turned toward the river and spoke.

"He doesn't want to let her go, Lieutenant," said Uncle Georg, "but he cannot think of that, as she has joy again in her eyes. He saw it for the first time when you appeared."

Rand looked at Stefan, who was gazing out over the water, his hands in his pockets.

"Tell him, please, that he will not lose her. He will gain a friend. My grandfather left his farm to my father, and when the war in the Pacific is finally over, I plan to work the farm and to teach at the college there. It is a large farm and I will not be able to work the fields alone. Maybe after we are settled, we can call for him. At least he could get a start there."

Uncle Georg turned to Stefan and told him everything the lieutenant had just said. Stefan turned to the lieutenant and smiled shyly; then he turned his gaze back to the river and spoke a couple of sentences. Uncle Georg turned to the lieutenant with a victorious smile.

"He thinks you should ask Leyna. Whatever she gives you for an answer will be his answer," said the old man.

It was early evening when the three of them got back from market with some food for supper. Leyna took the groceries and stepped into the kitchen. Uncle Georg was standing still by the front door. Stefan was standing by the living room window, and Rand was standing in between the two men. Leyna looked out into the living room as she took the vegetables out of the bag. She looked at Uncle Georg, then at Stefan, then at Lieutenant Kellam. They were all staring at her in silence.

"What's the matter?" she asked carefully.

Rand looked at Stefan, who nodded to him to go ahead.

Lieutenant Kellam pulled out a chair from the kitchen table, took Leyna by the arm, and sat her in the chair. By this time, she looked quite concerned. Rand lowered one knee to the floor and took her hands in his, while her uncle and brother looked on.

The week before he had left England, he had tracked down Lieutenant Trommler, who had patiently taught him one simple sentence in German. Rand swallowed hard and looked into her beautiful eyes.

"*Möchtest du mich Heiraten,* Leyna?" he asked her. "Will you marry me?"

Leyna raised her left hand and covered her mouth for a moment; then she held his hand again. She was shaking. She looked at her uncle and then over at her brother. Then she looked down into the lieutenant's eyes.

"Yes," she said in English. "Yes." She wrapped her arms around his neck.

He picked her up and held her close. After so many years of darkness and pain, this little moment in time was full of joy for everyone in the room. Uncle Georg, who had never been married, even lost a tear or two at the sight before him.

"I think your father and mother would be proud," he said to Stefan, patting him on the back. Lieutenant Kellam pulled a piece of blue ribbon from his pocket, took her left hand, and tied it on her fourth finger.

"*Herr* Hartmann, please tell her that I will replace this with a ring the next time I see her."

"It is Uncle Georg to you now, Lieutenant," replied the old man playfully. "I will tell her."

Leyna turned to her uncle. "When will this happen? How?"

"She wants to know how this will all work, Lieutenant."

Rand sat down at the kitchen table and folded his hands.

"Truthfully, I don't know how this is going to work. I did some investigation before I came. The military is taking applications for women who have married Americans here in Europe. I am told the process is long and difficult, with a lot of papers to fill out."

Lieutenant Kellam paused, and a tired look came over his face.

"They are not taking paperwork for any German fiancées yet," he said, continuing. "Uncle Georg, I will send you the papers. If you can help Leyna fill them out, I will send them in. They will reject them, and then I will get my commander and everyone I know to write to my senator to appeal this decision. It will, no doubt, take a long time."

Uncle Georg nodded. "That will give Leyna time to recover and time for you to prepare for her."

Lieutenant Kellam's smile faded. "It will seem like forever," he said softly, glancing at Leyna.

Uncle Georg proceeded to tell Leyna and Stefan all that the lieutenant had said. Stefan replied.

"Stefan wants to know when he can fill out his paperwork."

Lieutenant Kellam laughed. "I'm afraid that my oldest sister is only now eleven years old. He may have to wait a few more years."

Stefan laughed heartily when he heard the translation. Then he sat down and played a game of dominoes with the lieutenant while Leyna prepared their supper. Rand found Stefan to be a formidable opponent. Uncle Georg sat in his chair by the window and read the evening paper. It was a day Rand would not soon forget.

On Sunday, they all attended church services in an old cathedral and spent the rest of the beautiful, sunny day resting and enjoying each other's company. Early Monday morning, Leyna walked with Lieutenant Kellam to the train station. All of the birds along the way were singing sweetly, and the fresh mountain air had a sweet smell to it.

Leyna walked with her arm in Rand's. There was nothing left to say between them, as they both knew this would be a long and tenuous separation. They sat together on a bench on the platform. He held her hand tightly until the conductor called for boarding.

Lieutenant Kellam swallowed hard and stood to his feet, helping Leyna to stand. Leyna looked at the ground and tried not to cry. She did not want him to remember her with tears in her eyes, with the ugly scarf on her head, and with no hair, but such was her state at that moment. Lieutenant Kellam put his hand gently under her chin and lifted her eyes to his.

"I love you," he said. "I know you don't understand that yet, but you will someday."

Leyna listened to the melody of his voice. She did not much care that she did not understand his words. Leyna closed her eyes, and he kissed her gently. Finally, he tore himself away from her embrace and headed for the train. He paused as he climbed the first stair, turned, and smiled at Leyna. The train began to pull away, and he waved to her until she slid out of sight.

Summer 1945-Spring 1946

After a ten-day sea voyage back to the States, Lieutenant Kellam was on his way home for thirty days of leave.

Rand sat on the front porch of his house after supper, watching the sun slip down over the horizon. He could hear the crickets in the distance and see the soft glow of the lightning bugs as they hovered in the warm, evening air.

It was good to be home, to sleep in his old bed, to eat his mother's good cooking. His reunion with his family had been wonderful, filled with tears of joy and laughter. Rand would never forget the sweetness of those moments; his little brother and sisters clinging to him, and his mother standing at a distance, smiling through her tears. His father said very little but stayed close by with a look of pride in his eyes.

Mr. Kellam came out of the house, and Rand watched as his father crossed in front of him and sat down in the swing. His father looked out at the red, pink, and yellow sky, where the sun had been moments before. Rand stared down at the planks on the porch.

His father cleared his throat. "Pretty evening," he said softly.

"Yup," replied Rand. He looked over to the screen door, where his mother was drying one of the supper dishes. The faint light from the kitchen poured through the screen door.

"You fellows want something to drink out there? I have some lemonade left in here," she said as she finished drying the dish.

"No thanks, Mom," replied Rand.

His mother put the plate away and then swung the porch door open and took the seat next to Rand's father on the swing, resting the towel in her lap.

"We'll be having everyone over on Sunday, Rand. All your aunts and uncles and cousins want to see you."

Rand closed his eyes and breathed in deeply the familiar smell of the Iowa summer night. The moon came slowly up over the eastern horizon, and they all sat in silence, listening to the crickets.

Because of the nature of waging war, Rand had spoken sparingly of his experiences and had been able to share little of his life with his family over the years in his letters. Now he had something very important to tell them, but he was not sure they would understand. He was a very different person than when he had left home for college, and especially since God had spared his life that day over Germany.

Rand cleared his throat. Then he told his parents that he had something important to tell them. He told them he was engaged to be married to a girl they had never met, that he had plans to bring a German girl to the States to be his wife. His words were met with measured silence. Rand had expected that reception since he had crossed the Atlantic Ocean on his way home.

"I know you have never met her. I know this isn't going to be easy for you, or for me, or for Leyna, but I also trust that the Lord will see us all through this. I think you're going to like her, Mom," he said to her as she swung back and forth on the porch swing.

By now, his mother was holding on tightly to his father's hand.

"She reminds me of you," added Rand.

His father was processing the information carefully as they swung there. Rand could see that on his face. Finally, he raised his eyebrows.

"Son," began his father, stuttering over his words, "it—it is completely understandable for you to feel some, some kind of—of obligation to her. After all, she helped you out of horrific circumstances. You share the memory of that time and the intensity of it together. So, your feelings for her are quite natural. None of that, though, obligates you to marry a girl you hardly know."

Rand played with his hands for a while.

"I understand what you're saying, Dad. There are more reasons than that feeling of obligation. I came to terms with that a long time ago." Rand took in a quick breath. "You told me when I graduated from high school that when the time came, I should choose someone who would love, honor and respect me. Well, Leyna demonstrated that to me when I was her enemy. She had nothing, and yet she gave what she could to us without complaint. I have been in combat over Germany and not ever seen such a brave soul. On top of her resilience, she is selfless. But more than that, Dad, she has faith in God that moved mountains for us."

Rand paused for a moment, sat back in his seat, and ran his hand along his chin. "I understand that life is full of hardship, and there is no one I want to face the hardships with except her."

Rand had said his last words with such resolve that he wondered if his parents would say anything in return.

"Does she speak any English, Son?" came the next question from his father after a long silence.

"No," he replied honestly.

His father scratched the back of his head. "And you're the first American she has ever known?"

"I think so," replied Rand.

His father reached around and scratched the other side of his head. "You're sure about this, Son?"

"Yes."

"She's going to have a hard time here. Folks around here have lost a lot of boys over there on account of the Germans, and it's just not going to be easy. She's going to have to learn English and adjust to a different culture. She's going to miss home. How are the two of you going to communicate? It's hard enough to understand a woman when she's speaking plain English!" his father said, looking at his mother out of the corner of his eyes.

His father leaned away and braced himself for the expected impact of a punch that his mother did deliver.

Rand laughed. "Don't think I haven't thought about all of this. It's all I've been thinking about. But I really think you will feel better about all this when you meet her and get to know her. She really is terrific."

"I hope so, Son," said his mother at last.

To Rand's relief, his sisters, Betty and Dorothy, came screaming out of the porch door with their pajamas on and dropped themselves into his lap.

"Good night, Rand," they both said in unison.

He gave them each a hug and then watched as they kissed their father good night. His mother got up and followed them into the house to tuck them into bed.

The next morning, the sun beat Rand out of bed. While he was standing at the bathroom sink, shaving, his father poked his head in and greeted him.

"Dad? Do you have a straight razor?" asked Rand.

His father moved his head back, surprised at the question. "I might. Why do you ask?"

Rand turned around. "I actually prefer a straight razor," he said.

"Where did you learn to use a straight razor, Son?"

Rand smiled. "In Germany. Leyna taught me."

His father shook his head and turned to leave. In a few minutes, he returned with an old straight razor.

"I'll have to sharpen this up for you, but you can have it if you'd like," he said, handing it to Rand.

Rand took a look at it and handed it back to his dad. Rand thanked him and turned back to finish his shaving. He had gotten used to the straight razor, and he really did prefer it.

On Sunday, Rand put on the white shirt Leyna had made him and stood in front of the mirror as he put a knot in the silk tie she had made from the lining in her winter coat. Wearing the things she had made for him at least made him feel that he was closer to her.

After a ham and egg breakfast, he piled into the car with his family, and they drove off to church. It had been a long time since he had been at church. Rand found it to be a breath of fresh air to his soul. The words of every hymn had meaning now, and the sermon found room in his heart.

Relatives from close by came to their house for dinner that afternoon, and he had a good time with cousins he hadn't seen in years. When his uncle asked him what he was doing home, Rand finally told them all, without much detail, what he had been through in the past couple of years. Then he told them he had his orders to report to Sioux Falls, South Dakota, for duty at the end of July, where the second air division was going to be restructured and shipped out to the Pacific.

As soon as Lieutenant Kellam reported for duty, he was called in to see his commanding officer, who handed the lieutenant his promotion papers to captain and ceremoniously pinned his new rank on his uniform. Rand then began the arduous task of finding the proper channel for obtaining the paperwork Leyna needed to fill out to start the process for her to come to the States.

In a month's time, he had sent Leyna the papers, and her uncle had helped her fill them out. Stefan had traveled all the way to Engen to try to retrieve her birth certificate and identification. Though the French liberation forces had ransacked the town, he somehow managed to get the appropriate papers to return to Rand to submit. Another month passed. The application was finally rejected for a number of reasons. They were only allowing spouses of service members who were English, French, or from occupied territories to apply to enter the United States. They were not allowing those who were merely engaged to come. Most discouraging of all, there were strict policies against fraternizing with a German.

Lieutenant Kellam took the papers immediately to his commanding officer, who had offered to assist him in any way possible. His commander told Rand to take the papers to his senator's office and that he should have everyone he knew write in on the subject. Rand looked away from Colonel Hudson with a look of discouragement.

"Didn't you say she was in a concentration camp?" asked Colonel Hudson, leaning back in his squeaky chair.

"Yes," replied Rand. "Dachau."

The colonel's face brightened. "You should see if they won't let her in as a political prisoner. I have heard that they will sometimes make that exception. Also, don't forget to tell them that she worked for the German Underground." Colonel Hudson gazed out the window for a moment. "Why don't you have that other guy who got shot down with you take up the cause too?"

Rand thanked the colonel for his good advice and went back to his desk. He sat down in a slump and stared off into space. All he could think about were the tears he remembered sliding down her face the last time he had seen her. It was way too late for his government to warn him not to get involved with a German girl.

Rand set to work, going down every avenue he could. He had prepared himself for a long, hard road, but he hadn't expected the emptiness in his heart as he made his way through the red tape. He missed her.

Following the surrender of Japan in August, Rand served three more months with his unit. Then, in November, Captain Randall Kellam transferred to the Army Air Corps reserve unit in Iowa after serving three years and six months for his country.

Rand returned home and took up residence on his grandfather's farm. In his later years, his grandfather had neglected a lot of things around the farm, and there was a lot of work to be done to restore the property and the buildings to running condition.

Though the war was over, times were still difficult, and he knew that if he was going to bring Leyna to the States, he had to have a way to support her. He worked from sunup to sundown six days a week toward this goal.

Rand's second order of business, however, was to continue with his struggle to gain Leyna permission to come to the States. Rand wrote to her every week to update her on his progress, although most weeks there was nothing much to say.

He finally received a long and detailed letter that Lieutenant Owen had written in support of Leyna. Rand had painstakingly tracked down their debriefing report from when they had arrived back in England, and he submitted it, along with Lieutenant Owen's letter, with yet another re-application form.

Another month passed. The government then notified Rand that they were trying to find evidence that she and her father had been imprisoned in concentration camps because of their resistance to the government of Germany.

Early one evening, in the middle of March, before the sun went down, Rand made his way slowly to the mailbox at the end of the long driveway. His beagle, Able, followed faithfully at his heals. Rand and Able had spent the day sorting through his grandfather's old equipment in the machine shed, and he was tired, dusty, and grimy. He wasn't expecting anything in the mailbox and was surprised to find a single letter inside. It was from Washington.

With his grease stained fingers, he tore the envelope open and pulled out the notice. Leyna's papers had finally been approved. A sense of great relief rushed over him. Rand bowed his head and thanked the Lord. She was German, and the state department made it clear that they were making an exception in allowing her to enter the country because of her service to America in harboring her soldiers. Further, the government required that they file proof of marriage within three months.

The next morning, Rand was at the telegram office before the doors opened. He sent word to Leyna that she had to make it to Antwerp, Belgium by the thirtieth of March. She was to sail on the *Queen Mary* to England, where the ship would dock to pick up other war brides.

Leyna said a hasty good-bye to her uncle and her brother and boarded the train to Paris with one suitcase in hand, holding all of her worldly goods. Even after she was safely on her way to Belgium, she could still see the sad and lonely look on her uncle's face as he stood there on the platform. She knew she would probably never see him again on this earth.

Once she was on board the *Queen Mary*, she had time to wonder what her new home would be like. She had seen pictures of America, but that was all. The *Queen Mary* steamed her way out of Southampton, England, in foggy weather. The quarters on board the ship were crowded. Leyna shared a room with sixteen other women, most of them traveling with infants. All of the other women in the cabin were English. This was to be her first taste of being disdained because she was German.

For the last nine months, her uncle had spoken quite a bit of English with Leyna. Leyna was thankful for this now as she struggled to communicate with the women in her cabin. One afternoon, when she was sitting on her bunk, reading, Leyna looked up to see one of the infants rolling over off of a top bunk. Leyna dropped her book and quickly snatched up the child before she fell onto the floor.

The mother of the infant was hanging up laundry along the end of the bunk and had not seen the danger of the situation. When she saw Leyna grab her daughter, the mother stepped across the crowded room and angrily snatched the child from Leyna's arms. She called Leyna a Jerry and pushed her to the floor.

Leyna got up slowly off of the floor and made her way quickly to the door. As she left the room, she heard one of the other women explaining to the mother what had really happened. Leyna bit her tongue all the way up to the deck.

She understood their feelings toward her to a certain point. Leyna had suffered at the hands of the English, the Americans, and the Germans during the war. Leyna stood at the railing and stared out into the never-ending sea. The wind was whipping all around her.

She wondered what her new life would be like. She wondered if she would recognize Rand. She thought about the little she really knew about him, and she wondered why he wanted to marry her. In the deep places in her heart, she had admired him for all that he had done for her when he was with her in Engen. But the thing that caused her heart to melt the most was the picture she held in her memory of him standing there in front of her uncle's apartment building that summer morning. She couldn't have been more surprised or happy to see him. He had traveled so far and taken such a big chance for just one reason: her.

In each of his letters to her over the past four months, he had shared a part of his heart with her and always ended with a verse of Scripture he had been pondering. She almost felt guilty not feeling torn between her old life and the new. She was looking forward to being with him and to starting her new life in America.

She stayed up on the deck until she was almost frozen solid. She caught a glimpse of her face in a porthole as she headed below deck. At least her hair was growing back. She entered the cabin timidly, went directly to her bunk, and picked up her book. The room suddenly became silent.

The mother whose infant she had rescued came slowly over to Leyna. She swallowed hard before she spoke. "I owe you an apology," she said softly.

Leyna looked up into her tired eyes. "Apology?" she said back. She was not sure what that word meant.

"I'm sorry," she said, trying to simplify things, and then she looked away from Leyna.

Leyna leaned over until she caught the mother's eye. "It's good," said Leyna. "I understand. I am not the enemy. I want to be your friend."

The English woman reached out and hugged Leyna. The tension in the room left after that situation, and the rest of the voyage was easier on Leyna. After all, they were all in the same situation, sailing alone to a new country, leaving the trying times behind.

April 8, 1946

In the early morning hours of Sunday, the eighth of April, Leyna arose, dressed, and made her way up to the deck. She had heard that they would be sailing into New York harbor as the sun came up, and she didn't want to miss her first sight of America. She joined many of the women and children on deck in the fog, and they all waited anxiously as they sailed closer to the harbor. Before long, the sun began to rise lazily in the east, and the fog scampered away.

A ripple of excitement ran through the crowd as they entered the harbor, and they all cast their eyes on the Statue of Liberty. She rose before the ship like a beacon of light on a dark night, glowing red in the morning sun. Before long, the ship pulled alongside a dock. Then there was a mad scramble to the cabins to finish packing belongings and to gather up suitcases for disembarking.

Leyna brought her suitcase up to the deck and tried to find a place to look out onto the dock. There were swarms of men filling the dock area, waiting for their wives and children. Leyna waited as the crane brought the gangplank to the ship. Suddenly, there was a massive rush toward the center of the ship.

Leyna stood firm at the railing, looking out over the crowd. She wondered how she would find Rand. She had not pictured the pandemonium that she was watching before her. She scanned the crowd for his familiar face. Then she closed her eyes for a moment and straightened her blouse.

She picked up her suitcase and followed the flow of the crowd toward the gangplank. The crowd was making a tremendous roar. She held onto the railing as she walked down to the dock. She still did not see him. Once she was safely on the dock, she moved off to the side and set her suitcase down.

She watched the happy reunions, the kissing and the tears, for over forty-five minutes. Finally, most of the women had found their husbands and were wandering off the dock toward the building at the end, where they would be processed into the country and allowed to leave. Leyna watched as the men unloaded the cargo from the ship.

Although the crowd had thinned considerably, Leyna still did not see Rand. She picked up her suitcase and moved over to a crate that was sitting by the gangplank. She climbed up onto the crate, sat down, and dangled her feet over the edge. From this crate, she had a direct view of the line into the out-processing building and a side view of the cargo removal operations.

For two more hours, she sat on the crate, waiting. She had been too excited to eat much for breakfast, and now she was too upset to be hungry. As the minutes went slowly by, she began to wonder if Rand was going to come at all.

Behind her, she could see the tall buildings of New York City, and it all looked very large and scary to her. She had a small amount of money in her suitcase that her uncle had given her when she left. She shuddered at the thought of trying to find somewhere to sleep for the night. Leyna reached into her suitcase and pulled out the last letter Rand had written to her. She ran her hands across his return address. She had no idea how to get to Iowa.

Leyna's heart began to sink. Then she heard a still, small voice. "I will never leave you, nor forsake you." Leyna chuckled. How could she doubt the love and care of her Lord? He had brought her safely through the war, safely through the concentration camp, and safely to America.

Leyna watched as the out-processing line diminished. She picked up her suitcase and made her way to the building at the end of the dock. She stepped inside and surveyed the row of desks before her. She seemed to be the last person left to process. There was a short man sitting at the first desk to her right.

"Papers, please," said the man.

Leyna pulled out the papers that Rand had sent to her from

her coat pocket and handed them to the man. He looked up from his desk to take her papers.

"Where is your husband?" he asked, looking around her.

Leyna narrowed her eyes. "I have no husband," she responded. "I am here to marry."

The immigration officer shook his head. "Look, lady, you have to have a husband with you to leave this place, or we're going to have to send you back to—."

The man was talking so fast that Leyna could not understand anything that he was saying.

"Slow, please?"

The man rolled his eyes and sighed. "You have to have a husband, or we cannot let you leave," he said again, emphasizing each word.

Leyna looked around the room. She did not know what she was going to do now. She stuck out her hands, asking for her papers back; she picked up her suitcase and stepped back. There were others in line behind her now. She walked slowly back out the door and back to the dock. The sun was steadily warming the day, and there were puffy, white clouds in the sky. Leyna saw none of this. She set her suitcase down and sat down on the ground with her back to the building. She leaned her head back and closed her eyes.

When she had needed comfort, she knew that she could find it in the presence of the Lord. When she needed bread to eat, she always asked her Lord to provide. Slowly, she bowed her head and asked the Lord to help her.

Before she had even finished her prayer, a young man in a black overcoat came rushing out of the door of the building to her left. Leyna opened her eyes in time to see him rush past her and stop dead in his tracks at the sight of the empty dock. He was standing now with his back to her. He drew up his hands behind his neck and sighed. Leyna stood up slowly.

When he turned around, Leyna saw the look of despair on his face. Then he looked directly at Leyna, and the look of despair turned to a broad smile. Rand ran to her, took her up in his arms, and kissed her.

"I'm sorry I'm late, sweetheart," he kept saying. Then he pulled her back and took a good look at her. "You're more beautiful than I remembered. Welcome to America, Leyna!"

"Thank you," she said, and she smiled.

"Do you have luggage?" he asked excitedly.

"Yes. This is all I have," she responded, again in English, accompanied by a big smile.

"Leyna? Where did you learn English?"

Rand was a little taken back at her response in English.

Leyna nodded mischievously. "Every day speak Uncle Georg English to me."

Rand laughed and picked up her suitcase. They went together into the building, and Leyna handed her papers back to the same immigration official she had seen before. He looked up at her and took her papers.

"You again," he said.

Rand stepped up next to Leyna and put his arm around her waist.

The immigration official seemed to be a little surprised to see that she had found a husband so quickly. He looked down at the papers and began to stamp them. When he got to the third paper, he stopped and studied it closely.

"You two are not married, Captain?" he asked directing his question to Rand.

Leyna looked up at him.

"No, sir," he replied.

The immigration official wrinkled his nose and pushed his glasses back up. "Hmm," he said, looking troubled. "If you will excuse me for a moment," he said as he rose from his chair. The man took her papers and wound his way around two desks behind him to an older man in an office behind a glass partition.

Rand looked down at Leyna nervously.

They watched as the older man looked through her papers

and then exchanged words with the immigration official. The short man came slowly back to the desk, sat down, and then looked up at Leyna. "I see that an exception has been made for your entry to this country. I will need one more thing before I can process these papers. You are required to have proof of your stay in the concentration camp. Do you have any papers or..."

Leyna looked up at Rand. He drew in a breath. "I thought this was all in order," he said to the man.

"I'm sorry, Captain, but this says that she must present proof of internment at the concentration camp of Dachau upon entering the country."

Rand shook his head. "How is she supposed to prove that?" he said, raising his voice a little.

Leyna reached down and began to roll her left blouse sleeve up to her elbow. Then she extended her arm so that the man at the desk could see the tattoo of the prison number that was embedded across her forearm.

The man at the desk looked down at the papers and read off her prisoner number while comparing it with the numbers on her arm. Then he took his stamp in his hand and stamped the rest of the pages. Rand stared at her arm. There were a lot of things he had left to learn about her.

"Here you are, Captain," said the man, handing him her papers. "You are free to go."

Rand picked up her suitcase with his right hand and took Leyna's hand with his left. "Come on," he said to her with a smile. "We have a train to catch."

Leyna stared with amazement at her new country. She did not see a single bombed-out building. The buildings were big, the cars were big, and everywhere they went was full of life and activity. Rand ran with her through Grand Central Station to the ticket desk. After he had purchased their tickets, they went to the platform and boarded the train to Chicago.

They walked through the cars until they found two empty seats. Before Rand could put her suitcase overhead, the train began to move. Leyna lost her balance and fell against Rand, who caught her with one arm. Leyna looked up into his eyes and blushed. Rand did not waste his opportunity. He drew her close and kissed her softly on the lips.

Leyna looked down, embarrassed, and quickly sat down in her seat. She was not used to this. Rand lifted her suitcase into the rack and sat down next to her. After a minute or two, he took an apple from his coat pocket and offered it to Leyna. She thanked him and took it. She was getting very hungry now.

"Our trains are not like your trains in Europe," he said, looking down at her as she ate her apple. "We were a full two hours late getting into the station this morning. That's why I wasn't there on time to meet you, Leyna."

She looked up at him with a look of confusion. "Slow, please," she said.

Rand smiled. "I'm sorry, sweetheart. I'll slow down," he said, and repeated his earlier statement.

"I think you switch your mind," she replied.

"No way," Rand replied immediately. "I have thought of nothing but this moment since I left you in Zurich."

Leyna smiled shyly and took another bite of her apple.

Rand cleared his throat. "There is so much I have to tell you. I don't know where to start."

Leyna tried to listen hard, but she was only catching half of his words.

"The day you found us, before we bailed out of the plane, I told God that it was up to him to let me live or die, but that if he would let me live I would give my life to him and not live for myself any longer. Then you came along."

Rand paused as he had a lump in his throat. To date, he had shared this experience that he kept in the inner room of his heart with no one. Leyna stopped chewing her apple and looked up at Rand. She had seen that expression on his face before.

"Your faith in God was so real. I want our life together to be that way, Leyna." Rand paused and looked down into her beautiful eyes. He did not know how much she understood, but he could see that she was listening with all of her heart.

Rand talked with her about his family. He told her about all the work he had been doing on his grandfather's farm, and he tried to describe the place they were going to make their home. Then he laid out for her the plans that had been made for their Saturday wedding. Leyna listened with excitement until her eyes began to grow heavy. Rand slid his arm around her. Leyna laid her head on his shoulder and fell fast asleep. He knew it had been a long journey for her.

April 9, 1946

Monday morning, the express train from New York City pulled into Chicago, Illinois. Leyna and Rand stepped off of the train and soon boarded a slower train for Iowa. By late afternoon, they were pulling into the station at Davenport. Leyna had watched the countryside go by with great interest. She had slept all night, leaning against her husband-to-be, and she had tried, both successfully and unsuccessfully, to communicate with him.

Rand pulled her suitcase down from the rack and helped her put on her coat. Then he took her hand, and they made their way down the aisle. Rand had told her that his whole family was going to make the two-hour trip down to Davenport to pick them up. Leyna swallowed hard and tried to put on a smile, even though she was exhausted from her travels. She was surprised at how nervous she was.

Rand stepped down onto the platform and held Leyna's hand as she descended from the train. A warm and gentle breeze was blowing from the south. There were no clouds in the vast, blue sky that seemed to stretch out forever. Leyna looked farther up the platform at the train depot. The platform was virtually empty, except for a family standing at the door near the depot. Leyna looked at Rand, who smiled in recognition at them.

She noticed his father first. He was tall and handsome, just like Rand. His mother was quite a bit shorter than his father, and had a kind, round face. She was wearing a pretty hat. His younger brother was thin and tall. His hair was darker than Rand's, and he had it parted down the left side. He had the same big, beautiful eyes. His sisters were dressed in pretty dresses, and their hair was shining in the sunlight. The girls were both standing in front of his parents, looking quite serious and squinting in the sunlight. Leyna thought they were all very beautiful.

Rand brought Leyna directly to his family. Before he could clear his throat to make introductions, his mother reached out from behind his sisters and opened her arms to Leyna. It was at this gesture that Leyna began to cry.

She had faced so many unknowns in the past couple of years. She never knew when she would walk in and find her mother dead. She never knew if her father or brother would come home or, for that matter, whether they were alive or not. She did not know if she would live through prison camp, and she did not know how her new family would accept her.

Leyna clung to his mother for quite a while, and then she tried to compose herself. She didn't want them to think she was always a weepy mess.

"Welcome home," said his mother to Leyna as she tried to dry her tears.

Rand's father stepped forward and extended his hand to her. Leyna passed by his hand and gave him a hug. By the smile on his face afterward, Leyna knew that she had done the right thing.

Rand cleared his throat. "Leyna, this is my brother, Ted." Leyna reached out and shook his hand. He was a little taller than she.

"And this is Betty," he said, motioning to the taller of the two girls.

Leyna shook her hand and gave her a smile. "And the last one is Dorothy."

Leyna reached down to shake her hand, but she refused to. Leyna stood up and smiled. *I would not have wanted to shake a stranger's hand if I was that age,* she thought.

"It is an honor to meet you," she said slowly. Uncle Georg had taught her that phrase a month ago.

Rand's father and mother exchanged a glance of surprise and approval.

"Let's not stand here all day. We should get you two home," said Rand's father. "Is this all of her luggage?" he asked, reaching down for her suitcase.

Rand shrugged. "Yes."

Rand took her by the hand, and they all headed for the car. During the two-hour car ride to Dubuque, Rand told his parents all about his trip to New York and missing Leyna at the dock. Leyna was sandwiched between Rand and Ted in the backseat, but she didn't mind. She was watching out the window as the rolling countryside passed by. America seemed so big.

Rand's parents lived two blocks off of Main Street in town, on a corner lot. When they arrived at his parent's house, Rand took her into the living room and set her suitcase by the stairs. His mother took her hat off at the front door and went into the kitchen.

Leyna looked around the living room. There was a piano in the corner, next to the staircase. Leyna went over to look at the pictures that were sitting on top of the piano. She ran her hand down the picture of Rand in his uniform. Then she turned her attention to the picture beside his. It was a portrait of the whole family that must have been taken years earlier. Leyna breathed in deeply. She recognized that she had a lot to learn about Rand and his family, but she was determined to take her time. She knew that she could not fit into their family in a day.

"Come on up," said Rand, picking up her suitcase. "I want to show you my old room."

Leyna followed him upstairs and into his room. He set her suitcase on his bed. "This is where you will stay until Saturday. You probably want to wash up. The bathroom is right next door," he said. Rand showed her to the bathroom and then left her and went downstairs.

Leyna washed her face and put a brush through her hair. She stared into the mirror for a minute. Perhaps after a good night's rest she wouldn't look so frightening.

Leyna made her way across the squeaky floor to the stairs. She found Rand in the kitchen, talking and watching his mother get supper on the table.

"May I help?" she finally got the courage to ask.

Rand's mother looked at her as if she had asked her question in a foreign language.

Finally, she replied. "Sure, if you'd like to set the table."

Leyna froze for a moment. *Set the table?* she was thinking. Rand reached into the cupboard and handed Leyna the dishes. When she had finished putting them on the table, she turned to Rand.

"*Wo sind die Besteck*—? Where is the spoon?" she said, catching herself.

Rand smiled proudly. "Your uncle really worked you hard, I can see. I didn't expect this at all."

Leyna smiled.

Rand's mother called everyone to the table, and in no time at all, everyone was in their favorite spot. Ted ran to get an extra chair, and Rand sat Leyna down next to him. Then they all joined hands, and Leyna listened carefully as his father thanked the Lord for their food. It was in that moment that she felt at home.

It had not been too long ago that she had sat around the table at the farmhouse in Engen with her family and listened to her father pray. Leyna watched between bites as they all ate their food. The table was set with an abundance of good things to eat. Everyone was eating; no one was saying a word.

Following dinner, Leyna helped wash the dishes, and then Rand's mother beckoned Leyna upstairs. She led her into Rand's room and closed the door behind them.

"Rand says he has told you about Saturday?" she asked cautiously.

"Yes," Leyna replied, recognizing the word *Saturday*.

"I wanted to ask you what you are going to wear," she said, "for a wedding dress. Do you have anything?"

Leyna's mind was still processing the question. Then she smiled broadly and opened up her suitcase. She carefully pulled out a white roll that had taken up almost the entire suitcase. Leyna unrolled the dress, held it up to her shoulders, and tried to smooth out the wrinkles.

Mrs. Kellam's mouth dropped open at the sight of the dress. "Leyna," she said, "it's beautiful. Where did you get this?"

Leyna returned the question with a blank stare.

"Did you make this?" asked his mom at last.

Leyna nodded proudly and set the dress on the bed. Leyna raised her finger to her lips.

"Shh."

Rand's mother looked at her curiously.

"Do you have any gloves?" she asked, mimicking a pair with her hands.

"No," replied Leyna. "All that I have is this two dress."

Rand's mother stared at her empty suitcase and shook her head in disbelief.

"Leyna," she began, "I don't know how you are going to feel about this, but we have planned a simple wedding for you. I hope you don't mind."

"Don't mind?" she asked, not sure what it meant.

Rand's mother shook her head in frustration. "Tomorrow, I am going to invite Mr. Furst over for dinner so that he can talk to you," she said.

"*O nein,*" said Leyna, suddenly covering her mouth. "I forget. I have gifts," she said with a smile.

Mrs. Kellam took Leyna's wedding dress and hung it up in the closet as Leyna unrolled her other dress and removed several packages.

"I want to give," said Leyna meekly.

Mrs. Kellam turned to Leyna after hanging up her other dress and looked into her empty suitcase. She was having a hard time digesting the thought that her future daughter-in-law had come with only the clothes on her back and yet had thought to bring them gifts.

Mrs. Kellam nodded slowly, and the two of them went downstairs to the front room, where everyone had retired after dinner. Leyna, who was tired of speaking English by now, reverted to speaking German. She did not care if no one understood her.

"*Das ist für dich, Vater,*" she said in German, handing Mr. Kellam a rather large, square object wrapped in plain, brown paper. "*Und das ist für dich, Mutter.*" Leyna handed Rand's mother a smaller, flat object as Mrs. Kellam sat down in her rocking chair.

"*Jetzt für die Kinder,*" she said. "*Ja. Für* Ted *und* Betty *und für die kleine* Dorothy." Leyna handed each of them a package, and then she turned to Rand. "And you, my darling, will have to wait," she said mischievously.

There was silence in the room, as her German was received with confusion.

"Open," she said at last in English as she took a seat on the floor in front of Rand.

Mrs. Kellam turned to Mr. Kellam. "You go first," she said with a nod.

Mr. Kellam tore the paper from his box, and then he opened the lid slowly. His eyes grew wide as he pulled out a beautiful, Swiss watch. He looked up at Leyna and then back at the watch. He held it up to his ear and smiled.

"I don't know what to say," said Mr. Kellam. "Thank you, Leyna."

Little Dorothy began to tear at the paper on her present, and Betty, seeing her sister's actions, began to do the same. Ted was not far behind. The girls' eyes brightened as they each pulled out a small, German doll clothed in authentic Dirndl German dress.

Betty straightened the skirt on her doll. "This is a funny dress," said Dorothy, wrinkling her nose.

"I like mine," said Betty kindly.

Ted pulled a small pocketknife from his brown wrapping paper and surveyed it closely. "Is this from Germany?" he asked at last.

"No. Switzerland," replied Leyna. "They are good with the knives and the watches."

Ted smiled. He seemed happy to have something from a foreign country.

"Children, what do you say to Leyna?" asked Rand's mother, scolding them lightly.

A chorus of "thank you" rang out, and Betty even reached out, threw her arms around Leyna's neck, and gave her a hug.

Leyna looked up at Rand, who was smiling proudly. She was relieved to sense that she had done something to make him proud. Uncle Georg had insisted that she find something special for each one of them before she left Zurich. It had taken considerable effort on her part and by Uncle Georg and Stefan to make the gifts possible, but in that moment, the effort was nothing compared to the impact it had.

"Mom, open yours up," said Rand.

"Oh, yes," said his mother as she tore open the paper. Before she pulled out the lace table scarf Leyna had brought her, she looked up at Leyna and shook her head. "I'm going to love this, Leyna," she said as she held up the table scarf. "It's beautiful."

Leyna watched Rand's sisters as they played with their new dolls. In a special place in her heart, Leyna carried the memory of a doll her mother had made her for her fifth birthday. She had tried to faithfully recreate the doll for Rand's sisters, and, from the looks of it, she had succeeded.

Second Week of April 1946

The next day, after breakfast, Rand came and picked up Leyna in his truck and took her on a drive out to the farm. Leyna watched the town disappear behind them as Rand took her up and down some rolling hills. To Leyna's eyes, the land around them was strangely clear of trees, and the hills stretched on for miles.

About twenty minutes later, Rand turned left onto a dirt road at the top of a hill. "We're here," he said proudly as he drove up a tree-lined lane to a white farmhouse that stood to the south of a big, faded, red barn.

As she opened the door to step out, a cute dog greeted her with a chorus of barks.

"Able!" said Rand as he rounded the front of the truck. "This is your new mistress. You're going to have to get used to her," he said, squatting down to pet him. "This is Able, Leyna," he said at last, looking up at her.

Leyna let him smell her hand, and then he licked her fingers. She laughed. "We have a dog. He was Schufti," she said. "He left when father went away and did not come home."

Rand stood to his feet and turned toward the house. "Let's go inside. I want to show you our house."

Leyna followed Rand up the stairs to the front porch and then in the front door. The screen door made a comforting screech as it shut. Rand steered her through the front room and then the dining room that led to the kitchen and pantry. In the back room, he stopped for a moment and waited for her to notice the black sewing machine in the corner by a window.

Leyna drew in a deep breath as she saw it. "A Singer!" she said happily. Leyna went right over to the machine and lifted up the needle. Then she turned to Rand.

"It was my grandmother's. I hope you will be able to put it to good use," he said proudly.

Leyna smiled, and then she spoke in German because she did not know the words in English. "I have never had such a fine treadle machine to use."

"On Monday, I will take you to the store, and you can buy some material and some sewing supplies. I want you to get a very sharp pair of scissors too," he said, making a cutting motion with his hands.

Leyna's smile faded a little as she realized that Rand had taken careful thought of many details on her behalf.

Rand narrowed his eyes at her serious look, and then he took her to the stairs to show her the second floor. "The house has been shut up for five years, since my grandfather died, so it can sure use a good cleaning, but I hope you will like it. You can arrange the furniture however you want. It doesn't matter to me, as long as you are here with me," said Rand as he watched Leyna closely.

Leyna stopped at the bottom of the stairs and turned to him. "When will we marry?" she asked, slowly piecing her words together.

Rand looked at her a little puzzled. He sat down on the staircase. "We are going to be married on Saturday," he said, looking a little disappointed that she had not understood his long explanation on the train. "When do you want to get married? You haven't changed your mind, have you?"

Leyna ran her hands up and down the wall; then she climbed up two stairs and sat down next to Rand, looking as serious as she could. "Today," she said at last.

Rand chuckled, finally realizing she was teasing him. "We can't get married today, Leyna," he said, quite relieved.

"Why?" she shot back.

"Because we are going to marry on Saturday. It has already been arranged. I have just been waiting for you to get here."

"Saturday?" asked Leyna. She counted on her hands. "Four days," she said, and she sighed.

Rand took her by the hand, and they climbed the stairs. "I want to show you the rooms up here, and then we will go out to the barn."

It was out in the barn that Rand really began to feel that Leyna would make it in her new country and in her new home. She seemed at ease on the farm, and he was glad. With Able by his side, he showed her the wheat and corn seed he had purchased for planting, and then he showed her the tractor he had just finished repairing. She laughed when she saw Able jump up into the driver's seat. After a while, they went back into the farmhouse and sat down at the kitchen table to have some lunch.

Rand told her that he was going to buy some cows when they had the money, and that he would milk them. He told her it would be a while before they were on their feet financially. They needed to have a couple good harvests behind them. He told her honestly that he was not sure how they would make it through the first year.

"I can sew," she said eagerly as Rand was struggling to explain the current economic situation to her. Rand lifted his eyebrow. He was impressed, first with her offer to contribute and secondly that she seemed to understand what he was saying.

"In September, I will start teaching physics and math at the college in town," he said after taking a bite of his sandwich. "Then I want to see what we have to go through to bring Stefan over here."

Leyna reached out and touched him on the hand. "Rand, I, do you have a word book?" she asked with a little desperation in her voice. "I cannot understand."

Rand swallowed his bite and got up from his chair quickly. "I'm sorry, Leyna," he said as he disappeared out of the kitchen. "I almost forgot. I picked these up for you a month ago." He returned with two books in his hand. He set aside the dictionary. "This is an English grammar book," he said. "To tell you the truth, I never liked grammar much, but hopefully you will."

"What in September?" she asked him. After he repeated his

plans, Leyna looked up the words she did not understand, and then she set the dictionary down. With each passing moment, Leyna felt more and more as if her heart would burst with gratitude. She knew her Lord would take care of her, but she did not expect the abundance her eyes were seeing that day. Leyna looked at Rand. Above all of that, she could feel the love Rand had for her, and she did not understand it.

"Is something wrong?" Rand asked. He was confused by the look on her face.

Leyna did not want to resort to her old methods so soon, but what she had to say was too important to try to explain on her own. She asked him for a pencil and paper. After a few moments with her head buried in the dictionary, she slid the paper over the table to him.

She asked him if he remembered the day they had nothing to eat and *Herr* Krueger brought them bread. That is how she felt today. And, she wrote that she was not sure how she would be able to return the love he was showing to her.

Without a moment's hesitation, Rand took the dictionary and cobbled together his reply in German. "You have already done for me what I will never be able to repay."

Before supper the next day, Rand's mother called Leyna to the front door, where she was introduced to *Herr* Furst. He was a short, stout man who lived three houses down from Rand's parents. He began speaking with Leyna in German immediately.

"You will have to excuse me, because I have not spoken in my mother tongue in such a long time," he began.

"Neither have I," replied Leyna. "It has been over three weeks now."

Herr Furst laughed and turned to Mrs. Kellam. "Your future daughter-in-law has a good sense of humor," he said in English.

"Won't you come in, *Herr* Furst," offered Leyna, "and tell me all about how you came to America?"

Leyna was quite relieved to be speaking fluently again, and the two of them sat on the couch and chatted incessantly until supper.

At the dinner table, *Herr* Furst was kind enough to translate the details of the wedding to Leyna. Leyna was overwhelmed and overjoyed at the plans, and she told them so—through *Herr* Furst. Before the night was over, Leyna had made a new friend, and she thanked him for helping her to communicate with her new family.

To Leyna's great relief, *Herr* Furst showed up the next evening for dinner and even volunteered to accompany Leyna and Rand to see the pastor who would be performing the ceremony on Saturday.

Rand left Friday afternoon in his father's car to pick up some people at the train station who were coming in for the wedding. Leyna spent the afternoon helping Rand's mother bake and decorate their wedding cake. When they were finished, Mrs. Kellam beckoned Leyna to follow her into the attic. Rand's mom lifted the lid on a dusty, old trunk and took out a small hat. She placed it on Leyna's head, and then she lifted the veil over Leyna's face.

"This was my wedding veil, Leyna. You are welcome to wear it if you'd like," said Rand's mom, passing her a hand mirror.

Leyna peered through the netting at the mirror. With the hat and the veil on, Leyna thought she looked a lot like her mother.

"You want me to wear this?" Leyna asked.

Rand's mother nodded.

"I will wear it," Leyna said with finality as she removed the hat.

April 14, 1946

Leyna slept soundly that evening. She was still tired from the long journey from Zurich to Iowa and from trying to make conversation in English. Saturday morning, Rand's mother woke her at eight o'clock. Leyna washed her hair and tried to make it look pretty. Then she went downstairs and sat down for breakfast with the children. Rand was nowhere around, and Leyna wondered where he was.

There was a white box sitting on the end of the table, and when Leyna finished washing the breakfast dishes, Rand's mother handed it to her and took the towel from her hand.

"This is for you, Leyna, from us," she said, and she kissed Leyna on the cheek.

Leyna opened the box and peeked under the delicate paper inside. There was a brand-new pair of shoes and a pair of white gloves. Leyna's hands began to shake. She looked at Rand's mom.

"Is something wrong, Leyna?" asked his mother with concern.

"No," she managed. "No. Thank you." Leyna did not know how to tell her in English that it had been over ten years since she had had a new pair of shoes. She took the shoes out of the box and put them on her feet. Then she smiled.

"Now we go to the wedding," Leyna said.

Rand's mother looked at the clock. "We'd better get going, Leyna," she said in a rush. "Go on upstairs, and get your dress on."

When Leyna came downstairs with her dress, hat, gloves, and new shoes on, Mr. Kellam was standing at the bottom of the stairs, wearing a gray, pinstriped suit.

He smiled at her. "You look beautiful," he said. Then he

walked over to the kitchen door. "Laura, we are going to be late. What are you doing?"

Leyna made her way to the kitchen door in time to see Rand's mother braiding a silk ribbon into the stems of three roses she had just cut from her garden.

"Now I am ready," she said with a hasty sigh as she tied a bow on the end. "These are for you, Leyna," she said, handing the roses to Leyna. "Where are the children?"

"They are all out in the car, Laura," replied Rand's father calmly.

"And the cake?"

"It is in the trunk."

At ten thirty in the morning, Leyna was in the back of the car with Ted, Dorothy, and Betty, who were dressed up in their best clothes, and she was on her way to the church. She wished that her brother was there, and her mother and her father as well, but she just closed her eyes and thanked the Lord for all that he had done to get her to that day.

Leyna waited alone in a Sunday school room. She was sitting on a child's chair, holding her rose bouquet, and listening to the strange voices of the guests in the hall as they arrived. If she was nervous, it was only because she had to say her vows in English, not because she was afraid to marry the man that she would soon come to love more deeply.

Two minutes after noon, Rand's dad opened the door and beckoned for Leyna to come. She stood, smoothed out her dress, made her way to the doorway, and took his arm.

In Stefan's place, Mr. Kellam escorted the bride down the aisle. With the exception of *Herr* Furst, who was sitting on the second pew, and Rand's family, the church was full of people Leyna had never met. Leyna smiled as she took Rand's arm. At ten minutes after twelve, Leyna and Rand exchanged their vows. Then Rand slipped a ring onto her finger.

Leyna stood beside her new husband as they greeted the guests afterward in the church hall. Leyna tried to smile at all of the strangers as she shook their hands. Suddenly, she let out a shriek. Coming through the line was the unmistakable figure of Lieutenant Owen.

"This is your surprise, Leyna," said Rand, who was beaming.

After he had shook Rand's hand and congratulated him, Leyna threw her arms around Lieutenant Owen.

"Congratulations, Leyna," he said. Then he stepped back. "Where's the dictionary when you need one?"

"I have a dictionary in my pocket," Leyna said in English. Lieutenant Owen was shocked that she had addressed him in English, but he was pleased.

"Leyna, this is my wife, Sally," he said, introducing the woman behind him in line. She extended her hand to Leyna shyly.

"Thank you," she said softly. "Thank you for helping my husband."

"You are welcome," returned Leyna. "Who is this?" she asked, looking at the little boy at their feet.

"This is Charlie," returned Lieutenant Owen proudly.

"It is an honor to meet you, Charlie," said Leyna to the boy as he buried his head in his mother's skirt. "And who is this?" she asked again, pointing to the baby girl in his wife's arms.

"This is Leyna," replied Lieutenant Owen with a serious look on his face.

Leyna looked up at Rand and then back to Lieutenant Owen.

"A good name," she said at last, unsure of what else she could say. She was soaking in the honor that Lieutenant Owen had obviously bestowed on her.

Leyna continued to greet the guests as her heart was filling up with happiness. Rand told her that Lieutenant Owen and his wife had come from New York to Chicago to visit her parents, and they had made the trip out to Iowa just for the wedding.

Before they cut the wedding cake, Lieutenant Owen stood up and quieted the crowd. "I would like to make a toast to our wedding couple," he began, raising his glass of punch. "All of you know Lieutenant—Captain Kellam now—or you wouldn't be here. And there are not enough good things to say about him. I had the privilege of serving with him on our crew at Wendling. Rand, I wish you all the best in the years to come.

"But I want to let all of you know something about his bride. She is probably a mystery to you all. If it were not for her courage and daring, I would not be here today, and neither would Rand. Some of you may have your doubts about Leyna because she is German. But I assure you, because I have seen her first hand, that as you welcome her into your family, into your church, and into your community, you will not find anyone more selfless, more kind, or more brave."

Lieutenant Owen turned to the bride and groom. "Leyna, I owe you my life, and I wish you both nothing but the best in your marriage." Lieutenant Owen raised his glass; then he made his way over to Leyna and kissed her on the cheek.

Leyna tried to thank him for his kind words through her tears.

Epilogue, Spring 1984

"And that, ladies and gentlemen, is all we have time for," said the gray-haired professor as she glanced at the clock at the back of the lecture hall.

"In closing our character studies for the week, I would like to make one observation, students. In the portals of time, you can be assured that our maker and creator holds your life and everything that will touch you in the secret recesses of his eternal plan. There is nothing that you will face that he does not know about. You can plan your life, young people, but you must be brave. Always allow for him to direct you and you will not be sorry if you trust him, for he is the one who gives you life, and life more abundantly.

"Don't forget, your synopsis of chapter twenty-one is due on my credenza on Monday morning at ten. Have a good weekend, and I'll see you all, God willing, on Monday afternoon."

The professor waited as the students slowly made their way out of the lecture hall. There were not the usual raucous noises that accompanied their Friday exits from world history. She marveled a little at the lack of chatter. Then she gathered up her papers and made her way to her office.

It was five o'clock on the dot when the dean of the math department stuck his head in the door of her office. He had a small scar above his left eyebrow, but it was hidden now in the wrinkles on his forehead.

"Are we going to Stefan's tonight, sweetheart?" he asked.

"Yes," replied the professor. "It's his birthday."

"Are you about ready to go?"

The professor nodded. "Yes, I am," she said. Then her face lit up with an admiring smile. "*Terrorflieger.*" She stood up slowly and picked up a stack of books and some papers. As she reached for the light switch on her desk lamp, her hand passed a picture frame on her desk that held the remnants of a letter, written in broken German by the hand of the man whom she had met so long ago on the road to Engen. The only surviving part of the letter contained the passage from Isaiah 43:

> Be not afraid for I have redeemed you; I have called you by name: you are mine. When you pass through the waters, I will be with you; and through the rivers, they will not overflow you: when you walk through the fire, you will not be consumed. You are mine. You are precious in my sight.

LIVE

listen|imagine|view|experience

AUDIO BOOK DOWNLOAD INCLUDED WITH THIS BOOK!

In your hands you hold a complete digital entertainment package. In addition to the paper version, you receive a free download of the audio version of this book. Simply use the code listed below when visiting our website. Once downloaded to your computer, you can listen to the book through your computer's speakers, burn it to an audio CD or save the file to your portable music device (such as Apple's popular iPod) and listen on the go!

How to get your free audio book digital download:

1. Visit www.tatepublishing.com and click on the e|LIVE logo on the home page.
2. Enter the following coupon code:
   cb0b-2f94-be28-6bc6-0f76-8ddb-4f2e-351d
3. Download the audio book from your e|LIVE digital locker and begin enjoying your new digital entertainment package today!